I0728483

Doves
Love in Los Angeles Book 2

By Racheline Maltese and Erin McRae

Avian30
New York, New York
2017

This is a work of fiction. Names, characters, places, and incidents either are the product of the author's imagination or are used fictitiously. Any resemblance to actual events, locales, organizations, or persons, living or dead, is entirely coincidental and beyond the intent of either the author or the publisher.

Avian30
New York, New York
Doves by Erin McRae and Racheline Maltese
Copyright 2017
ISBN: 978-1-946192-05-9

www.Avian30.com

All rights reserved, which includes the right to reproduce this book or portions thereof in any form whatsoever except as provided by the U.S. Copyright Law.

This work originally published by Torquere Press, January 2015
First Avian30 Printing: May 2017
Printed in the USA

1

Paul has asked him, more than once, if climbing feels like flying.

"No," Alex always tells him. "It feels like being a very tiny bug on a very big rock. And a lot like almost falling."

"Please don't fall."

"The entire point is to not."

This high up it doesn't feel like bugs or falling. It feels like rock and his ropes and the wind in his hair, even if Paul will yell at him again for not wearing a helmet.

He slips, just a little, and his palm stings on stone. One more scrape for Zach, his character. Victor will be thrilled. For Alex, it's a reminder that he wasn't quite careful enough. For Victor, it's pain for one of his beautiful things, which, as a rule, he delights in. It's a mark of how long Alex has had this impossible life that Victor's inevitable reaction doesn't even seem that fucked up anymore.

When he gets back to the ground there will be a dozen things to worry about, from the *Fourth Estate* renewal that's taking longer than it should, to Paul's pilot that he's hoping anxiously for a pickup on, to the trip to South Carolina they're finally taking now that they both have time. But while Alex is up here, there's nothing to worry about except not falling. He happily puts all of his concentration into that and lets the rest of the world fade away.

On the descent, he startles a family of cliff swallows. Alex grins as they swoop away.

2

"Marry me?" Paul asks. Alex is at the bathroom sink brushing his teeth before bed.

"What?" Alex spits before he chokes on the toothpaste in horror. He meets Paul's eyes in the mirror.

"Marry me." Paul folds his arms over his chest. He's dressed for sleep, just in boxers, and his blonde hair is spiky from where he's been running his hands through it in frustration over a script all evening.

"Paul."

"Yes?"

"Nooooo."

Paul hides his disappointment well, but Alex is more horrified over the fact that Paul even asked the question than worried about his feelings. Paul laughs like it was all a joke and nudges Alex to the side so he can wash his face. Alex keeps staring at him. If he stares long enough, maybe Paul will explain whatever train of thought led them to this junction.

He doesn't disappoint. "Sorry," Paul says. He pats his face dry. "Momentarily overwhelmed by domestic bliss."

"Witty dialogue is not hiding the fact that you're crazy."

"I can only do my best."

They've been living together for almost a year now, and they've never talked about making their relationship legal. Alex doesn't see why they would. Paul's thirty-two, but Alex is only twenty-two. In a normal world, one in which Alex has never lived, he'd be finishing college this year. Instead he's the unexpected star of a hit TV drama, in a relationship with one of the show's writers. And he has no interest in carrying on this conversation further.

"You want to get un-overwhelmed and fuck me instead?" Alex asks.

"That's a sexy come-on."

"You asked me to marry you while I was brushing my teeth and we have a flight in eight hours. Go with it."

Paul laughs. "You're not too sore after your climb?"

"Sore, yes, 'too', no. Besides, I'm making you do all the work."

Paul swats Alex's ass as he walks past him out of the bathroom. Alex drops his toothbrush into the sink. When Paul does things like that he loses all ability to do anything but respond.

♦

Traveling with Paul is both more and less difficult than traveling on his own. Paul insulates him from everything invasive and unsettling about it, but they also draw attention when they're together. The world doesn't know Paul's face the way it knows Alex's…yet. Paul's been working hard to make himself a brand in preparation for what he hopes will be a long and successful run for *Winsome, AZ*, the show he's still waiting for the network's decision on. And while they don't do press about their relationship, it's no secret. Alone, Alex can be a guy who just sort of looks like J. Alex Cook. With Paul by his side, everyone knows exactly who they are.

In airports, people generally have the decency not to approach them. But the world is full of fans who are not as stealthy with their smartphone cameras as they would like to think; Alex has been considering starting a pinned map of airports from which blurry pictures of his sneakers have been posted.

He sits silently next to Paul as they wait for their plane to board. He has no interest in having yet another conversation that's going to be misheard and disseminated over the internet.

♦

On the plane, they're in coach, and Alex squeezes into his seat by the window as quickly as he can, pulling his beanie down until it covers his eyes. Paul smiles at the absurdity as he stows their carry-ons and takes the seat next to him. They'd bought the one on the aisle too, just to have a little more space and privacy, but there's no universe where Paul doesn't want to be pressed up against Alex as the plane takes off. When it leaves the ground, Alex twists in his seat so he can press his head into Paul's shoulder instead of against the window.

"Fuck, I'm in love with you," Paul whispers in his ear.

Alex snorts. By the time the seatbelt light goes off, he's asleep.

♦

Paul's mom greets them at the baggage claim. Alex hangs back, shy and unsure of his place, as she gathers Paul up in a hug.

Beth lets go of Paul and folds Alex into a hug, too. "It's good to see you."

"Good to see you too."

She pulls back and tweaks the beanie straight on his head. "How was your flight?"

Paul and his mom chat as they make their way to the exit. Alex stays quiet, content to let them catch up. Beth came out to L.A. last Christmas, when an avalanche of scheduling disasters made it impossible for them to get out of the city for the holiday. Alex likes her. But he's never been to South Carolina with Paul. He's glad to help get the suitcases into the trunk and then slide into the back seat to rest with his own thoughts.

Alex dozes through most of the two-hour drive, putting an occasional word into the conversation when Beth asks him something. He finally jerks out of a nap when they pull off the main road into the driveway.

Paul turns around in his seat, his smile gentle. "Hey there. You awake?"

"Mmm. Yeah." Alex rubs his eyes.

"Welcome to the family seat."

The driveway is long and winds up through a lawn somewhat in need of mowing to an old farm house. Weathered siding and faded shutters speak of old grandeur and care, but not much wealth. The verandah is the stuff of picture books, complete with ancient climbing roses. When the car pulls round the side to the garage, Alex can see a large vegetable garden in the back and rows of old fruit trees stretching down to woods.

When they get out of the car, the silence of the country evening is deep and peaceful. Alex takes a deep breath. The air here smells of earth and grass, and is deeply relaxing.

"So this is why you like it here so much," he says to Paul as Beth leads the way into the house.

Paul hesitates, just for an instant, before following. "I like it better with you here."

♦

Alex offers to help with dinner — strange places are always easier to manage if he can be busy — but Beth shoos them into chairs at the kitchen table and gets them iced tea. There's more chatting and catching up between Beth and Paul, and there's even more when Paul's sister Sarah and her son Jake arrive for the meal. Alex sits back and enjoys watching everyone else interact. One of his favorite things about this family is that they never treat him like a celebrity or indeed like anyone other than just Alex, Paul's boyfriend. Seeing them on their home turf is even more enjoyable. Everyone is relaxed and at ease. Even Paul, who Alex thinks of as pure L.A. in so many ways, softens somehow in this environment. Around his mother and sister his accent, which only comes through rarely at home, gets stronger.

"You boys sleep well," Beth says once Sarah and Jake have left for the evening. Night has settled outside, warm and filled with the soft hum of insects.

Paul leads the way upstairs to the guest room, which bears no particular personality of any resident, current or former. They could be at an inn as easily as at Paul's mother's house.

"Is this your old room?" Alex looks around the space and tries to imagine a teenage Paul living here. What sorts of trophies and decorations did he have? What books or magazines did he have on the shelves?

Paul, though, shakes his head slowly. "No. This was Sarah's. Mine's a craft room now."

There's something uncomfortable and weighty in Paul's voice that Alex can't figure out. Does Paul miss this house the way it was? Does he feel displaced?

"It's been a long time," Alex says.

Paul shakes his head. Alex isn't sure whether that's a no to his assumptions or a dismissal of the topic.

♦

The bed's narrower than what they have at home, and in the dark they're unavoidably pressed up against each other. In the southern spring night it's warm enough to be uncomfortable. Alex is just drifting off to sleep, finally, when Paul wanders a hand up his bare leg.

"Seriously?" Alex asks. He's hot and tired, and even if he weren't, they'd still be in Paul's mother's house. These walls aren't thick at all.

Paul hesitates but only a little. "Too long a day?"

"Too shared a roof."

"You can be quiet."

"Paul."

"Tell me no," Paul says.

"No." Alex is already getting hard. He's never been able to resist Paul. Or ever wanted to.

"Gonna be a long week," Paul points out.

Trust Paul to misunderstand. "I meant *no*, I'm not going to tell you no."

"Oh thank God." Paul has his hand around Alex's dick before he even finishes the phrase.

Despite his own objections about noise, Alex mewls as Paul starts to jerk him off. Embarrassed, he bites at the heel of his hand to stay quiet.

"No," Paul says gently. His free hand pulls Alex's away from his mouth and presses it up to the old wrought iron headboard. "Hold on, don't move, both hands."

Alex slides his other hand up his body to grab onto the headboard. He wants to tell Paul that he's being absurd, but Paul's hand on him — too steady, too slow — feels too amazing for him to be able to find any words. Whatever it is that he and Paul bring out in each other always seems to work exactly as it should.

He whimpers again. Paul shushes him.

"This isn't for you. This is for me," he reminds Alex. "And I want you to be quiet so I can hear you struggle."

The idea should piss Alex off, but it just turns him on more. He presses his eyes shut, panting and whispering *"Please,"* over and over again. Paul admonishes him with shushing noises and the occasional slowing of the hand on his cock. Whatever this started as, it's rapidly getting edgier than what they usually do. Alex doesn't want it to stop. He arches and squirms on the bed.

"So fucking needy," Paul tells him. Alex is distantly aware that the bed creaks. Why did he think a handjob would be quieter than anything else?

"What if I just stopped?" Paul asks.

The thought is terrible. If Paul stops, he might actually explode. So Alex begs even harder.

♦

Alex comes abruptly and with little warning. He rides the orgasm out in Paul's slick hand, and the second he's done he's on his knees, rubbing Paul's dick across his face before sucking it into his mouth.

Paul's never been with anyone who stays down in the moment of sex quite the way Alex does. For most people, an orgasm breaks the spell, but Alex just doesn't seem to be wired like that. He goes somewhere small and obedient and doesn't always want to come back. Sometimes it's glorious. Sometimes it's concerning. Usually, it's a little bit of both.

"Holy shit," Paul says, not quiet at all. The words break the madness of what they're doing a little, and Alex laughs with his mouth full. Paul joins him until he's too overwhelmed by sensation to do anything other than grip Alex's hair too tightly and pant as he fucks up into his mouth.

When Paul comes — it doesn't take him long at all — Alex flops back onto the bed, his temple pressed to Paul's hip bone.

"So, I'm thinking we really need to practice this quiet thing," he says.

3

They sleep so late Beth has left for work by the time they make it downstairs for breakfast. As much as Alex likes her, he's relieved. After the sex last night with Paul, he wants time alone just for the two of them. Also, they were loud, and he wants to pretend Beth didn't hear them.

Paul asks if he wants the grand tour as they work their way through coffee and toast. Alex agrees eagerly.

His body clock is off, thanks to the time difference, and the sun is higher than he expects when they step outside. It's still morning, but won't be for much longer. The whole outdoors is like a fairytale compared to the Indiana of Alex's childhood. Yes, there were fields and sky there too, but the land always seemed tired and worn out. Here things are fresh and green. There's an energy to the plants and birdsong Alex can feel as they make their way down a path that leads into the woods. He scuffs happily through the layer of pine needles and leaves carpeting the path and tries to name the flowers growing up shyly under the ferns.

Eventually he becomes aware of a sound rising through the trees he can't identify. It might be a stream chattering through the woods, but he doesn't think so.

"What's that noise?" he asks as they hike up a little rise.

"That," Paul says. "Is the cricket barn." His voice is a little strained.

"Excuse me?"

"The cricket barn," Paul repeats. He nods toward what was probably a rather nice outbuilding in much better days when the farm was fully functional. "Do you want to go in?"

"No." He neither wants to ask, or know, why crickets need a barn. Is it a very small barn, or are they very large crickets? Either way, the answer isn't appealing.

"Come on." Paul tugs his hand to get Alex to follow. "You can't conceive of the profound fucked-upness of this place until you see what we're willing to do to hang on to what we've got."

"What do crickets have to do with anything?" The question is better than reminding Paul that he's from Indiana, and has plenty of experience doing fucked up things to survive.

Paul lets go of him to unlatch the door and push it open for them. Alex shoves his hand into his pocket, so he won't accidentally touch anything he really doesn't want to.

"We've got seven hundred acres," Paul says as he steps inside. "We can't farm it ourselves so we rent out most of it. The money from that covers most of the taxes, but there's never enough to keep the place up, *hence*," Paul sweeps a hand dramatically across the warm, unlit interior of the barn. "Crickets. We raise them and sell them for bait. It's not a bad enterprise."

Paul's standing inside the door, but Alex hovers on the threshold, looking into the ratcheting darkness and feeling any number of crawly things shiver up his spine. The smell is disturbing.

"This is insect hell."

"Actually, they're quite comfortable."

"Paul." Alex wants to have his back to a wall, but he also doesn't know what is *on* the wall, so he shifts uneasily from foot to foot.

"Told you it was fucked up."

"*Crickets?*"

"Why? What was your job as a kid?"

"Farm work is nothing like raising demons in the family barn." Objectively, the jobs Alex had in high school and even middle school were worse than working with crickets. But he doesn't want to talk about that. Also, that was then and the crickets are now.

Paul grins and ushers Alex back outside so he can, to Alex's relief, close and latch the door again.

"I didn't know your family was having trouble hanging on to the land," Alex says when they're far enough down the path that he doesn't keep looking over his shoulder for a following mass of tiny, too many-legged creatures. It's awkward, as always, to talk about wealth, or the lack thereof. But Paul had never mentioned anything about his family struggling.

Paul reaches for Alex's hand again. Alex takes it out of his pocket to let him have it. Out here with no one around, there's no reason not to, and Paul seems uneasy without the contact.

"It's not terrible. Just the way it's always been."

His fingers tighten around Alex's. Alex looks sideways at him. "What?"

"Speaking of things that are the way they've always been, I've got lunch today with my father."

"This is the father who wanted to disown you and from whom you're now estranged?" Alex should probably be more supportive than sarcastic, but, really?

"I've only got the one." Paul tries to joke.

"More than I have," Alex points out. "Seriously, though. Why?"

"It's what we do," Paul says. "For Mom's sake. Things aren't good between them, and I hate that I make that worse."

"That's not on you." Alex doesn't say *because your father is a homophobic asshole*, even if he is, because he doesn't know anything about the bonds between fathers and sons. Fucked up as this family situation is, he's working on trying to be more understanding. Sometimes.

Paul shrugs. "I need to know that I can."

"Okay?" Alex says when Paul doesn't elaborate.

"Just to prove to myself that I can still be sane."

"Am I going with you?" Alex isn't sure if he should be freaked out by Paul's tone. He also doesn't know what being a good partner demands in this situation.

"Do you want to?" Paul asks.

"Is there a way I don't make that situation worse?"

"My beautiful, sharp, Hollywood boyfriend in the same room as my father?" Paul shakes his head. "Probably not."

"I would go," Alex says. He may be uneasy, but he's not afraid. He's faced worse than Paul's father, surely, in Indiana and in Hollywood.

"I know."

Alex squeezes his hand, and Paul squeezes back.

"He gave me a gun for my fifteenth birthday," Paul says abruptly.

"Yeah?"

"I wasn't very good at it. I'm not really into the whole shooting animals thing."

"So shoot cans." Alex shrugs. "It's a great way to deal with shit like your dad."

Paul shakes his head. "Yeah. Destroying things because I'm angry is not good choices for me."

"It's just blowing off steam."

"Maybe for you," Paul says darkly.

Alex looks over at him. Paul is occasionally cagey about things in his past but this is something different. "What's going on with you?"

Paul shrugs, looking helpless.

"Do you still have it?" Alex asks. It's been years since he's been near a gun. He's curious.

Paul nods. "One of the barns."

Maybe if Alex can touch it he can show Paul how not to be so uneasy around something he doesn't need to be. Maybe he can show himself, too. "Oh God, please tell me this is just a normal barn and not a demon insect barn," he tries to joke.

"Not more crickets, I swear."

Alex laughs. "Show me."

◆

"How do you know how to do this?" Paul asks. He had no idea Alex knew anything about guns. Above them in a tree, a mockingbird trills through its repertoire.

Alex has brought the gun out of the barn and is now sitting on the ground, examining it carefully. The sun glints in his hair, making the threads of gold in the red stand out. A morning outside has brought out even more of Alex's freckles. Paul marvels again at just how unspeakably lovely his boyfriend is.

"Indiana, Paul."

"Yeah, but —"

"My mom taught me," Alex says, his voice distracted but his hands on the gun sure like they are over his climbing equipment. "I had a lot of shit to get out of my system. It's relaxing."

"Okay," Paul says dubiously.

Alex asks if they have any earmuffs.

♦

When Paul gets back from the lunch, he can't find Alex anywhere in the house.

"Do you know where Alex went?" he asks his mom when he walks into the kitchen. She looks up from a recipe book spread out on the counter.

"Out back. With your old Winchester. I didn't think you'd mind."

She doesn't ask how Paul is, or how lunch went. She never does, even though Paul knows that she's glad he goes. Paul wonders if she's afraid of invoking the ghosts of all the things that have happened in this house if she speaks of them out loud.

"I'm going to go find him."

"Okay, dear."

She returns to her recipes, but Paul knows she's watching him leave and not without relief.

♦

Paul follows the measured sound of gunshots, disturbing only in their potential. Alex is on the old range that's been set up for generations, beer cans he must have raided from the recycle bin perched on an old stump. He doesn't hear Paul approach — he's got earmuffs clamped over his ears — but when he sees Paul out of his peripheral vision, he stops and pulls them off.

He doesn't ask anything, either, just looks at Paul.

"Keep going," Paul says. He picks a spot on the ground a safe way back to sit and watch.

Alex shrugs and re-positions the earmuffs before picking up the gun again.

It is profoundly strange, seeing his boyfriend use an instrument of destruction and use it well: Alex is very good at this. But it's not any stranger — and is far less awful — than lunch had been. So Paul lets himself relax watching Alex's movements and delighting in the fact that Alex never does stop surprising him.

He takes a few pictures, just to catch the moment — Alex's skill, and his profound *stillness* as he takes aim. Paul is aware that spending a week at his family's house is a prime opportunity to finally tell Alex things about his own history he probably should have shared years ago. But Alex, often ill at ease in other people's spaces, seems relaxed and happy. Paul doesn't want to risk ruining that just yet to tell him something he doesn't want to confess anyway.

♦

Eventually, Alex runs out of targets and decides that Paul has been sitting alone long enough. He packs the things up carefully, then flops down next to Paul on the grass and looks up at the sky.

"I had no idea you could do that," Paul tells him.

"Mmm. Not a thing to bring up in polite conversation. Especially not in Hollywood hippie society. But here?" he shrugs.

"You're really good."

Alex grins. "I am. I should be, even if I'm out of practice. I spent enough time shooting in high school."

"I got pictures," Paul holds the phone up so Alex can see. "Mind if I post one?"

"Knock yourself out," Alex says. He shuts his eyes.

Paul's not saying anything about lunch, which means either that Alex is supposed to ask or that Paul doesn't want to talk about it. Alex isn't going to press. If posting a random picture of him to Twitter is going to make Paul feel better about his day, he doesn't really mind.

He nods when Paul asks for his okay on a caption (*Look what Alex can do!'*) and is glad when Paul slips his phone back into his pocket and then lies down next to him in the grass.

"Done," Paul says.

"Cool."

Paul's phone chimes insistently as people retweet it until he thumbs the setting over to turn off notifications. Alex rolls his eyes. Paul always forgets that things tend to get out of hand when he tweets anything that mentions him.

For a long while they drift, not saying anything and watching the clouds sail by overhead. There's so much quiet to enjoy.

"It's really beautiful out here," Alex says apropos of nothing.

"Yeah?"

"Yeah. Makes me wonder. Is Indiana beautiful, but I just can't see it?"

"Probably."

"It's not beautiful to you here, is it?" Alex asks, turning his head to look at him.

"Mmmm, no. It is. Just horror coexists. Like the crickets. And I worked hard to get out of here. Nearly didn't."

Alex hums slightly, leaving space for the conversation that he thinks is coming.

"I almost drowned in the lake when I was a kid," Paul offers.

"Didn't you know how to swim?" Alex asks.

"No, I dunno. Something grabbed my leg."

"What do you mean *something*?"

"I don't know... I mean, weeds or something. It was dumb. My sister pulled me out. I'm a better swimmer now, although you couldn't pay me to go back in there."

Paul chuckles a little, and it makes Alex fond. They're of a type to be amused by the really dumb shit that's happened to them, even if a lot of it isn't supposed to be for laughing.

"I know you want me to tell you what happened," Paul says. "And I will. I'm just — working up to it."

Alex wants to say something, but at that moment his phone chooses to ring. It's Liam. Alex frowns at it before ignoring it. He's on vacation, and that includes from colleagues he sees way too much of, no matter how close their friendship has become. If it's important, Liam will call back. Over and over again until he answers, because Liam, Alex's friend, kind-of ex, and co-star on *The Fourth Estate* is annoying that way.

"What does he want?" Paul asks.

"Didn't answer it, so don't know," Alex says. He chooses to not comment on what now seems to be an immovable bit of edginess from Paul around the way Liam is unavoidably enmeshed in their lives.

"Could be secret early renewal news," Paul offers.

Alex shrugs. Paul's not wrong. Liam is likely to hear things off-the-record from Victor long before there's official news, but Alex is fairly sure he'd only share if the word were bad. It's too nice a day — despite everything — to interrupt it with that. And if it were news about Paul's show, it wouldn't be coming from Liam anyway.

Paul takes a deep breath. "So, I didn't exactly try to kill myself," he says.

Alex feels dizzy. Of course Paul tells him he's not telling him something right now and then manages to wait only five minutes after effectively waiting years. If it weren't so strange and horrifying, the whole situation would be hilarious.

"What were you trying to do?" Alex asks, keeping his voice neutral.

"I was having a fight with my father. One of those free-ranging arguments where you want to run away but you're not fast enough and the fight goes from room to room."

Alex wants to say he has no idea what Paul means. His house growing up was so small, and he hasn't had a fight like that as an adult. But that's not true. Because that's exactly what the fight when they broke up was like, until Paul had said how angry he was instead of actually being angry.

"What was it about?"

"Nothing. Everything. Girls. The lack of girls. My grades. The thing with the pot. My best friend. My clothes. Church. I mean, anything and everything. My attitude, and Lord knows, he wasn't wrong about that." Paul gives a strange little chuckle.

"I feel like the next question is 'What did he do?'" Alex says carefully.

Paul shakes his head against the grass. "No. Valid assumption, but I was so angry, and I remember wanting to hurt him, except that didn't feel like enough? It wasn't good enough? So what if he hurt? People hurt all the time without knowing they're wrong, without having to live with the consequences of it."

Alex reaches for his hand, but Paul pulls away, folding his hands on his chest and breathing evenly.

"No. Let me get this out. We wound up in the kitchen, and I just kept asking, I mean screaming, really, at him about what he wanted from me. Like, there was this list of everything that was wrong with me, but there weren't any answers."

Alex snorts. "I love those fights," he says quietly. He knows what Paul means, even if he feels increasingly non-resident in his body as the story goes on.

"I pulled a knife out of the block in the kitchen and cut my own wrists," Paul says. "I didn't know how else to show him that I hated myself enough that he could stop talking. There was blood fucking everywhere."

Paul pauses for a long moment. Alex feels himself shrink in sheer horror. He struggles to breathe.

"So," Paul turns onto his side to look at Alex, "that's why I don't tell that story. It's a lot easier to let people think the obvious thing that's not exactly true. Also, can't recommend psychiatric inpatient treatment as an exciting summer vacation, but so it goes."

"*Paul.*" Alex feels small, and numb, and very far away. He wants to grab for Paul again to anchor him — or himself — but he's afraid to touch him. He isn't sure his hand won't go right through him, here in this beautiful, terrible place.

"I love you," he says instead, desperately, like the words can call Paul back from the past and have made this have not-happened. In what world is suicide not the worst option? His voice is shaky. The small bit of his brain that isn't obsessed with the horror of what Paul's just told him is shocked and unsettled by that. He didn't tell it to be shaky.

Paul tries to smile and doesn't quite manage. "Love you too."

Alex's phone goes off. Again.

"Are you fucking kidding me?" Alex mumbles.

"You should at least see who it is," Paul says. He's not wrong. They're both waiting on too much incredibly important news.

"Victor." Alex drops the phone between them. Dealing with his boss, let alone his casual menace, is the last thing he wants right now. But he's not going to pretend he doesn't want to know about the renewal.

"You should answer it," Paul says.

Alex feels sick. Because there's no world where this call — whatever it is — should be more important than what Paul's just told him. But this is *now* and therefore, it sort of is. With the unanswered call from Liam earlier, he does not have a good feeling about this.

"WHAT THE HELL DO YOU THINK YOU'RE DOING?" Victor yells into Alex's ear before he can even say hello.

"Being on vacation?" Alex says. He's confused and whatever delayed reaction he's having to Paul's story is just starting to kick in. He is not okay to deal with whatever this is.

"Do you have any idea how crazy you and a gun have made the internet?" Victor says, the decibel level only barely reduced.

"Everything I do makes the internet crazy."

"My God, Alex. I am in the middle of some terrible fucking negotiations AND YOU'VE JUST

SINGLE-HANDEDLY REIGNITED AMERICA'S GUN CONTROL DEBATE."

"I sort of doubt that." Alex is still trying to catch up. "And Paul tweeted it."

"You two are *IDIOTS.*"

"Victor," Alex snaps to get his attention. "Your timing is not great. What can either of us do right now, and then we can all touch base later?" Alex reaches for Paul, who's looking at him with a ridiculous amount of pride in the middle of all this bullshit and misery.

Victor, of course, doesn't have an answer other than a list of things Alex and Paul shouldn't do next. The whole thing is, frankly, a little crazy. Alex feels bad for him — a little. Victor views himself as responsible for every one of the hundreds of people that work on *Fourth* and with its fate up in the air, that has to be hard.

"Is there anything else I can do?" he says once Victor has run out of steam.

"Yes. Call Liam back. Like a good little New York liberal, he's completely freaked out."

"You're fucking kidding me," Alex blurts before he can help himself.

"I am not. We will touch base later," Victor says threateningly before the line clicks closed.

Alex stares at the phone in his hand.

"Not good news?" Paul hazards.

"Apparently America doesn't like its darling little gay to have a gun."

"Technically, it's my gun."

"I think that makes it worse," Alex rolls his eyes as he scrolls to Liam's number.

Liam picks up immediately. "Alex? What are you doing?"

It's an odd repetition of Victor's initial reaction, except much quieter and less angry.

"I'm hanging out with Paul. How are you?"

"The internet says you have a gun." Liam sounds aggrieved.

"The internet is incensed about things that are not its business."

"Why do you have a gun?"

Alex rolls his eyes. "Liam. The internet being inappropriate is nothing new. This doesn't actually affect you. What the hell is your problem?"

Liam babbles his way through a paragraph of a response that is, at best, incoherent. Whatever has him upset, it's more than a principled, political objection to firearms. Yet it provides Alex no information he can use to soothe whatever inexplicable anxieties have cropped up in Liam's head.

"Okay, I don't really know what to say to that," Alex says when Liam finally winds down. "What do you need from me?"

"Can we hang out when you're back in town?" Liam sounds wary, of what, God knows.

"Sure," Alex says. "Now, I know Victor doesn't care, but I really am on vacation with Paul, so can I get back to that?"

"Yeah. Okay," Liam says. He sounds meek now. "Bye."

"*Goodbye.*" Alex hangs up and drops the phone on the grass.

Paul just stares at him. He looks like he doesn't know whether to laugh or cry. Alex can sympathize.

"So that was an interesting fifteen minutes."

Paul chuckles weakly. "You yelled at Victor."

"He yelled at me first."

"This is why I'm impressed."

Alex tries to smile. "Just priorities."

"What did Liam want?"

"To know why I've offended all of his sensibilities by having a gun. I can't figure out if he's more afraid that I'm in danger or putting everything else in danger." He takes a breath and lies back again with his arms folded behind his head. "This place is weird. I'm not sure he's wrong to worry."

"Maybe we should go back inside," Paul suggests.

"Oh, fuck no. Not yet."

"It was a long time ago," Paul says.

"I know. And in my head it was twenty minutes ago."

"Okay."

They lapse into silence again, until Alex says, "Psychiatric in-patient?"

Paul keeps his eyes on Alex. "That was not a good summer."

"Do you want to talk about it?"

"Given that I didn't tell you for almost two years, not particularly. It wasn't terrifying or traumatic or anything like that. At least not from this vantage point. But it was not my happiest time."

"And you had lunch with your father today."

Paul nods. "Yeah."

"And *I'm* the one that doesn't talk," Alex says. He's far more baffled than angry.

♦

They do eventually go back to the house, after Alex returns the equipment to its safe, locked place in the barn. Alex's head is a mess of confusion and a strange, dark grief for a tragedy that only almost happened. He also has a simmering anger that the world cares way too much what he does, especially when he's on vacation, about things that matter not at all. The timing of everything really is too awful.

Paul runs upstairs to check in on his email, and Alex finds Beth. She's in the kitchen and looks up when he walks in.

"Hey, sweetie. How'd the shooting go?"

"Good." He frowns at the absurdity of the day. He wonders if he should tell her about everything that's going on in the wider world because her son's boyfriend took his stress and introversion out on her gun range. Maybe Paul will.

"He told me," he says. "Just so you know. He hadn't before."

She meets Alex's eyes and nods. "It's about time," she says before going back to the cooking. "We repainted the kitchen together after he got home."

Sarah, her husband Mike, and their son Jake, come over later, and dinner passes without incident. Alex keeps looking over his shoulder for something else terrible to happen, and he and Paul stay closer to each other than they normally do.

Usually it's Alex who curls into Paul's side whenever he can, at least when they're not in public, but tonight it's Paul who keeps their legs pressed together under the table. More than once, Alex sees Paul's mother watching them as they bend their heads together to talk quietly, but Alex has no impulse to pull away or remove his arm from low on Paul's back.

They're all sitting out on the verandah together, watching sunset creep across the fields, when Alex's phone makes itself known yet again. This time, it's Margaret.

The whole conversation is ridiculous on any number of levels, but at least she's not shouting. Her calm, competent crisis-management mode is somehow even more frightening than Victor's wrath, and now Alex's reception of it isn't numbed by terrible stories. The liberals are furious that their sweet Indiana farm boy has the temerity to know his way around a gun. The right suddenly has to deal with the fact that their new, if inadvertent, poster boy is Hollywood's pet twink. No one is happy. Even beyond the fans who feel betrayed that J. Alex Cook would do something so terrible as shoot beer cans (he'd made Paul show him some of the choice replies), many, many people are angry.

"The NRA called," Margaret tells him.

"I'm on vacation," Alex moans.

"Have you talked to Paul's family about what happens when things like this happen?"

"Do things like this actually happen that much?" Alex asks.

"Are you planning on maintaining dangerous and politically sensitive hobbies?"

"I'm not going to defend a sport I like and I'm good at, because it makes people who say *flyover* nervous. I shoot targets, not animals, and I'm also not interested in being a spokesperson for a bunch of freaks who think the government is coming for their Jesus. Can't I just be a person who does stuff?"

"I'm taking that as a yes."

Alex swears. And then reluctantly explains that yes, he and Paul have had conversations with Paul's family about some of the realities of a relationship as public as theirs. Everyone has been gracious, but as welcoming as this family has been, Alex knows that by dating Paul he's making everyone's lives harder than they have to be.

Eventually Margaret talks him down from his pitch of righteous anger. He retreats around the corner of the verandah to keep Paul's family out of earshot as much as possible, because dumping all of this on them just seems rude. She lays out a reasonable strategy for dealing with it which amounts to much the same as Victor's: Do nothing, and do *not* do a whole lot of somethings.

"Hey, can't you just say you're trying to get me an action movie deal or something?" he jokes.

"I could," Margaret points out, "if we knew what the hell was going on with your show."

And with that, Alex finally gets why Victor was pissed. Because on top of everything else, they all live in some sort of crazy world where a tweet can be strategy and betrayal.

After he hangs up with Margaret, before he can even walk back round to the front of the house, Victor calls again. There's less yelling — and the timing is less awful — but once *that* call is over and Alex has finally slumped back into the chair next to Paul's, he's ready to never answer his phone ever again.

Which is when Paul's phone rings.

Paul looks scared. His mother looks like none of this is terribly out of the ordinary. Alex wonders if that's just because she's used to Paul's job or if her life transcended *strange* and *scary* a long time ago.

"Answer it," Alex hisses. He knows this is one of the two calls they've been waiting for and the one that will go a long way towards telling them the shape of the next year.

Paul answers it. Alex watches him closely as he nods and says *yes* and *thank you* a number of times, but he's so damn even Alex can't tell if the news is good or bad.

When he clicks off, he just stares straight ahead *breathing* for a moment. What Alex would have once taken as shock or admired as an even disposition now seems learned in the most unsettling of ways.

"Well?" he finally asks.

Everyone leans forward in their chairs on the verandah staring at Paul in the bug-filled twilight.

"Thirteen episodes," he says softly. "Option for another eight. And then we pray for season two."

The reaction from Paul's family is loud, but Alex sits there, still bent toward Paul and holding his hand, waiting for the moment to actually connect. When it does, Paul is out of his chair in a flash, hauling Alex up with him into a crushing hug.

"Oh my God, this day," Alex says in his ear.

Paul laughs in utter delight. "Will you marry me now?"

Alex laughs and shoves at his shoulder. "Staff your fucking show first."

"I have a show!"

◆

"Last bit of quiet we're going to have for a long time," Paul says once everyone else has left or gone up to bed and he and Alex have the verandah to themselves.

Alex hums, not particularly eager to break the precious silence. "I don't know, I'm still waiting for another crisis to erupt."

"So turn your phone off."

"Did after Victor called the last time. Can't control yours, though."

Paul takes the hint and digs his phone out of his pocket to silence it.

"Does this mean I have all your attention now?"

Paul smirks. He drags his eyes up Alex's body in a way that is entirely not helpful when they're outside on Paul's mother's front porch.

"Sooooo, wanna go upstairs?" Alex nudges his toes against Paul's leg.

Paul laughs, clearly delighted, and after a pause they practically chase each other into the house and up the stairs.

♦

"What do you want?" Alex shuts the door behind them and leans back against it.

Paul smiles at him. "You don't usually ask. You just do. Or let me take."

"Well, now I'm asking. What do you want?" Alex repeats.

"*Everything*," Paul breathes.

"Not helpful," Alex says. But he doesn't mind.

He winds up naked on the bed, knees tucked under him as Paul eats his ass forever, before deciding to fuck him. It's incredibly excellent. Alex is so damn glad they've done the whole testing thing and can skip the condoms and get right to the fucking. He feels amazing as Paul finally pushes his cock all the way into him, pulls back, and thrusts. Alex moans, probably louder than he should, just before the headboard slams into the wall.

"Oh shit," Paul half laughs against his back.

"Terrible choices," Alex manages. He's a little tipsy and a lot giddy. Apparently Paul is too because he goes for it, thrusting several more times and causing several more loud collisions of the bed and the wall. Laughing, Alex has to tell him to stop.

"We deserve to celebrate," Paul says even as he pulls out of Alex. He drags him into the center of the bed, turning him as he goes.

It's a decent idea — Alex sideways over the edge and Paul standing. Their momentum doesn't rock the bed into the wall this way, but the creaking is epic and the angle is bad. Eventually they wind up on the floor, laughing until Paul grabs Alex's hips hard.

Alex whines when Paul gets distracted by how quickly he can raise marks on his skin. He just wants to get fucked. Paul always, *always* wants to play first, whether it's to tease or paint him with scratches and even the faint bruises of his fingers. Alex doesn't mind — it feels amazing. He's grateful his skin is fragile enough to lead Paul into this thing and also, it seems, to stop him from ever going too far with it. Paul has never hurt him in a way he doesn't like.

But Alex has been made impatient as much or more than he's been designed to bruise, and oh, he loves Paul, but he is infuriating. Eventually, after he's begged enough, Paul grabs him by the hips as if they were grooved to his fingers and fucks into him from behind. Alex pants against the floorboards, ancient and smooth under his cheek.

When he comes, loose-limbed and messy across the floor and the edge of a knotted rag rug, it feels like an offering to the house.

"That's going to be awkward tomorrow," Alex manages once they find their way off the floor. It's dangerously tempting to drag the duvet off the bed and sleep there. Paul laughs as he cleans them up.

"I don't think I care." Paul frowns a little at the marks he's left. They both know those are more likely to deepen than fade with the day to come.

◆

After Paul hangs up from the third phone call he's gotten over lunch in the kitchen, Alex asks, "Should we talk about going home early?" He doesn't want to, but Paul's show is everything to him, and he deserves time to give it the attention it needs.

"No. Maybe. Probably," Paul says and frowns down at his phone. "We've been looking forward to this trip for a while."

"It's not a vacation if you're working the whole time."

"Does it bother you?"

Alex shrugs. "I get you no matter what."

They decide to stay. Extra time away from L.A. is worth the headache of Paul setting up shop in their room and not always being completely with his family.

The internet continues to be stupid, but Alex is happy to avoid it in favor of rambling around the property, alone when Paul's busy, with him when he's not. He loves the space and the quiet, and as spooky as so many parts of this place are — like the cricket barn and the pond that tried to drown Paul — he enjoys it.

Halfway through the week, he gets the call from his agent, Vanessa. The news isn't bad, but the call is somber. *Fourth* has been renewed, which is a relief. The terms of the renewal, however, throw everything out of whack.

"Victor only wanted another year, you know, like a normal person," Alex tells Paul, lying with his arms folded under his chin, stretched out on the bed in their room while Paul sits on the chair in the corner with his laptop propped up on his knees. "We got five more arcs."

"That's more than a year."

"But what happens after that?" Alex asks. A season and change makes no sense as a deal if it's not a clear message that the end is coming. Victor, he suspects, is furious.

"I wish I knew."

It's solving one uncertainly only by adding another. Now instead of fretting but not really worrying over the future of *The Fourth Estate*, they're facing down the prospect of it actually coming to an end one day. A world in which Victor and the studio disagree over what should happen to the show is not a stable world. Alex can feel the future starting to shift.

"I still have to go to fucking upfronts," he complains.

Paul laughs, until Alex reminds him that he has to go this year, too. And since they aren't on the same network, they won't be going together.

◆

On their last afternoon in South Carolina, blessedly uninterrupted by phone calls, Paul tells his mom about his show *Winsome, AZ* as they sit around the living room with the windows open and an ancient box fan whirring comfortingly.

She's interested in all the details of the production company he and Victor have formed to create the show: Paul has sixty percent ownership and creative control. Victor does not, but Paul gets to lean on Victor's connections and resources. Victor also gets to be sure Paul is actually out of his nest. The setup is a little unusual, but Paul is glad of it because everything is also a little terrifying. He hopes that if he works as hard as he can and has just enough luck, they can actually make his show work.

"What's it about?" his mom finally asks.

On the couch, Jake drowsing on his lap, Alex snorts.

Beth raises an eyebrow at both of them. "Yes?"

Paul says, "It's about a girl named Melissa who graduates high school —"

"This is Darcy DeRosier?" his mom asks. The name of Paul's lead actress has cropped up in phone calls.

"Yeah. She graduates high school, super smart, can't afford college, so gets a day job at a 7-11 and starts a business."

"That's a way to put it," Alex teases.

Paul smiles fondly at him. It's not like the subject of *Winsome, AZ* — named for the tiny crossroads town in the middle of nowhere it's set in — is one he's embarrassed about, since he's *running a show about it*, but this is his mom and Alex is being a shit.

"The town's on a truck route. Where there are truckers, there are prostitutes. Melissa decides she's the businesswoman to make an efficient empire out of all the inventory. Most of them are old enough to be her mother. Drama, black comedy, and strong female characters ensue." Paul loves talking about his story. He's spent more time than he cares to think about pitching various permutations of the idea to so many people.

"My son is running a show about whores," his mom says somewhere between amused and horrified.

Paul nods. Alex cackles.

She sighs and leans her cheek on her fist. "I won't say I'm not proud of you. Or that it doesn't sound fascinating. But it would be so much easier to watch if I didn't know you were running it, Paul."

By the end of the conversation Jake is asleep on Alex's lap, and Paul pulls out his phone to take a picture. It's not a conversation they're even close to having, but Alex with his nephew is just lovely.

"Going to post that one too?" Alex asks, voice quiet for the sake of the sleeping kid.

"No, this one's just for me," Paul says.

Alex smiles softly.

Paul's mom gestures him into the hallway.

"Well done, Paul," she says with a nod of her head back to Alex.

Paul smiles, so fond. "I don't know what I'd do without him."

5

As soon as they get back from South Carolina, almost before they're done unpacking, Paul starts office hunting.

The offices they used while shooting the pilot had been painfully temporary and aren't extensive enough for everyone. Not now that they're actually a real show with a real crew and cast and a full writing and production team. The list of individuals Paul is responsible for grows daily, and he starts to understand better some of Victor's neuroses when it comes to taking care of all of his people. They're here because of him, and Paul really does not want to fuck any of this up.

He feels like he's on his second chance already. The first pilot he had written — the one Victor helped him pitch more than a year ago after he and Alex had tumbled back together — had died before it had even been filmed. Now that he has other people's jobs and lives depending on *Winsome* succeeding, it's even scarier. That Alex has made clear that their mutual, yet separate, success and ambition is key to Paul getting the future he imagines for them, only ups the pressure.

At least things feel just a bit more certain when they find a space that works and start moving in.

The first time Paul visits his new office after he signs the lease, he spends five minutes standing in the middle of the empty space, spinning slowly on the spot and trying to take it all in. This is his. Paul's not sharing it with anyone else, and Victor, as a minority partner in *Winsome*'s production company, can use the admittedly shabby conference room when he visits. It's not a dream, or a bargain with Alex, or a favor handed down from Victor. This has four walls and a roof and it's real.

He feels as victorious as he did the moment he'd gotten the phone call saying this was going to happen. He takes a picture and sends it to Alex and to his mom.

◆

As Paul gets his working life in order, Alex spends his time sorting out his own next steps for the summer. He sits down with Margaret to talk about creating a brand for himself outside of *The Fourth Estate*. *Paradise Square* had been a cool thing he'd gotten to do because he was the guy from *Fourth*. If he wants to keep working, Alex needs to expand his opportunities.

Looking at life after *Fourth* means looking seriously at other projects now that have the potential to conflict with his shooting schedule, which remains in constant flux as Victor battles the season schedule out with the network.

"Victor will kill me," Alex says darkly to Margaret. It's not a happy prospect to consider. But he has to learn how to tell the world he's someone to watch regardless of *Fourth*'s fate.

"You haven't made any decisions yet," she says.

Alex shrugs. He doesn't have to explain to her how much, given circumstances, it's intent not outcome that matters.

The conversation ends with a new media plan that includes more press than he'd normally do for the ramp up to the new cycle. The prospect is annoying, but it will at least keep him busy while they wait for filming to start.

♦

The interviews, once he starts them over the next few weeks, are generally business as usual, but someone always asks about the fucking gun. Alex enjoys staring down the interviewer who asks him how he'd learned to shoot without a father at home.

"My mother taught me," he says. By a supreme act of will he doesn't add, "*Asshole.*"

But then they ask about his sister and growing up in poverty with weapons. Alex is sharp with his refusal to discuss that. Guns are bad enough. There are way too many reasons he never wants to talk about knives in kitchens or criminal records right now. Or ever.

His mom sees the interview and calls him, which leads to a long, strange conversation that touches things they've never really talked about. In the end, she asks how South Carolina had been, aside from the gun.

"Good," he says. The parts that he can tell her about were, and he doesn't want to talk about the rest.

"You and Paul aren't going to visit here much, are you?"

"No," he says, and then, "I'm sorry," because he is. For her feelings, more than any regret he himself has about Indiana. Laura tried to give Alex the best chance to get out of the hell that is their hometown, but that doesn't mean she's happy he's fled so very permanently.

◆

Alex goes out to lunch with Liam a couple of weeks after he gets back from South Carolina. They go to a little restaurant that has too much quinoa on the menu for Alex's taste, but it's small and they're not any more likely to be photographed together here than anywhere else.

After they order, Liam dances around the gun thing again. He's as twitchy and uncomfortable as Alex has ever seen him about anything, but he still can't seem to articulate why he's so upset.

Alex eventually gets the conversation away from guns. When Liam mentions that Carly's been house hunting, Alex asks if that means they're finally moving in together. They've been engaged for a year, but without a date set Alex has been starting to wonder if they would even cohabitate after the wedding.

After a rambling and surprisingly knowledgeable digression into some of the more arcane aspects of real estate — Alex has no idea why he knows or cares so much about floodplains and chalks it up to yet another random Liam thing — Liam asks how Paul and Alex's trip down South went.

"There was the creepy, haunted pond," Alex says. "That sort of set the tone."

He has no interest in discussing any of the things Paul had finally confessed to him there, even with Liam. After their brief and ill-fated *thing* together —

Alex still doesn't know what to call it — he trusts Liam more than anyone except Paul. Annoying as he can be, there's a bond between them now that goes beyond friendship.

But Alex suspects there's something in the dark history of the Marion farm, of which he has to acknowledge he's probably only gotten the first hints, that will appeal to Liam. After all, Liam once managed to sort of seduce Alex with trivia about *The Exorcist*.

Liam frowns. "Haunted pond?"

"Yeah. Paul said something grabbed him in it when he was a kid. I couldn't get him to go swimming," Alex opines.

"Why is it haunted? Did someone die in it?" Liam's bright blue eyes are wide, and he tugs at his too-shaggy dark curls.

Alex shrugs. "Maybe?" He'd meant this as a funny story to entertain and interest Liam, but he looks unnerved beyond what seems to Alex to be any reasonable proportion. "Why? It was just one of those things that happens to kids."

Liam shakes his head. "My grandparents passed away when I was like, thirteen. Back to back to back. It was kind of a mess and they didn't have living wills and we had to, like, decide stuff for them. Just because somebody can't talk doesn't mean they don't want things or can't feel things." Liam takes a deep breath and is briefly fascinated by his hands. "It was not a good time. I got really hung up on the details. So I don't do well with death," he says, sounding a bit exasperated with himself. "Or swimming," he adds with a rueful laugh.

6

Sunday brunches are one of the things that Paul tries to keep constant in his increasingly hectic schedule. Alex has long since stopped going regularly for a variety of reasons, including wanting more time for climbing and Gemma and way less time with Brian. But Paul still likes to put in an appearance when he can. Also, Shawna harasses him constantly via text about it. Mostly he enjoys them. This week, there's an odd sort of bittersweetness when Craig is there with Beau *and* his new boyfriend.

On his way out of the restaurant, Paul's phone chimes. It's from Alex, a picture from the top of whatever giant rock he's decided needs climbing today.

On top of the world, it says. *Wish you were here.*

Paul smiles as he types back, *If I were there you'd be only halfway up the mountain.*

He climbs with Alex occasionally, but he's not as good on the rocks and usually ends up slowing them down. It drives Alex — who always pushes for higher, faster, scarier — nuts.

I'd get to watch you from up here. Great views.

Paul chuckles. *Just come home in one piece. Then you can enjoy the views all you want.*

I always do.

◆

Alex gets home not long after Paul, happy and relaxed as he usually is after a climb. Paul decides he has plenty of time to take Alex back to bed before he has to get started on work for the day.

After, Paul gets his laptop and sits in the armchair with his feet on the bed, going through his email. Alex sits against the pillows working his way through a new set of knots he's learning for climbing. Todd, who crept in earlier when they had been distracted and now refuses to be dislodged, sits on the open book next to him, eyes fixed on the rope in Alex's hands and his tail twitching.

Paul watches them both. Quiet moments like this are always precious in their lives, and they don't get enough of them.

Eventually he asks, "Do you want to stay for the party next week?"

He hopes Alex will say yes. Thanking the pilot team and getting everyone ready for the upcoming half-season — and the hoped-for full-season order — means a get-together. This time Paul isn't acting as a proxy for Victor in keeping a team human: This is *his* team. While Paul has never had Alex's uneasiness in crowds, things are easier with him by his side. Plus, Paul wants to share this moment of triumph of bringing the *Winsome* team together in their house.

Alex considers for a moment, then looks up from his knots. "No," he says. "It's your empire, not ours."

Paul supposes the decision makes sense. Alex draws focus in any room he's in, and, aside from living with the showrunner, he has nothing to do with *Winsome*. It's just one more part of the ongoing conversation of how much they are willing to let their professional and their personal lives overlap. As much as Paul knows that this is how the business works — and how much it benefits neither of them to be seen as fucking their way to relevance — he still wishes he could have Alex next to him for everything.

But he knows — and has always known — that is never going to be the case. So he says, "All right," and stands so he can lean over and kiss him.

Alex kisses him back and goes returns his knots.

♦

The night of the party, Alex vanishes to go out with Gemma, and Paul hosts his people, crew and actors alike. Because of the nature of *Winsome* and all its drama about the desires of the aggressively average-at-best, the divide between the two is less obvious than it could be.

Victor had opted out from the party, throwing his hands up and repeating *minority partner* yet again. Then he gave Paul some good advice and reminded him that in this, Paul is his boss and not the other way around. Besides, Victor said, he has plans. From the look of his shark smile, Paul could only assume that meant Liam, or making some poor *Fourth* writer's life hell.

Paul thinks his cast is obscenely talented, completely gorgeous, and real in a way that's brave and often difficult in L.A. Looking at Ruth and Terry and Annette, it's obvious to him that they're stronger than him and all his compulsive exercise. All the charisma in the world doesn't change the deep lines and sad eyes that are just the shape of Ruth's face;

Terry's beer gut is completely non-optional; and Annette may be the prettiest of them, but Paul's seen her resume. He knows the sort of roles Hollywood makes black women play. In a way, *Winsome*'s no better for her, but he's trying. At least everyone on his show is a whore.

Darcy is the room's one traditional beauty. As she bounces around the event, her blonde curls flying and her green eyes sparkling, it's obvious to Paul and probably everyone else that she knows it and thinks it a moral good. Sometimes he worries that she has a crush on him, but mostly he knows it must be hard to be eighteen in L.A. and career-oriented and successful as opposed to party-happy and insane. Paul likes her, but she makes him nervous in a way oddly not dissimilar to Liam. He assumes it's the child star thing.

When he's not playing good host and Darcy isn't trailing along in his wake, he hangs out with Ruth, whose soothing, not-unkind deadpan is decent at settling him in Alex's absence.

Ultimately, it's a long night but a good one, and at many points Paul looks around the room and remembers the first pilot party he ever went to, hosted by Victor. So many things started that night for all of them. He wonders what things are beginning now.

◆

Paul's standing at the sink rinsing out dishes, the house finally empty and quiet around him, when Paul hears Alex's key in the lock.

"Hey, you," Alex breathes in his ear as he slides his arms around Paul's waist.

"Hey." Paul leans back against him and sets the down dish he's holding. Alex is hot-skinned and a little sweaty from wherever he'd gone with Gemma. He's irresistible.

"Mhmm," Alex presses his face into Paul's shoulder, his damp hair rubbing against Paul's cheek. "Missed you."

"Missed you too," Paul says. Alex has his hands on his hips swaying them both, and it's hard to think of anything but him.

"How was your party?"

"Mm." Paul turns around into Alex's arms and rests their foreheads together. "A resounding success. Everyone has been thanked and now hopefully feels appreciated."

"I'm sure they do," Alex says.

Paul groans. Alex wrapped around him like this shorts out everything else in his brain. "I want to take you to bed."

"How traditional." Alex bites his ear.

"Fuck, you want it," Paul breathes.

"I want you," Alex breathes as he walks them towards and then up the stairs.

When they get to the door of their bedroom Paul grabs his face and kisses him. Some traditions are damn well worth keeping.

7

Now that Paul has a large and growing production team, he should be able to ease up a little and let his people take over. But *Winsome* is compelling, he is enamored of the work, and there is always some new and exciting thing he can give his attention to. Paul does his best to balance the reality of *Winsome* with his life with Alex, but it's the nature of the business that it's a losing battle. It doesn't take long before he's working six a.m. to six p.m. in his new offices before coming home for dinner and another several hours of work in the loft space that used to be Gemma's living area.

He freaks out before every table read over scripts that are done and solid and *fine*. Victor always shields his writers from so much network bullshit. Now Paul knows he must pay the debt by taking those hits for his own team.

The problem is, he's convinced he can somehow get the scripts tight enough that there won't be any hits, but it doesn't work that way. Network executives object to things to remind writers and showrunners who God really is. The battles Paul is determined to fight are largely losing ones.

As difficult as things are now — Paul is getting five hours of sleep on a good night — he knows they will become next to impossible once Alex starts filming again. There's a difference between seeing each other when only one of them is fully functional and never seeing each other conscious at all.

At least Alex has finally learned to cook something other than pasta. Which Paul finds himself enjoying for reasons that range from having one less thing to worry about to thinking that Alex looks absolutely adorable in their kitchen puttering around in a stupid apron Carly bought him as a joke. When Paul is foolish enough to tell Alex this, he gets a dry and unpleasant comment about housewives and kept boys. It screams of some sort of defensive inner narrative that Paul is hesitant to inquire about. He doesn't have time for a crisis — or a lack of indulgence — from Alex right now.

Unfortunately, that means he also doesn't have time to indulge Alex, and that's far less good. Filming on *Fourth* is still a couple of weeks from resuming, and Alex is restless and bored. Sure, he climbs as much as he can make time for between the meetings and interviews and events that pepper his days. But the act of making magic on film is what drives him. Without that center, he's clearly a little bit lost.

And Alex lost has always been, from even before it was a legitimate option, an Alex who looks to Paul. Which means he interrupts Paul's home office time constantly.

Paul knows to grit his teeth, smile, and be grateful for something in his life that is not *Winsome*. But it's hard. With every day seemingly bringing a new crisis, it approaches impossible. Paul has no idea how far Alex's patience is going to ultimately extend.

◆

Just because Victor opted out of the *Winsome* party doesn't mean he has any intention of opting out of his own yearly event for *Fourth*. The party at his house for the cast, crew, and staff is one of the rare times Victor allows anyone but his intimates into his home. It is, by necessity, much larger than the event Paul hosted.

This year, it's also considerably less happy. Were it a smaller event, Victor probably would make a speech about everyone's concerns, about his own unhappiness with the network and what they have to work with. He'd spend some time talking about how this is going to change all of their lives as they figure out how to tell the story they want to tell with a whole new set of constraints. But Victor's house is currently packed with people and all their attendant plus-ones, and Victor wants to say nothing about what he has planned — or his own anger — anywhere it might leak.

The semi-official silence on the topic doesn't stop people from talking in corners, and the whole crowd feels uneasy. Which makes Victor even more angry with the network. His people are good — no, his people are the *best* — and while Hollywood offers no one any guarantees, they deserve better than this strange situation.

♦

"Jesus, Alex, your back," Paul says into his ear as they strip out of jeans and T-shirts down to their swim trunks at Victor's house for the *Fourth* party. Alex knows he's covered in scratches from Paul. This isn't the first time the ease with which his skin marks has made things conspicuous, but it might be the most awkward.

Alex cranes his neck to look even though it's useless. He'd already caught sight of it in the mirror this morning. "It's fine," he shrugs.

Paul presses his palm against his lower back and looks worried. And guilty. "Are you okay?"

"It's *fine*," Alex repeats. He doesn't want to start this discussion. The marks aren't anything new. "But if Liam gives me shit for it, I'm blaming it all on you."

"I would hope," Paul says. Alex bumps his hip before leading the way to the pool deck. Paul doesn't seem to know whether to hover or give him his space. The third time he asks if Alex is okay or if he needs anything, Alex huffs and pushes at his shoulder.

"Oh my God, I'm fine, Paul. Believe me, I'll tell you when I need you," he adds in a whisper, and gives him a look on the right side of wicked when Paul's eyes go wide. Finding new ways to play with his boyfriend is a joy.

When Paul doesn't move from the spot Alex adds, "I see Carly — I'm going to go say hi." He kisses his cheek before he saunters to the edge of the pool, where she's floating, lazy and regal, on a bright green raft.

Across the pool from her Liam sits fully dressed on the lounger furthest back from the water. He gives Alex a wave hello.

♦

Paul stares after Alex. He has no idea what to make of any of it.

Victor appears suddenly at his elbow. "How's he doing?"

"He's good," Paul says cautiously. He's beginning to notice that Victor never asks after Alex when they are in *Winsome*-related space.

Alex jumps into the pool and disappears under the surface, kicking his way toward Carly. Paul is still wary of saying anything of great detail about his boyfriend to Victor. Especially when he's not entirely sure how, exactly, Alex is, other than happy, which shouldn't throw him as much as it does.

"And how are you, other than taking it out on him?"

Victor sounds amused enough that Paul doesn't bother to engage the insinuation. "Good. Okay. You know how busy. I don't know how you manage to sleep."

"I don't." Victor shrugs. Paul wishes that felt more like a joke; he's exhausted. "It's not going to get easier for you two once *Fourth* ends."

Paul has heard plenty about the uncertain fate of the show from Alex. He's felt superstitious about asking Victor about it, however. He doesn't work on the show anymore, but hearing it stated that directly makes him feel like some beloved relative is terminally ill. He wonders if Victor is beside himself and tamping it down in their twice-weekly calls as he tries to keep Paul's sanity afloat.

"His job, not mine," Paul says.

"Mhmmm. And what do you think he's going to do once he's done with that?"

"Victor, the first time you offered me advice about Alex, it didn't exactly go as planned. The Chinese walls you and I have going on right now?

Work really well. Let's not tempt that. And how do you even know what's going to happen?"

"He's thinking about it," Victor says.

Paul has no idea what *it* is and isn't sure he particularly wants to find out.

"Nothing is certain," Victor muses. "And Alex is very good at making his own way through uncertainty."

"I've noticed," Paul says, looking for some sort of foothold in the conversation.

"Notice better," Victor says before heading off toward the corner where Liam is.

Paul sighs and goes to look for a drink. Victor is exhausting.

◆

Alex hauls himself up onto Carly's raft while she laughs and curses and threatens dire retribution if he dunks her. He doesn't, though, just stretches out next to her while she complains about him dripping everywhere.

"It's a pool, Carly," he snarks. She pushes wet hair out of his face so he can tuck his head into her shoulder without getting her too cold and damp. "There's supposed to be water."

"Yes. In the pool. Not on me."

"Diva."

"Yup. Baby boy, what happened to your back?" she asks, feigned concern all over her face. She wraps an arm around his shoulders and cranes her neck to get a better look.

Alex smirks.

Carly runs a thumbnail along a scratch that ends in a bruise on Alex's shoulder. Some of the marks are fresh, while others look older. It's quite a patchwork. "Jesus. How'd you talk him into that?"

Alex shrugs, looking smug. "It's what we do."

"Well, that's hot," Carly says, tracing another scratch. "And mildly surprising. You gonna give me any good details?" Certainly, it's not a thing Paul ever did with her.

Alex snorts. "Unlikely."

"Well, that's a shame."

◆

It takes less than two hours for the party to go from nervous and falsely discreet business chatter to people happy to cut loose out of the public eye. Some get drunk fast, while others entertain themselves by ambushing colleagues and throwing them into the water. There's not a lot of overlap between the two groups thanks to the party two seasons ago when Victor made good on his threat to publicly humiliate anyone who attempted to drown in his pool.

The more fun people have, the less polite they get. As a cast and crew they already know way too much about each other even as they don't always like each other. Which is how Alex winds up, ridiculously, having to explain the state of his flesh to someone he neither knows well nor likes.

"Climbing mishap," Alex shouts across the pool area when one of the crew guys shouts something more than a bit obscene about the state of Alex's back.

"Didn't know rocks could fuck," Dan hollers back.

"Fuck off," Alex calls, his head still resting on Carly from where he's been zoning out from the rest of the party for as long as possible. There's an edge to his voice now that makes the words half question and half threat.

"Daniel, if you don't shut up I will not stop Alex from laying you out, and if you think he can't, you are far too stupid to work for me," Victor drawls, loudly, from the corner where he's still holding court with Liam. It shuts Dan — and everyone else — up.

Conversation quickly rushes back in, too fast and too loud, in an apparent collective attempt to forget Victor's rather relaxed, but perfectly sincere, threats.

"Thank you," Alex says crisply from the pool, the words for Victor only.

Victor shrugs. Inexplicably, Liam offers Alex a thumbs up.

"I don't understand anyone," Alex whines into Carly's neck.

◆

"Paul, come here," Victor says as Paul idles with a drink in his general vicinity, watching Carly experimentally pinch Alex in various places to see how easily he does or does not bruise.

As much as he's not in the mood for another unsettling conversation with Victor, Paul is happy to go. As a former colleague and potential source of work at a time of significant upheaval, most people here are being weird around him in a way he doesn't yet know how to navigate. For all the challenge of his presence, Victor is a known quantity and something of a refuge.

Victor shoos away the people he's been talking to at his approach. Paul fistbumps with Liam before he takes a seat on the edge of the lounger he's spread out on.

"We need to look at our teams and make some moves," Victor says without preamble.

Liam ignores them in favor of spinning a disc-shaped charm hanging from his latest ridiculous hipster necklace. This far into the party, he and Victor are the only ones not in swimsuits. Victor may be ordinary looking, with tan skin, plain black hair, and fine wrinkles around his mouth and eyes, but even in street clothes and surrounded by this much poolside Hollywood fabulousness, he radiates charisma.

"Like what?" Paul knows better than to agree to Victor's pronouncements without gathering additional information.

"We're not going head-to-head, and my fate may be sealed. Even if it's not, everyone thinks it is, so I need to consolidate. *Winsome* should staff up more. My problems are going to solve your problems."

"Did they cut your budget?"

"No, but I need to keep people from jumping ship."

"By gifting them to me in what seems like a creepy power grab?"

Victor shakes his head. "I recommend — and you hire — people I don't use all the time. You get a crack team. I get left with a team that assumes they are all my very special favorites. Everyone thinks our allied empires have done them a massive favor."

"And I owe you for life."

"You think you don't already?"

"I can't tell when you're joking," Paul says cautiously.

"At least I tell you what my intentions are."

"Fair."

"So what do you need that you haven't had the sense to tell me about yet?" Victor asks.

Paul has a list, and he and Victor work through it for about thirty minutes, Victor making occasional notes into his smart phone.

"I'll send you this later," he says, waggling the phone and then setting it down. "We'll get it done."

◆

After Carly loses Alex to a gaggle of people he can't ignore as much as he probably wants to, she wanders over to Liam's corner.

"Why so quiet?" she asks. It's one thing for Liam to hang back from the edge of the pool, but he's hardly talked to anyone all day, even Victor.

"Hard afternoon. Hard crowd." Liam frowns.

Carly scootches over to sit next to him on the lounger. "Everybody's pissy," she agrees.

"Yeah. Going back to work is not going to be fun."

"They'll be fine once they have a routine again." Carly combs her fingers back through his dark curls.

Liam's shoulders sag as he relaxes into the touch. "Maybe."

"Are you staying tonight?"

"Yeah. I think so." He shrugs. "Too many people for everybody."

"The worst is almost over."

"Shhhh, you'll jinx it," Liam admonishes. He catches her hand to kiss it obnoxiously.

"We'll live. Did you see Alex's back?" she asks. Despite the smiles, Liam is still tense and a subject change is clearly necessary.

Liam laughs and wraps his arms around her. "*Everybody's* seen Alex's back."

◆

Ellen, one of Victor's prized directors, laughs when Alex whines to her about being bored and wanting to go back to work. "Speak for yourself. The rest of us are going to miss being able to take a goddamned vacation."

"Our last vacation involved crickets. I'll be okay."

Ellen raises an eyebrow, but doesn't ask. "You think that now. See how you feel when you've shot two arcs back-to-back and there's still no end in sight. Insects will start to look good."

Alex laughs. He likes Ellen. She can be as sharp as he is and has none of Victor's more manipulative tendencies.

"We'll see," he says. Everyone else seems to know what the new deal means for them, but Alex is still deciding.

◆

Much later, when the crowd is starting to thin out, Carly drops heavily into the lounger next to Paul's. "Alex is a fucking beauty."

"Don't let him hear you say that," he says wryly. He looks across the pool to where Alex is standing in a little cluster of people, including Natalie and Raphael, two of his other co-stars. Paying his respects, probably. While there are a handful of people on the crew and in the cast Alex is genuinely friendly with, including Raph, Natalie is not one of them. Then again, Natalie isn't genuinely friendly with anyone as far as Paul has ever been able to tell.

"I already told him," Carly says.

"And he didn't shove you into the pool?" Paul asks.

Carly raises her eyebrows at Paul over the rim of her glass. "We have an understanding."

"You certainly looked like you were enjoying yourselves out there."

"Are you jealous?" Carly purrs and leans against Paul's shoulder.

"Of my ex-girlfriend and my current boyfriend?"

"Stranger things have happened. Actually...." Carly presses a finger to her lips in exaggerated thoughtfulness. Paul wonders how drunk she is. "That one isn't that strange."

"Maybe not in *your* life."

"He's very cute. And warm. And cuddly," she says. "I never see him stick close to you, I didn't think he had it in him."

"Should I be jealous?"

She lifts a shoulder. "I don't know. You can't say it's not a pretty picture."

"Picture, yes," he concedes, because as much as it is in the past, there really is something about Carly that had attracted him, and Alex is Alex. "Somehow I don't think he's really interested. Hell, I don't think it would even occur to him."

"Are you sure?"

There's both an offer and a tease in her voice. The conversation has officially become drunk and absurd, because there is nothing about the idea Carly is oh-so-coyly presenting that isn't working for him.

"Did he say something?" Paul doubts it. Alex does chase the new and the unknown, but this is a whole different place they're talking about.

"Alex never says anything."

"He does sometimes." Paul is extraordinarily pleased with himself for all the ways he's able to get Alex to speak.

"Oh, really?" Carly drawls.

"Maybe I should ask him," he says.

"I think you should." Carly rolls onto her side on her lounger and gives him a long look from under her eyelashes.

"This is ridiculous," Paul says with a disbelieving laugh.

"But it's hot," Carly counters.

Paul laughs loudly enough for Alex to catch the sound. He turns around from whatever conversation he's having to raise an eyebrow at him.

"Really fucking hot," Paul muses.

"Merely some food for thought, *darling*," Carly says in imitation of Victor's most condescending cadences.

Paul chuckles and lifts a hand to wave Alex over.

♦

"What?" Alex asks, amused and indulgent when he walks over and Paul grabs his hand.

"Carly and I were just talking about you," Paul tips his head toward Carly before he pulls Alex into his lap.

"Were you?" Alex leans lazily back against Paul's chest.

"Mhmmm. We had an idea."

"Do you want to hear it?" a giddy Carly asks.

Paul shoots her a look.

"Do I?" Alex watches as Paul slides a hand over his knee, intrigued just enough not to cut this off.

"I think so," Paul breathes.

Then, as Carly watches them both, he leans closer to whisper in Alex's ear. About Carly and how Alex would look with her, about what the three of them would look like together, and about how hot it would be if Alex were ever curious.

"You're not serious," Alex says.

Paul slides his hand higher on his leg. "Aren't I?"

Paul's tendency to tease has always frustrated and delighted Alex, but he has never offered anything he wasn't interested in. As insane as this idea is, it's on the table if Alex wants it to be.

"Think about it," Paul tells him.

The conversation is both compelling and a little unsettling, but Paul's hands are on Alex's thighs and his mouth is brushing his ear. Carly watches them with interest.

It's weird, but the weirdest thing is that he's not laughing off the idea. He's as eager as ever to play along with Paul's ideas to see how far they can explore together. But Alex is in a swimsuit, and he needs to get out of here before his humiliation escalates way beyond a scratched back.

"Bathroom," he says and bolts.

♦

"Alex," Victor says when the pool area is almost empty.

Alex looks up from where he's sitting next to Paul on the pool deck, both of them dangling their feet in the water and sitting in companionable silence while the sky fades from gold to black in the west. Liam, Alex notices, is up now, talking quietly to Carly by the door to the house.

Alex leaves Paul with a squeeze to his shoulder and joins Victor by the gate in the side yard, where Victor has one eye on the driveway as people leave. "What?"

"What have Paul and Carly been conspiring at?"

Alex squints evaluatively. "Nothing to do with you."

"Does it have something to do with you?"

"Yes."

"Okay," Victor drawls, stretching out the word 'til it snaps.

"I'm not going to tell you what it is," Alex says. Victor should know better than to expect him to.

"Have you told Paul what *you're* planning?"

Alex blinks at the sudden change in subject, but he's more than happy to move away from Victor inquiring after the drunken fantasies of his boyfriend. "How do you know what I'm planning?"

"You never get tired of testing." Victor turns away from Alex to shake hands with a pair on their way out. Alex smiles at them. Once they're out of earshot Victor turns back to him. "I told him to keep an eye on you."

"Victor," Alex says sharply, frowning. "I don't know what your deal with Liam and Carly is, and I don't care. But don't tell me what to do about Paul."

"I didn't," Victor says mildly.

"Or tell him what to do about me."

"I don't think he's going to make that mistake twice. I'm telling you this so you know what's going on."

"Am I supposed to thank you?"

Victor smiles dangerously. "It wouldn't be amiss. But no."

As much as Victor infuriates him, not even Alex is immune to the lure of that smile. "Then what is the point of this conversation, except to remind me of all the ways things tend to go wrong around here?"

Victor shrugs. "Make it big, Alex."

Alex doesn't respond verbally, just tips his head and smiles. Victor smiles back.

8

By the time everyone leaves, it's late and Victor's kitchen is a mess. In the morning, long before Liam has any intention of being awake, professionals will come and clean it, taking away the rental glassware and everything else. By the time Carly shows up for brunch, because Victor likes to putter around and make them omelets in the mornings after Liam stays, it will be as if the whole thing never happened. Until then Victor is, Liam knows, likely to be his usual slightly irritated and insomniac self. And for now it's just the two of them.

"I don't understand why you have these things at your house if you hate the invasion so much," Liam says, settling himself on Victor's couch. Victor pulls the blinds closed on the big sliding glass doors, shutting out the night.

They have been having this conversation for years, in part because it's one Liam knows how to have and in part because he's never gotten a satisfactory answer. Victor can say it's the done thing 'til he's blue in the face, but Liam thinks it's guilt and some sort of strange check-in with the universe: *Am I like other people now?*

"Because it would annoy me more to do it somewhere else, and my neighbors have the good sense to call the cops on the paps."

Liam nods. He's never met Victor's neighbors. On the odd terraced hills that are part of any celebrity-worthy neighborhood in L.A. that's not uncommon. He likes them all the more for their mix of invisibility and benevolence.

Liam scrolls through movie options on the flat screen as Victor drops onto the sofa, head resting on Liam's thigh. It's always movies and never TV because TV is work. Movies — too short to be anything but ephemeral, too outside of day-to-day life to define people's decades and desires — never are. They hold no professional interest for Victor and, generally, little personal interest. They're background noise and flickering lights while they make out until Victor gets too bored or Liam gets too desperate.

"You do realize this is just a very well-telegraphed cancellation notice," Victor says after twenty minutes of ignoring *Bladerunner* and not making out with Liam.

"Yes." Liam's voice is clipped because sometimes when Victor's upset he forgets it's a tuning issue with Liam and not an intelligence issue.

"You don't have to worry, though."

Liam huffs. "I've been on TV since I was a kid and still get checks from stuff I shot when I was eleven. I only work because I like it. Yay, another syndication deal." There are ways that Victor fusses over him that are essential to his being. This is not one of them.

"I will always hire you, you know."

"I know. You shouldn't tell me that when you have your head in my lap. People will think things."

"Terrible habit," Victor drawls. "They should stop."

Liam raises his eyebrows. "Do you need to be irritable and pretend I'm lost without you —"

"You would be lost without me," Victor deadpans. "And Carly."

"Or are you just bored?" Liam continues, as if he's not been interrupted by Victor's finely honed and mostly joking cattiness.

Victor crosses his arms over his chest and drums his fingers against his lips. "I don't know what's next. I don't know how to exact vengeance. I don't know how to take care of you all. And I definitely have yet to figure out how to blow this up in the network's face."

"Give it an hour," Liam says.

Victor finally deigns to sit up and kiss him.

♦

Liam leads them to the guest room he's come to think of as his, although he keeps nothing of his there and there is nothing in it to indicate it has any particular owner. It's just white. White walls, rustic white-painted bedframe, fluffiest white comforter on earth. Victor used to frown over it, saying he'd always meant to do something with the room and then stopped, fascinated at the accidental cross between minimalist modernism and princess fantasy.

To Liam's knowledge, no one else ever stays there. There's another guest room for visitors that aren't him. As far as he has ever been informed, Victor has no other lovers. Liam isn't sure if he's technically supposed to consider himself Victor's lover at all, because he just doesn't…they just don't.

Victor does *to*, not *with*. Liam has never found it odd so much as interesting. Which is, he supposes, why they are six years into this and going nowhere. Liam fell in love with Carly when she thought it was lovely, and they are now some ever more tangled snake of a family. He's not sure where Alex fits in, although he knows that he does. Paul either comes with Alex or was already here; he's not sure about that either.

They start the way they usually do. Victor kneels beside the bed in which Liam lies naked and jerks him off, while Liam begs for kisses and Victor reminds him how much he likes to watch and how little he likes most everything else. It's not voyeurism, Victor's told him — not sexual voyeurism, anyway. It's just Liam's face, apparently, his liquid blue eyes, and the way that in sex he loses the language through which he has taught himself to interact with the world. Hearing Victor talk about it is frightening sometimes, but that doesn't make it less true. Liam knows his mimicry falls away when he is in bed with anyone. Perhaps it happens so acutely with Victor because of the degree to which they are not, in this act, in the same place at the same time.

Tonight, though, Liam wants more. He's feeling things and doesn't have the words for them, so he needs his hands. When he tries to sit up and puts a hand on Victor's shoulder to kiss him harder, Victor pushes him gently back.

Liam frowns, but Victor shakes his head. Liam wants to obey more than he wants to push, at least for now, so he lets himself fall back on the pillow.

Victor runs a hand over Liam's forehead, and nods before kissing him again.

After Liam comes, Victor kisses him until his mouth goes drowsy. Occasionally Victor's breath even hitches when Liam isn't interested in being tired at all, but he pulls away and smiles as if everything in this world is a trick of the light.

♦

Victor excuses himself when Liam is halfway to unconsciousness and returns carrying too many things: His laptop bag slung on his shoulder, a damp towel to clean them up, a glass of water to leave on the night table by Liam's bed, his metronome, and coffee in a travel mug for himself — he's learned the hard way about spilling things in this ever so white room.

He has no interest in what other people consider sexual activity for himself, but he's happy to provide experiences like this for Liam so long as he never has to be subject to the sensations of sex. It is a thing that is true and that is complicated only because the rest of the world — and the way Liam is wired to do love and relationships — make it that way. But Liam is beautiful always and most beautiful when he wants. He's never asked for anything Victor couldn't give him. Yet.

Victor has no idea how long that can last. But once he is sure Liam is settled — clean and unconscious, duvet pulled up around his shoulders and face half buried in it — Victor sits on the floor, back to the wall, laptop open on his legs stretched out in front of him, and writes to the soft tick of the metronome and the sound Liam's breath and his often fussy sleep.

Sometime late in the night, Liam wakes enough to ask what he's working on. Victor shrugs in the dark glow of his words, smiles, and says, "Whatever's next."

9

Because nothing about scheduling is ever easy, Alex's upfronts obligations are at the beginning of the last week of May, and Paul's are at the end. Neither of them can afford to take a full week away from L.A., and Paul is generally surly about the entire thing. With the ongoing death of pilot season, the sanctity of upfronts increasingly seems nonsensical to him.

Paul watches dolefully as Alex packs and promises they'll figure something out in the middle. Although they both know there's a damn good chance they'll be together for little more than a couple hours between when Alex returns and when Paul has to leave.

Alex shrugs it off. When he has to travel for work he tends to go quiet. Paul worries sometimes that's as much about what happened when they were still trying to get their shit together and Alex had to be out of town for two months, as it is about Alex needing to protect himself from the onslaught of his life.

Paul doesn't even have time to take him to the airport. It's just as well. It's not like they can kiss goodbye there without being documented, and Paul knows Alex hates that. Some days, every fan is a thief.

♦

Alex texts Paul briefly when he lands to let him know he's safe. He follows up an hour later with *I'm on a bus*. It takes Paul a full ten minutes to realize Alex isn't taking public transit. He's being weirded out by New York being covered in ads promoting upfronts, some of them with his face on them, as if they weren't an industry thing civilians shouldn't give a shit about.

I wish I were on a bus, Paul texts back.

No you don't.

On a bus to you.

It takes five days. You really don't.

♦

New York is, as ever, bracing. Alex is scheduled hour by hour — and in some cases, minute by minute — for his three days in town. Media; meetings; upfronts for fans; upfronts proper; an after-party that's still an official party he's contractually obligated to be at; dinner with Victor, Liam, Natalie, Raphael, and the rest of the people doing the roadshow that someone will surely call the paparazzi about; and then six whole hours to sleep before he has to get up and do it all again. Liam loves it, Victor devours it, and Natalie measures it in obsessing over her gains in social media followers. Alex endures it. He does his best to never look ungrateful, because he isn't, but he's pretty sure he's more offended by the process than anyone else involved.

The first night, when they've already been up for way too long, they all have dinner together, public and intentional. The paparazzi are outside the restaurant. Alex assumes that's Natalie's doing until Victor gives him a sharp look as he holds the door to usher his ducklings in. Victor seats Liam on his right, as he always does — Alex makes a point to notice these things now — and Natalie gets pride of place on his left. That leaves Alex either having to make conversation with her throughout the meal or sit next to Liam, which would be fine except for the fact that the internet exists.

Alex lets Raphael take one for the team and situates himself between him and Liam with a grimace. Raphael gives him a look back, clearly amused at the proceedings he doesn't particularly want to be part of either. Raphael may play Zach's chief rival on *Fourth*, but he's easily the mellowest of the cast present, and Alex is glad for his buffer of sanity.

Throughout the meal that follows, everyone avoids eye contact in favor of looking over their conversation partners' shoulders to see who might be listening to or documenting them. It's a strangely false performance of intimacy considering the many very genuine connections between them. Nearly three years into all of this, Alex still feels out of place at these occasions.

"Stop looking at your cutlery like it's going to stab you," Liam teases, kicking him under the table.

Alex has to force himself not to startle. Sometimes Liam is uncanny. "I'm trying to remember which fork to use," he snaps back.

"Hey," Liam says softly.

Alex sighs. "I'd be more comfortable being stared at while doing normal things if it were more explicit," he says by way of apology. He still hates when people gawk to his face, but at least it's better than this strange theater.

Liam shrugs. "If people were capable of being more explicit, they would be."

◆

"I would like to inform you that former child stars are very, very hard to deal with," Paul says when Alex calls him late that night. He's upstairs in his office, going over notes and scripts for tomorrow's filming.

"Did you have dinner with Liam too?" Alex asks dryly.

"You had dinner with Liam?" Paul tries to keep the alarm out of his voice. Alex will likely be pissed if he expresses displeasure at the idea, and Paul doesn't particularly want to have that argument right now.

"With everyone," Alex corrects. "I'm sure the pics are on the internet by now if you care."

"Do you look cute? Then I care."

"I always look cute. And slightly surly. What did Darcy do, and do you want me to talk to her?" Alex asks.

When he had initially cast the Broadway starlet as an eighteen-year-old girl determined to make an empire out of a truck-stop prostitution ring in Nowhere, America, Paul had despaired of how to give Darcy all of the background information she'd need to play the part. Eventually, he'd asked Alex to talk to her. They connected fiercely enough that they have kept up a semi-regular email correspondence since. Paul is pretty sure Alex likes her because neither of their lives make any sense.

"She sent her parents a script," Paul says. "Which she now knows is a thing she should not do."

"Shit. Seriously?" Alex, reasonably, sounds incredulous.

"Yeah. She does even better puppy eyes than Liam when she's getting yelled at, by the way. It's unnerving. But apparently darling Darcy also never told her folks what *Winsome* was about."

"Oh God."

"Yeah. They are now distraught at her and pissed at me because how could there be *hookers, Paul,* and how will Darcy's baby sister ever get to play little Cosette now?" Paul sighs heavily. "They're fucking nightmares and don't understand that she's eighteen and that they are not her managers or agents."

Alex laughs. "Are you going to have to change your phone number? And will you remember to give me the new one?"

"I love you," Paul says, amused and deeply sincere. "Come home."

"Soon as I can. Although we're gonna be ships passing in the night."

"Don't remind me."

◆

Victor thinks about hiring a car, but there's a certain mercy to dealing with Penn Station and taking the train. It's ordinary and grounding. How people live and move who are of not Los Angeles remains of fundamental importance to him, even if he exposes himself to it not nearly enough.

Besides, anything but the train, and Nigel will mock him. This isn't a new condition, but as fond as Victor is — Nigel is family as much as anyone — there have always been times he's wanted to strangle him for insisting on acting like a big brother. Just because Victor ultimately has little physical interest in Nigel — and Nigel is stunning enough, well-built and with luminously dark skin, that if Victor doesn't want to fuck him he doesn't want to fuck *anyone* — doesn't mean he thinks of him as a brother. It annoys him that Nigel thinks he's the wiser of the pair.

Mainly because, on some level, it's not untrue. Victor goes to Nigel for advice, and Nigel rarely returns the favor. They may have wrestled through Victor's asexuality together, but Nigel's interest in men, greater interest in women, and ridiculously perfect marriage to a wife far prettier than Victor thinks he deserves were all met with a shrug from both of them. Nigel's not the only person Victor's ever been lost in front of, but he's the only one who knows it. Mostly, Victor thinks the power differential is hilarious. The alternative would most likely be damaging to their friendship and many of the carefully constructed architectures of their lives.

So Victor takes the damn train, lest Nigel let it all go to his head.

◆

After dinner and once the kids have been put to bed, Priscilla sits in the living room with Victor and chitchats while Nigel fusses with tea in the kitchen. It's such an absurd thing to Victor and irrelevant to the worlds both of them have come from. Beyond their shared personal history, his bond with Nigel has absolutely been predicated on the fact that they are both men of color from working-class families that never understood their passions or had much kindness for their empires of lies. Nigel is in advertising, which is exactly like making TV shows but with much shorter episodes.

Victor smiles and hopes he doesn't look uncomfortable. He's known Priscilla for years; he likes her. She is as aware of his various personal and professional aggravations as anyone, but all of that is, and has always been, because she is Nigel's wife. Victor doesn't keep secrets from Nigel because he can't and never could. During their failed hookup the first time he'd been in New York for upfronts, he'd tumbled out everything he'd been struggling with for years.

But Priscilla, who Nigel didn't even meet until a year later, knows everything only because she's there and lovely. So Victor can stall her, even if just for a little while. With everything roiling in his head, he's happy to do it for as long as he can.

"He knows he doesn't have to do that, right?" Victor asks Pris at one point.

She laughs. "It makes him happy."

"Allow a man his pleasures," Nigel says, entering with a tray and cups, everything arranged to precision. It's the attention to details of the sort that no one else thinks to care about that is one of the things that makes he and Victor friends.

"So, how are all of your charges?" Nigel asks now that they're not at a dinner table populated by impressionable young minds. "No more fucking in the trailers?"

"More or less," Victor says half-heartedly. "No one's making any headlines they shouldn't."

"How's Liam?"

"Fine," Victor says.

"That's a remarkably few number of words for your favorite," Nigel says.

"Upfronts is an ordeal. Everyone's worn out."

"Bullshit. You never sleep. Is he not handling it well?" Nigel asks, conspicuously leading.

Priscilla uncrosses and recrosses her legs in the corner of the couch, the rustling of her dress commentary on Nigel's benign query that's anything but.

"He's handling it beautifully," Victor says. Liam's conduct — in public, at least — is as much a concern as it ever is, which is usually not much. The world finds him charming, and he has remained, somehow, impervious to scandal through being a very good judge of people.

"Is it Alex again?"

Victor laughs. "No. Thank God. Not that the two of them did not make my life very interesting for a month, but no. You know Liam's engaged."

"It was in *People*," Nigel nods, waiting for Victor to get to the point.

"You don't read *People*."

Pris props her temple on her fingers, a smile tugging at the corner of her mouth. "He thumbs through it at the grocery store."

◆

Victor had called Nigel in the whirl of media attention that had followed Liam's surprise announcements over a year ago that he was, one, bi, and two, engaged to Carly. Nigel may not approve of the way Victor sometimes conducts his relationships, in public or in private, but the pride in Victor's voice when he'd spoken of Liam's bravery had been exasperated and very real.

Now, Victor doesn't say anything. He just looks distracted.

"I can't imagine that changing the way he does things," Nigel suggests.

"I don't *know*," Victor bites back.

Nigel blinks. Priscilla laughs.

"Surely you've talked about it," Nigel says.

"He's not my boyfriend," Victor snaps.

"You are a ridiculous human being," Priscilla says while Nigel stares at his friend. "You've been dating him for *years*."

"Human beings are baffling, irritating, and, rarely — and only if I'm very lucky — somewhat interesting," Victor says.

"I've heard this all before," Nigel says. Liam is one of Victor's favorite conversation topics. "And I can't imagine what you have to worry about now if he's been content for years not to go to bed with you."

Victor shifts in his seat and coughs.

"Wait. Are you actually fucking him?" Nigel asks.

Victor briefly passes a hand over his face. "That's a complex philosophical and logistical question to which I can easily say no and he should probably say yes."

"Should I ask what you're doing exactly?" Nigel asks, more out of a desire to be irritating than anything else. Certainly, Victor deserves to be judged for whatever this outburst is.

"No, you should not," Victor snaps.

"But?"

"I may be feeling increasingly generous towards him," he says.

"Victor," Nigel chides.

"What?"

"That doesn't seem very fair to either of you."

"I so appreciate your need to defend a man you've never even met," Victor says snidely.

"He's in your life," Nigel says simply. "So I imagine someone has to. And if it bothers you so much, perhaps you should introduce us, if you've decided he's staying."

"Liam is in my life because he does not do or expect what every other person I have let into my life does or expects. And now the great worm of romanticism that has found its way into my heart means our arrangement may need to come to an end, because I am two decades well past trying to figure out how my sexuality is relevant to anybody else's needs," Victor says sharply, before finally looking away from Nigel. "I know how this goes. I discuss my feelings with him and he starts asking for things I have no interest in providing. So how's Liam? Fine, until I damage the fuck out of his already precarious little world."

10

Alex finally curls up in the armchair in his room at the end of his second night in New York, and he calls Paul. "I thought I'd continue the tradition of ill-advised late night phone calls," he says without preamble when Paul picks up.

"Hey there. How's it going?" Alex can hear the smile in Paul's voice.

"Only one person blatantly suggested I have sex with them today."

"Are you relieved or disappointed?"

"Am I Natalie?" Alex snarks before feeling guilty about it. It's not really her fault she knows how to play the very shitty game Hollywood lays out for women. It is her fault she's mean, but that's a different and not necessarily unrelated issue.

"No. You have different styles. Why aren't you out with everyone?"

"Officially off duty until morning media."

"Surely there are adventures?" Paul leads.

"Victor muttered something about social obligations in New Jersey, and I assume Liam is harassing friends or family. Don't know what anyone else is up to. Thought I'd be a good boy and stay in."

"Mmmmm, which is why you're calling me?"

Alex barks a laugh. "You know you don't have to actually be subtle about the phone sex, right?"

"I do now."

"Get your dick out," Alex says, laughing.

Paul chuckles. "Let me go be not here."

"Are you still working?" Alex asks, a little disbelieving.

"I'm home, but it's barely after nine."

"Ugh. What are you doing?" Even with the time difference, Paul's being overly dedicated.

"Storyboarding," Paul says.

"Well, don't come all over those."

"Hence moving to the bedroom, impatient one."

Alex hears Paul thump down the loft stairs and jog up the other flight to their bedroom. The door creaks open and closed — Todd is banned for all sorts of reasons, including shedding and a fascination with swinging objects, including those attached to their bodies. That had been a particularly unfortunate evening, although at least Alex now understands why Craig only took the dog.

As much as it's Alex who starts them off, phone sex still isn't something he really thinks of as his thing so much as an almost in-joke (a very pleasurable, filthy in-joke), thanks to the time Paul had gotten Alex off on the phone when Craig was back in Paul's bed and Alex was being crazy.

Paul, though, loves it, would love it with anyone, that much is entirely clear. Alex is grateful for that, because it means he doesn't have to do most of the talking. The sex that works the best for him leaves him distinctly non-verbal. Masturbation and too much distance aren't really an exception. And right now what he wants, more than getting off, is Paul's voice and the way it makes him go quiet and his heart stand at attention.

Paul is happy to oblige, and Alex isn't even startled when he mentions Carly. Because the biggest problem with that incredibly weird moment sitting in Paul's lap by Victor's pool was that Paul whispering to him was hot and the timing was terrible.

It's ridiculously arousing when Paul tells him he's going to hold his head down between Carly's legs and make him lick until she gets off twice. Alex can almost feel the pressure of his wide palm across the back of his neck. The only thing he can hear other than Paul's breath and voice is the slick, wet sound of his own hand on his cock and a distant siren on the street below.

After they both come, they chuckle, but they don't talk about it at all. Alex isn't sure if that's the natural end of the topic or if there's a discussion to be had. Either way, it's something they need to talk about. It raises some questions about How They Do Things which they've never really talked about before, because *not like Liam* has always sufficed.

◆

Alex barely makes his flight back to L.A. He lets out a relieved breath only once he shoves his carryon in the overhead bin and slumps into his seat. As much as there are planes after that may even have seats, it's bad enough that he's landing at nine at night. Paul has to be at the airport at four in the morning. Between waiting for luggage and driving, that's maybe five hours they'll be in the same house, and five minutes after that they'll both be unconscious.

But before Alex can even text *landed* to Paul as his plane wanders LAX looking for a gate, his phone chimes.

Airport Westin. 2132.
???
Get your bag, get a cab, get here. Leave your bag if you want.

Alex laughs with delight, and then looks around sheepishly as he tugs his hat lower on his head. *Okay...*, he texts back, still marginally puzzled.

He's a lot less puzzled when he gets to the hotel and bangs on the door. Paul, hilariously, grabs him by the front of his shirt and yanks him inside.

"What —?" Alex blinks, startled, as he adjusts to this sudden and very welcome change in circumstance.

"I know you're exhausted —" Paul starts.

"Slept on the plane," Alex interrupts.

"*I know you're exhausted,*" Paul repeats, "and I know I should sleep, but this buys us a couple of hours and —"

"This is the most awesome thing you have ever done," Alex says when Paul trails off with a look of uncertainty.

"I'm sorry I didn't discuss it with you first?" Paul says meekly.

Alex cackles, even as it stabs at his heart a little. After everything in this absurd life they live together, he doesn't want Paul being afraid.

"Oh my God, just fuck me so we can order room service," Alex says. "Wait, how late does room service go?"

"All night," Paul says as they both start shucking clothes.

The sex follows the same pattern it has been between them lately. Alex isn't sure of the word for it. *Violent* seems wrong. As does *aggressive*, because sometimes Paul hurts him slowly, twisting bruising pinches into his thighs as he blows him. It's certainly a natural progression of what has always worked for them — Paul pushing Alex until he feels so much it hurts in the best way possible. It's just a little bit more explicit than it used to be.

That is, Alex supposes, a feature of growing up, or intimacy. Either that, or they're the perfect stereotype of *young, bored, and famous*. But they're too fucking good — and everything in their charmed lives has been too hard won — for Alex to write it off like that.

♦

Paul marks him everywhere, with mouth and nails, sucking and pinching. He bats Alex's hands away over and over again, wanting to watch what he does to him. The bruises bloom — red to white to the first flush of purple — and he refuses to let Alex pleasure him until he is wrung out and gone. It makes Paul smug to have Alex distant-present with desire. In these moments he could make Alex do anything, and that matters in the worlds of what they do.

Alex is so fair and so easy and eager to certain types of pain. That Paul gets to keep something of the history of those moments — it's amazing. But he keeps wondering when he's going to finally hit Alex's wall and find a *no*. He keeps wondering how bad of a conversation that's going to be.

"I should document these," Alex says after they've fucked and eaten, turning this way and that in the mirror on the bathroom door to see the marks. "Every time," he continues on, fascinated with himself in the way Paul supposes all actors are. "I really should."

"Isn't that dangerous in our lives?" Paul asks.

"I don't know if I care," Alex says, but the fact that he hasn't pulled out his phone to take a picture certainly makes it clear that he does.

"Com'ere," Paul says, shoving the room service tray a little bit more to the edge of the bed. He grabs Alex's hips when he stops in front of him. "Let me document it," Paul says.

"How?" Alex is wary.

"With my hands."

11

At work the next day Alex gets the tentative shooting schedule for the first block and his pages for the first week of filming.

"Oh my God, no," Alex blurts.

It's bad enough that he's come to the lot straight from seeing Paul off at the airport. But that the first sequence back that's going to be filmed is a love scene with Zach and James is just *no*.

Standing next to him, having just got his own pages, Liam chuckles. "It's not going to be that bad."

Alex moans.

◆

"I don't care about the nudity," Alex snaps, when Victor attempts to mollify him. Actually, he's fairly sure the nudity is going to be the most awkward thing ever. Even if there isn't full-frontal, precedent says Victor can get away with a hell of a lot on their network in their timeslot.

Victor folds his arms. "Then what's the problem?"

"You controlling what I do and how I look."

"That's not anything new, and you're hardly being singled out."

"*This* is new," Alex says.

"You're beautiful, Alex. Why are you upset about this?" Victor asks, obviously curious.

"Stop saying that," Alex says sharply.

"Why?"

"I have one condition," Alex says instead of answering. He has no words to explain to Victor, or anyone, how dangerous being *beautiful* can be.

"What's that?" Victor asks.

"Zach isn't the one getting fucked."

Victor's eyebrows go up. Alex knows he's being judged and doesn't care.

"That's not particularly going to change how I make you look. Or what I make you do."

"No" Alex's smile is small and absolutely evil. He's not Zach, and he's still angry about Victor missing the point entirely, but if the narrative theme here is going to be gross anyway, at least it can be gross in his favor. America can seriously go fuck itself.

♦

"Hey, man, why'd you ask Victor if Zach could fuck James?"

Liam slides in across the table from Alex at lunch. Alex stares at him. Why does Liam know about that? "Excuse me?"

Liam shrugs. "I mean, it's not your thing. What does Zach fucking James get you?" He inexplicably takes a knife and fork to a slice of pizza. Alex has no idea why he does that, but he has bigger concerns than Liam's cutlery habits.

"The most awkward day at work with you ever?" he offers.

"Alex," Liam says reproachfully.

"It's going to be awkward." Alex pokes at his pasta with his fork.

"You're not answering the question."

"The question is weird." Also they're in the cafeteria, and Alex has no desire to discuss this where they might be overheard.

"I ask lots of weird questions," Liam says as if this line of discussion is entirely reasonable. "And you're the first person I've ever done a love scene with who I've actually fucked, so like, I'm trying to figure out how this all works."

"What about Natalie?" Alex asks.

Liam looks confused. "What about Natalie?"

"You had a thing and your characters had a thing."

"Oh. That was different. Marjani and James had their thing first. Actually, that's kind of how Natalie and I happened."

Alex stares. "What the fuck?"

"Not, like, on set," Liam explains patiently. "We went out for drinks after. Sort of like you and I did, although not in my hotel room. And you're way more fun."

"Liam!" Alex hisses.

"What?"

"Could you not? With the outloud voice?" Alex pleads.

"Oh," Liam looks around a little sheepishly. "Sorry."

"Whatever. Just…be quiet, oh my God."

"You still haven't answered," Liam says.

Alex sighs and pushes his plate away. "I don't want to expose myself for this any more than I have to, okay? You and me, fine. Me being gay, fine. Discovering, with you, how much I like to get fucked? Something I'd prefer not to share with the viewing public, thanks."

"You're a really good actor. And this is all just bullshit choreography in a cold studio. Nobody could mistake it for real. Even you. Promise."

Alex ignores Liam's pep talk and moans. "It's still going to be so fucking awkward."

"Worse than the pancakes?"

Liam cracks up when Alex glares at him.

◆

The sex choreography meeting is awkward as hell. The fact that there's such a thing as a sex choreography meeting at all is mind boggling to Alex.

Ellen is directing this episode. If he's going to be miserable in this particular way, at least it's with her at the helm. Although when she starts talking about how many seconds of thrusting the Department of Standards will allow, Alex puts his head down on the table and groans. Liam rubs his back soothingly, but he's laughing too hard to really mean it.

Zach and James have gotten hot and heavy on screen before, but they were always wearing clothes. The stripping and Zach shoving James down onto his back on the bed is orders of magnitude more awkward than the making out they've become accustomed to. Not to mention the goddamned hair pulling. Alex is fairly sure Victor put that there out of spite.

"You boarded the love scene, too?" Alex complains when Ellen brings out the storyboards. Bad enough the fans are going to be compulsively rewatching this frame-by-frame and in slow motion. He doesn't need to know the official planning material will live in the network's archives forever too.

She raises an eyebrow. "Did you want me to draw curtains blowing in the wind like a fucking Sirk film?"

Alex frowns. "What's a Sirk film?"

Ellen and Liam exchange disbelieving looks. Alex then gets a five-minute, digressive history lesson into German cinema and melodrama that does nothing to make this day less absurd.

"Alex," Ellen says as they're wrapping everything up. "A word with you on behalf of Makeup. There's a lot of skin here —"

"I hadn't noticed," Alex says drily.

"We can cover bruises. But if we cover bruises on you we cover freckles, and if we cover freckles then we have to cover *all* the freckles because putting freckles back on you is a pain in the ass we don't have time for. No climbing 'til after we shoot this, and tell your boyfriend to play more nicely, 'kay?"

Alex gapes. Liam covers his mouth to hide a grin.

"Just say 'Yes, Ellen,'" Ellen prompts.

Alex closes his mouth and settles for glaring at her. The state of his flesh should be no concern to the show, and he hates all of the ways that it is.

On the phone that night with Paul, he doesn't mention any of it. Bad enough that he has to battle Victor for his body and what it means. He doesn't need Paul's irrational Liam-jealousy on top of it all. Paul doesn't need the distraction anyway.

◆

Paul isn't the talent or even a well-known brand and personality the way Victor is. Unfortunately and unpleasantly for him, he still has to be at upfronts to convince people that he can be — and convince them to spend money with *Winsome*. Initial ad buys, as much as whatever the early viewing figures prove to be, are essential to a full season and the show's survival. Paul's not convinced he's charismatic enough for the job.

Thankfully he has Darcy and enough enthusiasm from the network that she's doing some of the stage show hosting; her theater career means there's no question she can handle the live audience. It's all bullshit, even if he's a little jealous of the actors and their crisp, preternatural ability to turn joyfully toward any camera. It'll be nice to commiserate with Alex later.

He's fairly certain, however, that for all the hell that Alex has had to deal with at upfronts over the years, he's never been faced with a crisis quite like Darcy's parents. Paul is sure they're perfectly nice people and appreciates, in principle, that they're supportive of their daughter. But constantly calling Darcy to spend time with the while she's in New York and camping out on the sidewalk outside of the fan-oriented part of upfronts, is really way too much. He wonders at what point they're going to become a liability as well as a nuisance. Also, how he should conduct the intervention at the point it becomes inevitably necessary?

Victor, when Paul calls him about it during the dead space between the stage presentation and the first round of parties, tells him sternly not to do anything, because they are the type of people looking for purchase to make a scene.

Paul asks him repeatedly if he's sure. Victor's answers get shorter each time until Paul eventually says, "You're giving me the eyebrow, aren't you?"

All of that is nothing, though, to seeing the three-minute *Winsome* trailer played onscreen at The Beacon for a live audience. Even though Paul spends most of his waking hours bogged down in the most mundane minutia of production, the final product is still magic. It's amazing.

Despite having clearly been raised by crazy people she now finds mildly embarrassing, at the parties Darcy is charming, bubbly, and way too chatty with the stars of some of the other shows. They are not there to party with their peers, but to flatter their way to economic viability. Ruth watches her, dryly amused, and Annette laughs when Paul sighs and goes to have what feels like a very necessary chat about where her attentions need to be focused.

Darcy may be a pro, but she's a theater kid pro. Which means she can't even begin to imagine the level of attention that's already started to come her way and the consequences of even the most normal of slightly ill-advised choices.

"Look, it's awesome you're making friends, but don't annoy anybody, and please, I'm begging you, don't sleep with anyone." Paul feels way too weary for this already.

Darcy frowns prettily. "You're not my big brother, Paul. Even though it's sweet, so thank you. I'm networking for you, go away."

"Make friends with the ad guys," he hisses.

"Do you think if I barter my virginity we can get a full-season pickup *and* a renewal?" she asks like she's not being appalling and inappropriate.

"I did not need to know that," Paul says, pointing at her wanting very much to back away and rejoin Annette.

Darcy frowns at her rum and Coke, which Paul probably should have also yelled at her for.

"No, you probably did," Darcy tells the drink, before putting her game face back on and bouncing over to the nearest cluster of ordinary, boring people to convince them that a show about an eighteen-year-old girl-pimp who has a day job at a convenience shop in the barren wastes that are most of America is the perfect platform for selling…well, anything. But probably particularly cleaning supplies, erectile dysfunction drugs, and cat food.

♦

"I never appreciated just how good you are at navigating this shit before," Paul tells Alex that night. It's incredible to him that Alex was only two years older than Darcy is now when he was doing all of this for the first time and with far less preparation. "Thank you for being well-adjusted."

Alex laughs.

The rest of the week isn't easy. The media is constant, the schedule is exhausting, and Darcy's parents remain obnoxious. But nothing turns into a crisis, and by the time he gets to the airport Paul is profoundly grateful that he's gotten through his first upfronts with his people and his show intact.

He wants to sleep on the flight. He's getting his hands on Alex once he's finally home, and he'd like to be awake enough for that to be worth both their whiles, but Darcy wants to post-mortem everything. While dealing with the newness was part of why they'd agreed to book seats together Paul largely wants to pretend the whole thing never happened.

Darcy puts her socked feet up on the empty seat between them and recounts every completely insane thing she said to someone older than her parents. Which doesn't change his mind. When he blanches at the pussy joke she apparently told everyone after he'd scolded her for her excessive flirting, she reminds him that their show is about whores.

She blinks owlishly at him. "Was I supposed to pretend it's not about whores?"

♦

By the time Paul gets his luggage and gets home, he's shrugged off most of the in-flight exhaustion. He struggles with his keys at the door, unable after all this time to tell the ones for the top and bottom locks apart.

When he finally fumbles the door open, Alex is leaning against the wall with his arms crossed over his chest.

"Problems?" he asks.

"Not anymore." Paul drops his luggage to reach for him. He unfolds Alex's arms and runs his hands up and down them.

"Was the flight terrible?"

Paul opens his mouth to tell him that working in Hollywood should be banned as unhealthy for any man, woman, or child, but then he shrugs and shakes his head. "It's over now."

Alex smiles one of his crinkly smiles that almost closes his eyes. "Upstairs?" he asks.

Paul doesn't have to be told twice. He's halfway undressed by the time they get up to their bedroom.

◆

Alex wants it just as much as Paul does, but he always marvels at Paul's need to write out his day on Alex's flesh. It's not something that goes both ways, even if Alex adores it in sensation and emotional weight.

"Let me ride you." He pulls Paul away from his neck by his hair and pushes him over.

Paul gasps, tilts his head back, and mumbles a thousand yeses. Alex grins smugly because he knows every time they do this, Paul is remembering the first time they were apart, and, more importantly, the first time they came back together. It will also, hopefully, keep Paul from marking the hell out of him without ever needing to have a discussion as to why.

Unfortunately, Alex is wrong. He can sit up straight and keep his neck tragically out of range of Paul's mouth as he fucks himself on his cock. But there's nothing he can do about Paul's nails raking deliciously over his chest and back but ask him to stop. And he does, eventually, because he has to.

"Don't." He grabs for Paul's hands.

Paul freezes, but that unfortunately includes his hips.

Alex whines. "Not that too," he pants, lifting up and sinking down aggressively to make his point.

"But?"

"The nails, not the nails," Alex says.

"Sorry. I never —"

"Shhhh. Makeup's pissed. I like. Show doesn't."

"You sure?" Paul grabs Alex's hips to still them.

"Yes," he says insistently. "I said yes. Now stop being scared and fuck me."

♦

The relief of upfronts being over lasts only until the next morning, when Paul is up at five while Alex grumbles under the covers because he doesn't have to be at work 'til eight. Alex knows that this is the life they signed up for — and has his own schedule keeping him busy — but he wishes Paul would take at least a morning off before they don't see each other awake for a week. Plus, he has to shoot the love scene today and wants to ignore the impending awkward of that for as long as possible.

Alex grabs at Paul when he walks by the bed on his way to the wardrobe. "Five more minutes?" He kneels up and tugs Paul toward him by the hand.

Paul looks like he's going to say no, but Alex smiles coyly at him and leans closer for a kiss.

He gets ten minutes.

◆

It's a supreme irony — and an inevitable outcome of one of the many misunderstandings *Fourth* fans have about reality — that Alex and Liam have actually fucked. That said, acting their characters fucking is absolutely not sexy at all. Thanks to the bathrobes between takes and the socks on dicks and the fact that set is for some reason fucking freezing, it's a long way from Alex's favorite day in front of the camera.

At one point Ellen yells at Alex for clenching his ass, because heaven forbid anyone have cellulite that shows. When Alex snarls back, because this day is just terrible, Liam collapses into laughter.

"Shut up," Alex snaps at him.

"Oh my God, your face."

"Lee," Alex pleads.

"Hey. Be glad it's your face I'm looking at."

As awkward as the day is, only some of that has to do with their history. A lot of it is simply the nature of the job and how much Alex hates some of the things it demands of him.

But it could be worse. If Alex has to trust his body to someone else in this ridiculous and somewhat humiliating way, he's glad it's Liam. Who has always been nothing but kind and peculiar and so matter-of-fact about all the vagaries of desire.

◆

Back on the lot, despite the grogginess from the too-short night with Alex, Paul is beginning to feel anxious. They've survived upfronts, but now that he and his people have done their part to ensure the economic viability of *Winsome*, the work feels way more high-stakes. In order to keep surviving, they have to make sure that the craft is the best it can be.

That means a full day on the lot, both on set and in the offices, the first day back. As much as he wishes he and Alex could both stay home, something akin to panic is setting in. From now on, every day is important, and he can't afford to fuck any of them up.

As late as Paul stays, because he wants to make sure everything goes perfectly, he still beats Alex home. He's relieved for the few quiet hours to get a few last things done and make sure his head is even more in the game.

♦

When Alex finally does get in, he yells from the front door that he's home. The day has been exhausting and he doesn't want to expend any more effort looking for Paul than he absolutely has to.

"I'm up here!" His boyfriend's voice comes from the loft after a delay that might have been him getting his headphones off but is probably just a lag in processing.

Alex pulls on the railing as he climbs up the stairs to Paul's office. When he gets there, he drapes himself over Paul's back and buries his face in Paul's shoulder. After a day spent way too tangled up with Liam, he wants Paul's body and his attention and to not have to talk at all.

"How was work?" Paul asks but doesn't stop typing.

Alex shrugs and loops his arms around Paul's neck. "Fine. What are you working on?"

"Script edits."

"Want a break?" Alex teases, running his thumb along the collar of Paul's sweater.

"Once I get this done," Paul says.

"Oh my God, you just got back yesterday, there is no way you are behind," Alex says, more disbelieving than annoyed.

Paul shrugs. "Don't you have anything else to do?"

"Who are you and what did you do with my boyfriend?" Alex is taken aback by the dismissiveness in Paul's voice. "We were apart for a week. Then we were at work. Now we are home from work. Come fuck me and then we'll make dinner."

"You go ahead, I've got to finish this first."

Alex makes an annoyed noise. Paul's tendency to get lost in his work is nothing new, but this is mildly ridiculous. *And they were apart for a week.* Alex wants, and he knows the buttons to press to get it.

"Fine," he says mildly. "I desperately need a shower, I smell like Liam. Sure you don't want to come?"

Paul's shoulders go tense in Alex's arms. "Why do you smell like Liam?" he asks tightly.

"Zach and James scene," Alex says.

"Love scene?" Paul asks. He sounds horrified.

"Yes." Alex sighs, pushing himself off of Paul and straightening up. If he'd wanted a reaction out of Paul he's certainly succeeded, but now it looks like this is going to turn into a thing and that makes him want space.

Paul spins around in his chair to face him. "You didn't tell me you were filming a love scene."

Alex folds his arms over his chest defiantly. "Does it matter?"

Paul is frowning darkly in a way he hardly ever does. Alex would feel more sympathetic if the whole premise of the burgeoning argument wasn't so stupid.

"Of course it matters!" Paul says. "Is this why I couldn't mark you up the other day?"

"I also couldn't go climbing this week because they were afraid I'd bang myself up. This isn't just about you."

"You told me Makeup bitched to you."

"They did."

"And then you lied about why."

"Paul, it's a scene. I'm an actor. Liam's an actor."

"And your ex."

"He hardly qualifies as my ex. He dumped me when he thought I wanted him to be my boyfriend." Alex stomps toward the stairs. Paul is being ridiculous.

Paul grabs his wrist. "You did want him to be your boyfriend."

Alex stares at him but doesn't try to get away. "You weren't there. You don't know, and you are being a jealous asshole. You have been a jealous asshole about Liam for *years*, possibly even regarding him and Carly, I'm not sure, but this is a new level of stupid."

"It's not that stupid when you're lying to me."

"When did you start writing an after-school special parody? I didn't lie."

"You omitted," Paul snaps.

"Yes, I did," Alex jerks his hand out of Paul's grasp and starts downstairs again. He wants out of this whole stupid fucking argument. "And you omitted Carly and your father and your *wrists* and the goddamn crickets!"

"What do the crickets have to do with anything?" Paul sounds both angry and bewildered as he shoves away from his chair.

Alex spins around at the bottom of the staircase and glares up at where Paul is hovering three-quarters of the way up. "I didn't tell you before that we were shooting Zach and James fucking because I knew you'd flip out. Go me, I was right."

"I am pissed at you. And I want to yell at you."

"Well, are you going to yell, or are you going to come take a shower with me?" Alex is never sure if Paul's recitations of the reactions he wants to have are a substitution for Paul actually reacting, or a threat. Either way, they're unsettling.

◆

In the bathroom, Paul crowds Alex back into the shower as soon as he gets the water on. He knows Alex wants or he wouldn't have asked, and Paul is happy for a distraction from work and the argument he's fairly certain isn't over. He shoves his hands into Alex's hair and his tongue into his mouth. Alex's head falls back and away under the spray, his body tense and his mind clearly somewhere else. Paul chases him, even if he knows the way he's kissing Alex is even less of a conversation than what they'd had in the loft.

Paul slides his hand around to the back of Alex's head and drags it up. "Hey," he says, biting at his collarbone. "Stay with me here."

He half expects Alex to shove him away lest Paul bruise him, but apparently that's no longer a concern or Alex has just decided it's not. Either way, Paul is happy to push it. It's got nothing to do with Liam right now and everything to do with the fact that Alex is naked in their shower and not totally present. Paul wants his attention back, and of all the things that get good reactions out of Alex, this is one that really works for both of them.

"I am," Alex mutters in response, but his eyes are still closed and his mouth is slack, like he's trying to will himself into the moment. "Keep going," he says when Paul doesn't do anything, his voice barely audible.

Paul bites again, this time at Alex's neck, and again, until Alex grabs at his shoulders and whimpers. It will feel cruel, later, how much Paul enjoys this part of it, but all he feels right now is Alex coming back to him, drawn by something in the pain or in Paul's hands giving it to him.

"There, that's better," Paul murmurs. He slides his hand down to Alex's cock. Alex smiles with his eyes still closed and begs for more.

12

The strain of the fight lingers. Alex wishes they could clear the air, but there's never time. He's working five or six days a week. When Paul takes a day off it never overlaps with Alex's downtime. The *Fourth* renewal deal really does mean no breaks for anyone. Alex — and everyone else — are wearier right from the get-go.

A handful of people depart for *Winsome*, per Victor and Paul's agreement, which means that even as *Fourth* is entering its terrible year of shooting with no vacations that's only going to end in the death of the show, work on *Winsome* is going into full swing. Alex finds it incredibly odd that colleagues of his are leaving Victor's show for his partner's. He feels like Paul made a deal with the devil, even if he's aware Paul doesn't see it that way and deserves a good staff. Alex still finds it incredibly weird that Victor and Paul are business partners.

That's probably unfair, given how entangled their work and personal lives are. One night Alex manages to pry Paul away from his desk long enough to get him into bed. They spend the afterglow wrapped around each other, and Paul mentions that Darcy's character on *Winsome* is getting a gun.

"Apparently it's the summer of firearms." Paul chuckles darkly.

"At least tell me someone's going to teach her to shoot properly," Alex says. No one on TV seems to ever know how and it frustrates him no end.

"Is someone volunteering?" Paul runs a hand down Alex's side. Alex stretches and then curls into him.

"If you're not going to get anybody else to, yes."

♦

Alex calls Darcy to set a date to go to the range and finds her as enthusiastic about shooting as she is about everything she does. Alex's own younger sister is unpredictable at best, and he's not sure if Darcy wants an older brother or a friend in him. But, despite her Broadway-turned-L.A. dysfunction, Alex likes her and finds her irritating only in ways that are fun to push back against.

Darcy is inquisitive as they walk into the range, not just about the mechanics of what they're about to do, but about what it all means. Alex has spent enough time telling her about what life in the ass-end of America is like that her questions are, by now, useful ones.

The media is still in love with Alex's Cinderella rise from Indiana. But the story has become so packaged and oft-repeated that the parts of it that are important to him never get talked about. Most of the time, he's perfectly happy with that. Paragon is not a place he ever wants to return to.

But Darcy has gotten the full story, or as much of it as anyone has. Including all the awful, little details none of the interviewers ask about and no one really wants to know anyway. America prefers its poverty to be romantic. There is very little romantic about growing up in a town of seven hundred people where everyone is divorced or unmarried, people live in houses worth less than Alex's trailer on set, and at least one kid in his high school class died every year in a DUI or farm accident. It had been satisfying to watch Darcy's eyes go wide at his recital of those statistics, and it is satisfying to know that the world is going to get parts of Alex's story it doesn't want or like, even if it never knows that's what's happening.

Darcy doesn't bat an eye at the sketchiness of the area the range is in. Alex doesn't know if that's because she's very even or has no barometer for what's 'normal'. Inside the range she's curious and attentive, and by the end of the session she's doing reasonably well. Alex can't help but text Paul to tease him: *Your starlet is a way better shot than you.*

She does, however, ask a number of prying questions about him and Paul. She's being nosey, and she may be as bad a gossip as Liam. Glad to have someone removed from the situation to talk to, Alex confesses that things have been strange since Paul got back from upfronts.

"He seemed fine in New York," Darcy says.

"Paul is very good at seeming fine," Alex says darkly, remembering crickets and kitchens.

Darcy bites her lip and doesn't ask anything else.

At the end of the day, Alex takes a picture of himself and Darcy to send to Paul, but decides to tweet it instead.

"Are you sure you want to do that?" Darcy asks uncertainly as Alex futzes with his infrequently used account. "After everything in South Carolina?"

"Are you worried about your reputation?"

Darcy shakes her head. "No. Nor the show's, really. I mean, you're J. Alex Cook. Any gossip about this is gonna get you way more attention than it does me."

Alex stares at her, then grins fiercely. "I can't fuck up *Fourth's* renewal deal anymore, and I am so done being America's sweetheart." He punches send on the photo. "That's your job now."

♦

When Alex gets home from the range that night Paul isn't there, and the internet is already going on a mini rampage over Alex and guns. Again. As entertaining as that is, Paul's absence is irritating. This is Alex's one day off before another six-day block of shooting, and he wants some time. They're not going to be awake and together for more than an hour a day for at least the next ten days. Sometimes, their jobs suck.

Paul, though, is not making their lives any easier. Whatever panic he'd brought back from New York and upfronts is clearly still alive and well weeks later. His twelve-hour days at the office are getting longer.

On the rare occasions he is home, he rarely leaves his office except to go to bed. Even that he does reluctantly. To Alex, it becomes something of a game: how naked does he have to get — and how obnoxious does he have to be — before Paul loses focus and chases him.

Their days are exhausting and their schedules are punishing, but when their hands are on each other the rest of the world disappears: it's just them as they work best. Once they're in bed everything is fine. When they're done Paul always kisses Alex sweetly, if, increasingly a little distractedly, and then Alex drags them back to their room or under the covers. They still curl up in bed every time for as long as they can, but as the weeks go on that time gets shorter and shorter. Alex will rest his forehead against Paul's, and Paul will grab his hands, and they'll both try to start conversations that aren't "Wait, did *you* feed Todd today?"

For a while it works, but as they get into the middle of summer, Paul's hours get even longer, and the relentless *Fourth* schedule starts to take its toll on Alex. Everything turns into a discussion of their jobs or their friends or the future. Of course, on some level, it's all really about Liam. Meanwhile, Paul remains hurt that Alex keeps saying no marriage. Alex can't believe Paul, not when he keeps bringing up the issue when Alex is almost asleep or halfway out the door.

Eventually they give up trying, and the conversations in the dark stop happening. The time they do have together is much better spent quietly and peacefully in each other's arms, in this one room that belongs to them and nothing else in the world.

◆

"Are you coming to bed at all, or are you going to sleep at your desk?" Alex shouts up from the living room where he's putting the last touches on the pack for his climb tomorrow. He has a day off, and he would like to take advantage of the rare chance to sleep in with a late night with Paul.

"Yeah," Paul calls back down distractedly.

"Yeah, you're coming, or yeah, you're putting Victor to shame with your insomnia?"

"Can you give me thirty minutes?" Paul's voice is tight.

"You mean the thirty minutes that looks like an hour?"

"Alex —" Paul starts, sounding somewhere between guilty and warning.

"Okay," Alex closes the last buckle on his bag viciously. "Waiting up for you."

Alex falls asleep reading. When he wakes up in the morning his book is still open on his chest and the other side of the bed is empty.

He finds Paul in the bedroom that Alex still thinks of as Gemma's, asleep on top of the covers.

"Hey," Alex sits quietly on the edge of the mattress and nudges Paul's shoulder to wake him. "Didn't think you were actually going to pull a Victor."

Paul blinks blearily. "Came in here to rest my eyes."

"Hope they're rested; it's morning now."

"Ugh, not really. Do you have any idea how loud the wind is in here?"

"All the more reason to come to, you know, actual bed," Alex runs a hand over Paul's shoulder. The house backs up onto a canyon and sometimes when the wind howls down it, it sounds like voices. Alex doesn't mind much, but it's always freaked Paul out a little.

"It sounded like someone was dying. Are you leaving?" Paul squints at the faded jeans and T-shirt Alex wears for climbs.

"Yeah. Wanted to see if you were still here first."

"I am," Paul says, pushing himself upright and reaching for his glasses on the nightstand. "What time is it?"

"Almost eight."

"God, I need to —" Paul trails off, frowning and clearly scrambling to remember his to-do list for the day.

"You need to take a shower." Alex grimaces and kisses him briefly before he stands up.

"Be careful," Paul calls after him as Alex leaves with a wave. "Love you!"

Alex laughs from the stairs. "I'll be back tonight. Don't forget to eat."

◆

When Alex gets back, he's not sure Paul's left his office at all.

"Are you seriously still working?" he asks, grimy and sweaty and glad to be home. He nudges Paul's papers aside so he can sit on his desk. He's been gone all day, didn't share a bed with Paul last night, and wants nothing more right now than time with his boyfriend. "Come to bed with me."

Paul, to Alex's annoyance, rolls his eyes as he catches a stack of script pages before they can fall. "Can it wait?"

"Not asking for sex," he says with more shortness than he should. "It's past midnight. Come sleep."

"I need to get this done," Paul protests. "There's a table read tomorrow and the guys need notes on the script early enough to have time to fix it before the big guys hear it."

"You know this would be easier if you'd accept the reality of a head writer who isn't you." Alex nudges at one of the little wheels on Paul's chair with his foot.

"Since when are you an expert on show running?" Paul asks.

"Paul," Alex says. Everything about this hurts, from Paul's tone to the fact that Alex has to beg for Paul's attention. "You always have something to get done. I never see you awake anymore. Please?"

"Sorry." Paul doesn't bother to hide his impatience. "This work is important, not just for me. I don't have time to indulge you tonight."

"I am your boyfriend, not an indulgence," Alex snaps, stung. Paul may hedge and postpone and forget, but he's never outright refused. Alex levers himself off of the desk.

"Where are you going?" Paul turns around in his chair to look at him.

For a moment Alex thinks he's going to get called back for an apology. This conversation is strange and scary and not how they work at all. "I'm going to sulk."

"Sulk quietly."

Alex doesn't know if that's supposed to be a joke or not.

◆

That night, Paul doesn't go to bed at all.

The next night, he does, dragging Alex upstairs as soon as he gets home from work. Alex laughs, and Paul feels guilty at how relieved it sounds.

Paul fucks him, hard. That's a relief too, although a less guilty one. Alex throws his head back while Paul bites bruises into his neck and drags heavy fingernails down his back. Paul feels a little crazy with how much damage he wants to do. Alex doesn't stop him, whimpering instead and urging him on.

When they're done, Paul is left on his knees on the bed while Alex blinks dreamily up at him from the sheets. His skin is a riot of marks, spots of purple and wider patches of stinging red. The play is more intense than anything they've ever done together, and Alex can't seem to make words even as he's smiling.

Paul traces the edge of a cluster of bruises at Alex's collarbone carefully and flinches when Alex hisses.

"I'm so sorry," Paul breathes. Alex is beautiful and in pain; Paul is a little horrified to be responsible for it.

Alex frowns. "It's okay," he gets out. Paul doesn't know whether he should believe him.

♦

As time goes on Paul finds it easier and easier to sleep in the loft. At first he tells himself he's just napping, but when naps are all he ever has time for it starts to look different. Alex is a slippery slope of so many things: Jealousy, obsession, and the way Paul always fucks everything up either at work, because he can never stay on top of it, or at home, because these things happened with Craig too.

He wants to believe, like so much other pain in his life, that this period of time is something he — and Alex — can wait out. That this is an inevitable cost of what they have, professionally and personally. But it only takes thirty days to form a habit — Paul heard that on some talk show once — and it becomes easier not just to sleep on the other side of the house, but to have clothes and a toothbrush there. It becomes Paul's command center. Not for his work, but for his life.

◆

Alex assumes, at first, that this will blow over. That, terrible as it is, Paul is going through a patch of temporary insanity. He'll spend a few days running too much and sleeping too little but come out on the other side more or less intact, and more or less Alex's. Lonely and hurt as Alex is, the alternative, at first, doesn't even make enough sense to consider. He and Paul have been together, in one way or another, for nearly two years now. Paul's eagerness to give him attention has been a star around which Alex has revolved even longer, ever since the day Paul busted him for making out with Nick in front of the coffee maker.

But as the nights go on with no sign of thaw or explanation, Alex starts to doubt. As far as he can tell they're still together. Certainly the situation looks nothing like the one when they broke up before. But that the state of their relationship even crosses his mind as a question is jarring the first time it happens. Realizing his certainty in Paul is gone is frightening.

When Alex puts it to himself that way it seems dramatic, but then, he has never gotten a no from Paul before. Without any other relationship experience to go on, he can only assume it means something terrible. And Paul, who has always taught him how to do these things, has declared he has no time for him.

13

Paul comes home one night in June to find Alex sitting on the couch. There's nothing dire about that in and of itself, but he's sitting still with no sign of book or script or laptop near him. Paul watched Alex learn to act, wrote Alex into what he is now — and perhaps always was — so gifted at. He knows he's been practicing, composing and waiting, if not in his spot in the corner of the sofa's arm, then in his mind. Probably for days.

"Are you moving out, or have you actually moved out already and didn't bother to tell me?" Alex asks without preamble.

"I don't know what that means," Paul says hesitantly, even though he feels like he's been punched.

"Yes, you do. I've been sleeping alone for weeks."

"I certainly haven't been sleeping anywhere else," Paul says. He's tired, and he's annoyed, and he's frankly furious at Alex for having so deliberately chosen a moment. That's some sort of cryptic, additional insult that Paul can't even begin to figure out.

"Our bathroom and closet are still functional. Or should I say my bathroom and closet. Tell me what I should be reading into this, other than that the honeymoon is most definitely over?"

"The honeymoon is hardly over when you won't marry me." Paul knows it's a mistake as soon as he says it, but he can't take the words back. Alex's face twists in disgust.

"Oh my God. What the fuck?" Alex says. "I am twenty-three. Your parents are separated because your dad badgered you into slitting your wrists. I don't even know my dad, and this is how you try to convince me to change my feelings about an institution which, by the way, has been irrelevant to our people for, like, ever…until advertisers decided we had to be normal enough to market to? You are out of your fucking mind."

"When did you become a queer radical?"

"When you tweeted a picture of me with a gun," Alex says casually.

"After that bullshit, you think I care about *normal?*" Paul can't follow whatever strange thread Alex is weaving. "I care about you. And I would like to marry you, if you could wrap your fucking millennial brain around the concept."

Alex sighs. "I am not a child. Not any more than you, anyway. And is that the deal, you only want me if you own me? Sleeping in separate rooms…. Not even talking about the sex here, but this whole thing is feeling a bit medieval."

Paul snorts. "I would like more of you than I have, yes. Especially considering how much of you Liam still has."

"Oh my God. I AM RIGHT HERE. I am right here for the taking, and you have been ignoring me for a *month.* I *work* with Liam. He is my friend. And in case you haven't noticed, we have both made families out of our friends because our families are fucking broken, and I don't understand why you get to have pajama time sleepovers with Carly and then get pissed when I talk to Liam *at work!*"

"I don't fuck women," Paul says dismissively.

"You suggested we have a threesome with her."

"Because you'd be hot with her!"

Alex gapes. "Okay, can that, like, be beside the point while you stop and listen to yourself?"

Paul runs his hands back through his hair. "Our friends and their issues are not the point," he says wearily. "I'm sorry I've been busy, okay? But, fuck, Alex, you know what this life is like. You wanted me to do this. You made a big deal out of it. Don't be pissed at me because you suddenly don't like the costs."

"The other half of that deal was that we would make a go of a relationship," Alex says. "And, frankly, I'm not sure we're in one anymore. By the way, have you always had this ability to rewrite and forget events, or did you learn it on purpose? Or by accident?" His voice is oddly sharp, and Paul winces.

He has, however, no idea how to respond to any of that. "Do you know how many people depend on me?" Paul asks, frustrated.

"I depend on you!"

"You have a job and resources regardless of whether I fuck up," Paul says. "They don't. You're also probably the most resilient person I've ever met. My time is limited and I am trying to do the right thing at every fucking miserable second of this shit."

Alex looks away. "Maybe I don't want to be that resilient anymore."

14

Alex gives up and stops asking Paul to bed. It hurts far too much when he knows the only answer he's going to get is no. Paul doesn't go back into their room except when Alex is out to grab more of his clothes. Alex knows because he starts to check the closet.

Alex sleeps badly, whether from the stress of the situation or from having to sleep alone. To make it worse, Liam badgers him at work when he starts dragging in pale and exhausted. Alex is sure Liam can tell what the genre of problem must be without Alex having to confess anything, but it doesn't stop him from asking.

"Are you not talking because you don't talk, or are you not talking because of our history?" he asks one morning.

Alex wishes he could sit in the courtyard and drink his terrible coffee in peace and maybe go back to sleep.

"What are you even talking about?" Alex tries to deflect. He wishes Liam would learn to do small talk.

Liam sits down next to him on the bench, way inside Alex's preferred bubble of personal space. "Dude, I know something's up with you and Paul."

"Leave it."

"Look, I don't mean to be an asshole here, and I suppose this may be like all sorts of bonus terrible coming from me because I don't actually know how your brain works, but I kind of know how to do relationships, so you should, like, maybe talk to me?"

Alex considers telling all in an effort to make him go the fuck away. He does not care about the exact number of days Liam has been with Carly or Victor or whoever. And he doesn't want advice; he wants to focus on being someone fictional whose life sucks less than his real one.

"Things at home aren't good. No, it's not that Paul is busy. And no, it's not blowing over. We tried that theory," Alex says, clipped and terse.

"This is all just stuff you have to learn how to do." Liam worries his teeth over his lip. "It's okay that you kind of don't know how yet. Although it's sad that Paul doesn't. You should make him look at that."

Alex gives Liam a sarcastic *thank you* before going to hide in his trailer where he finds himself wondering if Craig actually took the dog because Paul didn't have time to walk him.

♦

"Is Alex going to come visit set again?" Darcy asks from her perch on top of the low bookshelf that runs the length of the wall in Paul's office. Paul has no idea why, but she's claimed it as her spot whenever she's in here for a meeting. Or to pester him.

"I don't know. Why?" Paul sighs. Alex has been disruptive enough to his work at home. He can't imagine it would be good to have him at the office as well.

Darcy shrugs. "I like him. He's fun to have around."

Paul frowns. "What has he been telling you?"

Darcy swings her foot gently against the shelf. "Nothing."

Paul suspects that's a flat-out lie — the rest of their friends' loyalties he can predict, but Darcy tries to play all sides. Sometimes, frighteningly, she even succeeds. Right now, though, he doesn't even have the energy to care what ulterior motives she may have.

After an interval where Paul clicks through work on his screen and Darcy is blessedly silent, she twirls the end of one of her braids around her finger. "Are things okay with you two?"

Paul considers lying, but the effort is too much. "No," he says shortly.

Now that the separate bedrooms aren't just a logistical shortcut but part of the ongoing fight their relationship has become, sleeping apart from Alex is awful and a constant reminder of how bad things are. Paul rubs absently at the back of his neck; his head is starting to ache. Even during their first separation, when Alex was on the opposite coast and Paul was a mess not knowing what they were, Paul woke up for weeks expecting Alex to be next to him. Nearly two years of living together doesn't make Alex's absence from his bed — or his from Alex's — any easier even if it's quite nearly by his own choice.

"What's wrong?"

He looks at her over the top of the computer screen. She looks genuinely concerned. Paul's vaguely aware that he shouldn't be telling one of his employees any of this. Especially not an eighteen-year-old virgin who has very little experience of real people in real relationships that have an arc longer than two hours and don't involve singing. But then Paul has never been in a place where work and personal lives aren't impossibly entangled, and it's not like he's been able to talk to Alex effectively about any of it.

"What isn't wrong?" he says.

"Are you guys breaking up?"

Paul chuckles darkly. "Way to be blunt."

"Are you?"

"No. Not yet."

"Why?"

Paul slumps back in his chair. Paul misses Alex desperately and resents missing him. It's just one more way Alex is taking his attention when it really needs to be elsewhere. Their terrible conversations are terrible, and he's constantly terrified that the next one may be the last one. "This show is a full-time commitment. Alex wants way more of my time than I can give him because I can't give him any of it."

Darcy raises an eyebrow; Paul wants to laugh at her judgmentalness. "Not any?"

"If the first thirteen episodes don't go well, we're finished. I've already sunk so much time into *Winsome*, if I give up on it now it's a waste. And I'll fail."

"Way to have faith in the rest of us." Darcy folds her arms over her chest.

Paul shrugs. If *Winsome* tanks, it really will be on him. He's filled this show with the best he could find. "I love him, but every day I think about how much easier my life would be if I did pack up and leave."

"Would it really be easier?"

"More painful, maybe, but yes. It might not be up to me anyway — Alex is thinking of leaving, too."

"Is he really? Did he say something?"

"He doesn't have to say anything." They may have fixed fewer of their communication issues than Paul could wish, but he still knows Alex. This, he's sure of, even if the prospect frightens him less than the idea of his own exit. Other people have never been Paul's worst enemy.

"How did this happen?" Darcy asks. "You used to be awesome."

Paul sighs. "Life happened. The show happened. Somewhere along the line I decided the story was more important."

"Idiot," Darcy says. Her voice is affectionate, but she looks hurt and worried. "Alex is your story."

◆

Paul still makes an effort to go to brunch, because having friends is an important part of being human. Paul desperately needs to still be human, even if, and especially because, he's a miserable failure of a boyfriend. Among other things, Alex is starting to look like a data point.

But sitting in the parking lot at their usual place, tapping his phone off the steering wheel, Paul frets. Alex left for a climb this morning but hasn't texted to say he got to the mountain safely, and he always texts. Paul thinks about walking inside and facing their friends. He can't do it. Brian will be snarky about Alex not coming because he's always snarky. Shawna will be worried because Paul's been avoiding her. Craig will be there with their fucking dog.

Paul starts his car again. Maybe he's driving home to wait for the end of it all, but, at the moment, that's a far better option than having to sit and smile and lie.

◆

Carly lets herself into Victor's house with her key. She feels weird about the fact that she, in addition to Liam, has keys to Victor's house. Any time she's raised the subject, though, Victor says that he resents interruptions so intensely that he'd rather trust them than have to bother with the door when they come over.

"Okay, we need to talk," Carly calls as she nudges the door closed with her foot and makes her way to the kitchen. Victor nods at her from the stove where he's making omelets.

"About?" he asks blandly. He crumbles cheese into one of the pans. Carly kisses Liam hello where he's sitting at the bar that divides the kitchen from the next room, his bare feet hooked on the crossbar of the stool.

"I just got off the phone with Paul. What the fuck is going on with him and Alex?" she says, dropping her bags down and leaning into Liam's side. He snakes an arm around her waist and frowns.

"Nothing good," Liam says.

"Obviously," Victor says. They all sit there silently for a long moment, listening to the faint gas hiss of the stove and Victor occasionally scraping the pans against the burners as he flips the omelets.

"I think it's Paul," Liam says.

"Don't take sides, Lee," Victor chides. "Alex is likely being unhelpful, stubborn, and possibly mean. But Paul is insecure, and that's dangerous."

They eat brunch at the circular black iron cafe table out by the pool. Carly helps ferry things out — utensils, napkins, a pitcher of juice — while Liam sits and fidgets, squinting into the sun.

"I assume at least one of you knows more about this than me," Victor says as he slides each of their plates — pesto and goat cheese for Liam; sun-dried tomatoes, spinach, and mushrooms for Carly; and summer squash for himself — onto the table.

Carly and Liam glance at each other without turning their heads. Victor laughs.

"Well, tell me what's happening," he says, "or start talking about the weather."

Liam goes first. Victor frowns through the not very informative story.

"Why didn't you tell me?" he asks.

"It's not your business," Liam says with a shrug.

Victor narrows his eyes. "Yes," he says with a smile. "But why didn't you tell me?"

Liam puts his utensils down as he considers what to say. He brushes the fingers of one hand across the other, almost as if sketching small figures in front of him. This is what he does whenever he finds himself looking for words.

"The story hasn't turned yet," he says eventually.

"What do you mean?" Carly asks.

"You're worried about what's happened," Victor says pointing at her. Then he points at Liam. "He's telling you that the thing to worry about hasn't happened yet."

15

Solo climbs are, as Alex's various instructors have insisted on telling him, riskier than partnered ones. Free climbs are even worse. But there's no one Alex trusts who also has time enough to meet him as a regular climbing partner, and he's hardly in the sport for the companionship.

He's not free climbing today because the weather looks iffy and, while Alex likes the physical risk and challenge, he does not actually have a death wish. He is alone, however, on one of the routes he hasn't been able to complete yet. He's grateful, as always, for the silence and the solitude. Home is way too quiet, but it's impossible to think there anymore because the silence between him and Paul is so damn loud. Alex is dreading the day when he finally comes home and finds Paul's car and everything gone. He's never regretted pulling his own version of that stunt on Paul years ago more than he has in the last few weeks.

His misery at work is, at least, solidifying into something actually useful. His work on *Fourth* is far from over — he, Liam, and some of the rest of the cast are headed to D.C. soon to do exteriors — but the show's days are still numbered. Alex can either get out now or wait to go down with the ship. Either way, he's not worried about finding work. But, now that he's had to start thinking of the future he can't unsee the opportunities either. There are new things to do and try and be, none of which can happen while he's still Zach Reagan and tied to Victor's behemoth.

Zach's due for his next big adventure anyway. He wiggles his fingers into a crevice and braces his weight carefully to dig his foot into the next toehold. Victor will be pissed, but Alex will hardly be the first star to jump ship for other things. He'll enjoy the challenge of finding Zach a good send-off. Liam probably won't like it, but losing Zach in one way or another will be good for James.

He's unbalanced, or the foothold isn't as strong as he thought it was, because Alex loses his footing, banging into the cliff face and getting rocked, yet again. He swears at the bite and sting of it and the way it's always scary, even with safety equipment. As he lets the ropes hold him for a moment as he comes down from the adrenaline spike, Alex giggles. He knows exactly what Zach's end is going to be.

He can't wait to tell Victor.

◆

Alex wants to tell Paul, too. Talking things out with him is part of how Alex has come to process the world, even if words with everyone else are often so damn hard.

But Paul's car isn't in the garage. The house is empty and quiet except for Todd, who winds around Alex's ankles looking to be fed. Alex is annoyed. Not even at Paul's general absence, which is nothing remotely new. But because he's not here when Alex actually has something to talk about that isn't one of their eight hundred fucking problems.

It's late already. Alex's call is early, and there's no point waiting up, so he doesn't.

♦

Alex waits to talk to Victor until shooting is done for the day. And then he waits longer. He has no urge to go home, and it feels right to do this when no one else is around to witness it.

He doesn't bother to knock on Victor's door, just leans into the office.

"Victor," he says.

"Yes?" The other man looks up from his desk.

"I need to talk to you."

Victor waves him into the room. Alex drops into the chair on the other side of the desk without further invitation.

On some level it's bizarre to sit across from Victor in this same office, in the exact same chair, where his whole new life began. Except that now, unlike then, he understands his job and is sure of what comes next.

"I'm out," he says.

"Really," Victor drawls.

"Yes. Don't act like you're surprised."

"Surprised, no. Curious, yes. Why now?"

"Because I know how it ends. And why you're not going to be pissed at me for quitting." Alex leans forward in his chair, wanting to be closer to Victor for possibly the first time ever. "At the end of the third arc, you're going to kill Zach, and it's going to be *awesome*."

Victor sits back in his chair and laughs. "This is why you are my other favorite."

Alex smiles, fierce and sly.

"Who else have you told?"

"Nobody."

"Not even Paul?" Victor asks. The question is leading.

"No. I will."

Victor pauses at that only slightly. "And Liam?"

"What do you think?"

Victor looks surprised. Probably because Alex asked an honest question instead of giving a sarcastic response. He has no idea what to do about Liam.

"When you're ready to," Victor says, "tell him you're quitting. I'll tell him about Zach."

Alex nods.

"This is going to make your D.C. shoot interesting."

"D.C. shoots are always interesting. And rarely good," Alex says.

Victor frowns. "D.C. is fine. It's the messes you drag after yourself that are not."

Alex shrugs, as if lying to Victor, or to himself, is no big deal. They both know what D.C. means to him and that there are only some days when he enjoys the sensation of a thumb pressed into the bruise.

◆

The night before Alex leaves for Washington, an appallingly hot night at the end of July, Paul is actually home, in the kitchen, when Alex finally comes in from work.

"Hey," Alex says softly, because Paul's *there* and not, for the moment, working. He's a little surprised and a lot grateful.

"Hey." Paul turns around and leans against the sink.

"I'm leaving tomorrow," Alex says. It's almost a question.

"Are —"

"The shoot. I just meant the shoot. But we should talk."

"Okay." Paul braces his hands on the edge of the counter.

Alex laughs, awkward and wet. "Can we not... in the kitchen?" He feels guilty for asking.

Paul nods and drops his chin onto his chest. "That is... fair and awkward," he tries.

Alex smiles, almost, and heads into the living room. Once there he doesn't know where to sit and stands a little uncomfortably by one of the big bookcases in lieu of figuring it out.

"Is this a you telling me things conversation?" Paul asks when he finally walks into the room.

"No. Yes... I have some things to tell you, but that's not what this is. I don't think," Alex says.

"Go ahead." Paul petulantly drops onto the couch.

Alex works not to grit his teeth and ball his hands into angry fists. He can't help but feel like Paul is trying to make trouble when they already have enough.

"I'm quitting," he says. "*Fourth*," he adds, before Paul can interject, again.

Of the roster of things Paul might have fairly expected Alex to come home with, Alex quitting his job was clearly nowhere near the list. He looks a little stunned. "Is this because of me?"

"No," Alex says. It's a vain and obnoxious question, but he also recognizes that it's not an unreasonable one. "I won't say I'm not thinking about shit differently because of whatever is going on with us, but I don't want to wait 'til the end. I want to have choices."

"That feels incredibly ominous." Paul's voice is more than a little snide.

Alex folds his arms over his chest. "Yeah. Well, right now, every time I come home feels a little bit ominous. Does it for you too?"

"Considering that you're avoiding me and we didn't talk about this?" Paul asks, leaning his elbows on his knees and looking up at Alex sharply. "Yeah."

Alex frowns. "You get that you're the one who moved into the other bedroom, right?"

"I thought maybe that would be clearer and less disappointing to you."

"What is going on in your head?" Alex asks. Every time they touch this mess it seems to make less sense than the time before.

"*You*. You're quitting your job. I didn't even know you were thinking about this —"

"You should have," Alex puts in, unhelpfully, but it's true. Victor knew, and Paul hasn't been home to tell.

"You don't get to ask me to be psychic," Paul says. "Everything else may be fucked, but I thought we had had that one thing cleared up thanks to the Great Thanksgiving Disaster."

"I didn't know it had a name," Alex says. "When did it get a name? When you liked me and it was funny or when you apparently started keeping score?"

"I can like you and not us, and I am always keeping score."

"What the fuck?" Alex starts pacing. He doesn't understand or really even recognize Paul right now.

"On me. Not you," Paul says.

It's no less horrible, but it at least makes slightly more sense. "You shouldn't do that," Alex says quietly.

"When's your flight?"

"Tomorrow at noon."

"I'll be at work."

"I assumed," Alex says shortly.

"When are you getting back?" Paul asks.

"I don't know. The schedule's still iffy. Will you even be here when I do?" It's the one terrible question. Alex is both glad Paul is actually here to answer it, and terrified of the answer, because he has absolutely no idea.

"I don't know either."

"Okay then," Alex says and sinks down onto the chair across from Paul. "Okay."

"I think we either need to make a decision now," Paul says carefully, "Or agree that we won't, until you're back."

Alex bites his lip and nods. "What do you want to do?"

"Frankly? I don't even have time to break up with you right now."

Alex thinks about throwing him out right then and there. It's not that the loss of the relationship hurts, although it does. It's that everything Paul is saying makes him feel so small.

"Trial separation, then?" he asks quietly.

Paul nods. "Something like that."

"Can I call you?" Alex asks. "When I'm on the road."

"You always do," Paul offers. It's not kind.

"Is that a no?" Alex says tightly.

"It's a maybe. You do what you want, no matter how ill-advised, and there's never an instant where I can even imagine saying no to you. That scares me to death, and it was there from the second I laid eyes on you. What if that cost me Craig and a normal, boring life —"

"You work in TV. Normal and boring weren't ever going to be an option."

"Yeah, and my number-one obsession has to be this show. That might have been possible with someone else, but it doesn't feel possible with you. I can't let you cost me this."

"That's a whole lot of irrational and unfair," Alex says. "I'm not going to cost you your show."

"You have no idea what it's like to be in love with you."

"Then tell me about it." Alex isn't fishing for compliments, nor is he hoping Paul remembers; he's hunting for clues.

"You overwhelm me. And I'm already on my second chance. If I fail at this because I never said no to you, you'll hate me. I'll hate myself."

Aside from offering reassurance he's fairly certain won't actually make a difference, Alex wants, very desperately, to tell Paul he is not cut out for this. That he should be the head writer and let someone else be showrunner and producer and all-around mad emperor. He also knows that, no matter how potentially accurate it may be, it's not a sentiment Paul wants or needs to hear right now. It certainly won't help their relationship.

"I know," he says. "You're also not Victor."

"If I could just be disciplined enough —"

"And what? Play with people like flies to rip the wings off of?" Alex asks.

"You think better of him than that."

"Not really. I don't make moral judgments about it, but I know what he is. I'm not sure why no one else does, but that doesn't matter. Everybody needs love, even flawed, controlling, funny, creepy Victor. And certainly even you."

"He doesn't," Paul says. "And it makes me feel like maybe I shouldn't either."

Alex folds his arms over his chest. "You are being ridiculous. Victor hates humanity and yet has some fucked up thing with Liam. You're being a crappy boyfriend, and you both work in TV. That's it. That's the whole similarity, *your jobs*. Emulating Victor is not a good choice for you."

"I miss you," Paul says.

"Yeah? Well, I miss you too. And I've been missing you since before you left for the other side of the house. But I can't keep having conversations about your pain where mine doesn't exist." Alex gets up to head upstairs.

"That's it?" Paul asks.

"If you have anything else to say to me right now, Mr. Trial Separation, you can do it in the dark, in our bed, with your clothes off. With words or sex. I don't care which. Otherwise, I'll see you when I get back."

♦

As miserable as he is, Alex feels a little bit proud. He didn't storm out. He didn't even slam the bedroom door. It all feels final, though. He doesn't start shaking until he sits down on the bed.

The last thing Alex expects after he's turned out the lights — bags packed and a worried email composed to Carly, who is possibly the only person who understands Paul better than he does — is the door to open. He doesn't say anything at first, merely watches Paul undress in the dark. When Paul lifts the duvet and climbs into bed, Alex is shocked and a little ashamed at how automatically his body moves to tangle itself with Paul's. It feels like water to be touched by someone who isn't paid to do so. He's long since given up trying to explain to people what it feels like to be an object for hair and makeup and wardrobe, for the cameras, and for the fans. Even Liam doesn't understand, because that's also how Victor loves him.

"This is unexpected," Alex says softly. "And really good."

"I'm sorry, I know," Paul says, smoothing a hand over Alex's hair. "I thought if this is really only going to be a trial, we should make some rules, not make everything worse."

"No fucking other people," Alex says.

"Agreed. Not what this is about. That includes Liam."

"Still not the issue you think it is." Alex says. It's weird how, pressed together in the dark, even all this misery is suddenly just funny and so them.

"No decisions about living arrangements until you're back," Paul says.

"You can't tell someone not to make a decision," Alex says. "That's not how decisions work."

"Okay," Paul says. Alex can hear in his voice it's not easy. "We're the first to know in any decisions about living arrangements. Don't fucking call movers without calling me first."

"Paul?"

"Yes?"

"Among other things, it's my house."

Paul cracks up and rolls onto his back, fist to his mouth as he apparently tries to figure out in which direction his hysteria is about to go.

"We have to fix that," he says, clearly without thinking. Then he sobers. "I mean, if we fix the rest of this."

"Yeah. Okay," Alex says. "That's…we can do that."

"Wait. Did you just agree to marry me?"

Alex blinks. It's the same leap Paul has been making over and over again. First, because he thought that *actually making a go* of their relationship when Paul started pursuing his own show meant getting married once he actually got it. Second, because Paul thinks them putting his name on the deed to Alex's house means the same thing. "No, Paul. I agreed to paperwork considerings if I don't leave you. Don't make this weirder."

Paul chuckles wetly. "That's probably fair."

"You think?" Alex decides he should also not also point out that Paul is talking marriage again an hour after considering, very seriously, breaking up with him. He wonders if Paul has always been this volatile, or if it's just something Alex is bringing out in him now.

"Can I kiss you?" Paul asks.

Against his better judgment, Alex nods.

The kiss isn't wet or deep or sexy, but it also doesn't feel like goodbye. It is solemn, though, and after, Paul presses his forehead to Alex's. It feels like a promise.

Paul isn't there in the morning when Alex wakes up, not that Alex is surprised. They are, for the first time in months, on the same page, even if it is a terrible one. As he leaves for the airport, he almost feels okay. He certainly feels older, which he doesn't mind at all. He needs all the tools and strength he can get.

He texts Paul when he lands to let him know he's gotten in safely and actually gets a reply. Once he's checked in, he texts Liam to the same effect but with clear instructions to not call, appear at, or otherwise consider the existence of his hotel room. They can hang out tomorrow, after they've seen each other on set. While Alex has no particular interest in fucking Liam again, outside of his agreement with Paul he still needs to be sure his costar isn't some sort of refuge — sexual, emotional, or logistical — for him right now.

D.C. is strange and haunted and odd, even when Alex isn't being someone else. As a bonus, this is probably his last time here as Zach. It makes Alex thoughtful and sadder than he had expected, both for Zach and for what he himself will be losing.

That they aren't doing night shoots this time is a godsend, but they're still outside all day in the terrible heat and humidity of summer in D.C. Given that they're trying to use every hour of daylight possible, that means pre-dawn calls and shooting through sunset. The days are long, exhausting, and disgustingly sticky.

Alex doesn't mind the physical work of it, but there is absolutely no magic in sweating through his costume before the sun is up. To make matters worse, people will not stop fussing over him and making sure he's drinking enough water. Which, fair, maybe, but Alex has no desire to revisit that particular ordeal and is perfectly capable of keeping himself hydrated. Not that that ever gets taken into account in a job where he is an asset but not quite an autonomous person.

The first day is less terrible than it could be, weather aside. That Raphael is there too is a relief, because that means Liam has someone other than Alex to badger in between takes. Alex doesn't feel like talking to anyone. For now he's happy to get absorbed in the work and be alternately amused at — and frustrated by — the fans and curious passers-by who stop to watch.

"Maybe we should kiss to keep them entertained," Liam muses during a long wait.

Alex smacks him on the arm and doesn't yell only because he knows Liam is not anywhere close to being serious. Liam has been very clear that he's looking forward to Victor joining them for a few days later in the week. Alex suspects that's likely to be more peculiar than he can currently anticipate.

◆

"So, we get to hang out now, right?" Liam asks once they've wrapped for the day and Alex is cursing mosquitoes.

"You've been looking forward to this, haven't you?"

Liam loops an arm through his to drag him off.

Alex grumbles.

"Oh, like you haven't."

Alex lets himself chuckle. Like everything else in his life right now, the answer is complicated, but complicated is something he knows how to do with Liam.

Alex has no patience for people or public right now, although he suspects his preferences may have to change later in the week in order to placate Victor. For now, he's more than happy to tag back to Liam's room with him. He wants somewhere quiet, without people and with air conditioning.

"Dude, do you want a shower?" Liam asks, when Alex drops into the armchair and props his feet over the AC vent.

Alex makes a face. "Between the trailer shower and yours, the trailer is actually preferable."

"Dude, ow."

"Also my room is next door."

"Okay, point." Liam hands Alex one of the bottles of water from on top of the dresser — ridiculous, the things that stay the same — and sits down on the edge of the bed. "How are you?"

Alex shrugs.

Liam swings a foot into his chair. "Alex," he says quietly.

"We're on a trial separation," Alex says, picking at the label of the water bottle. Liam will nag him until he says something and saying it out loud won't change the reality of the situation. But it does feel different — worse — to say.

Liam frowns. "That doesn't sound good."

Alex chuckles darkly. "It's actually better than it has been."

"How the hell does that work?"

"We had an actual conversation. No one yelled. No one wants this? Like, I know I'm whatever I am, but he is not okay."

"And separation is the solution?" Liam asks warily.

"I don't know, Liam," Alex says too sharply. It's not Liam's fault. "I don't know how this works. All I know is that I'm in this fucking city again, and I have no idea what happens when I get home."

He considers telling Liam the rest of it, about quitting, at least. He doesn't know how Liam's going to react to that, other than badly, and he wants at least one twenty-four-hour period in his life without a crisis to manage. "But I learned things here last time. Maybe I will this time too."

"That sounds less dire," Liam says carefully. "Even though it freaks the hell out of me to think about you and Paul not being together. But I still don't understand why this is happening."

Alex blinks at him. It's not Liam's to understand. "Join the club," he says.

Liam says nothing else, because Liam's an asshole and seems to have absolutely no circuit in his head that reminds him it's quiet and he's been staring for too long,

"A lot of it is time," Alex says to break the silence.

"Not enough time?"

"I don't know. No. I mean, it's not like anybody has enough, but — no."

"Then what is it?"

Alex tips his head back against the chair and squeezes his eyes shut. Liam is still staring and it's disconcerting. "Attention. Focus. Plans. It doesn't matter what we call it, we just *aren't*, anymore. At least we're actually naming it."

"And that feels good?"

"It feels terrible. Now, it's a terrible that might have a solution. So that's what we're going to try to focus on. If Paul ever picks up his phone."

"He will," Liam says. "Like, I can't imagine him not."

"You don't know what it's been like."

"Well, no, because you're not telling me, but I know he loves you."

Alex shrugs again. He adds Liam's optimism to the list of things he dislikes about him.

Liam frowns. "Okay, see, now you're acting like that part isn't important or grounds for a solution, which means we may both be out of our depths here."

Alex tilts his head back to laugh at the ceiling. It feels unsettling, even to him.

"We're so different," Liam says. "And I really regret that right now, because I want to help."

"You are one of the things we fight about," Alex says. "I shouldn't tell you that, but it's true."

"He jealous?" Liam says simply.

Alex shrugs again. "He thinks he is."

"What do you think?"

"I think he thinks if he's jealous of you, then he's not responsible for the fact that I feel like I've been left for a TV show. And he is jealous of you."

"Have you been left for a TV show?"

"He lives on the other side of the house."

"Okay," Liam says. He folds his legs up to sit cross-legged. "Why are you two monogamous again?"

"Lee! Not helping."

"No, no, no, that's not what I mean. Just, he met someone new, and he's really into her. Now you're feeling neglected because you don't know how to talk about it, and I'm feeling kind of Poly 101 at you, except she's a TV show about hookers, and you're both fucking dense."

Alex stares at him.

"Are you gaping at me because I'm right or because I'm wrong?" Liam asks.

"I don't know, keep talking," Alex says although he realizes he may regret that later.

"Okay, so, New Relationship Energy. One, *Winsome* is a bright, shiny object. It is something Paul's wanted for a long time. It makes him feel sexy and smart and powerful, so he is doing everything he can to make sure it sticks around. Two, he's got you, he's been really sure of your place in his life. He starts to focus on this other thing because you love him and he loves you and everyone knows that —"

"Yeah, that's called taking me for granted."

"Three, don't interrupt me."

Alex laughs.

"It's only called taking you for granted if you didn't discuss it and figure out how *Winsome* fits into your relationship."

"What's to discuss? It's work," Alex says. "You know we all sign away our lives to the dream."

"No, I don't know that. I've been doing this most of my life. I'm getting married to a wonderful woman. I've known my best friend since we were eight, and I've got a man who doesn't even like sex or want to need anyone thrilled to take me to bed because it makes me happy."

Alex wants to whine about it all being too much information, because it is, but Liam also has a point. "You're making me feel incompetent," he says instead.

"That's because hierarchies only work if they're flexible."

"Explain."

"I've been with Victor six years. I'm marrying someone I've been dating for four. Who's the winner?"

"Carly," Alex says automatically. He keeps to himself the fact that he's been half assuming Liam's thing with Victor will end with the wedding.

"No, idiot. *Me.*"

It's a lot to think about — and challenging. Following along with Liam isn't always easy. But Alex is starting to see, if not a solution, at least the roots of his and Paul's problems a little more clearly. He and Paul *haven't* been talking. Not usefully. And that's on Alex as much as it is on Paul. Whether it's fixable at this point is a different question.

When Alex finally goes back to his room, he thinks about calling Paul, but decides he's not ready yet for whatever that will or won't be. He texts him instead, to tell him he's thinking of him.

A reply comes, but over an hour later, as Alex is falling asleep, his phone on the pillow next to him as his only company.

Thanks for this, it says. *Thinking about you too.*

♦

Alex waits until the end of shooting the next day to find Liam and say, "There's something I need to tell you."

Liam frowns. "Okay. Your room or mine?"

Alex sighs and stalks off.

They end up in Liam's room again, though Alex detours for a proper shower first. He'd be perfectly happy to put off breaking the news for longer, except that Victor is coming in tomorrow. Alex has no idea when Victor plans to tell Liam about Zach, but he does know he'll be pissed if Alex doesn't hold up his end of the deal. Besides, direct communication seems to be a thing that's working for him right now.

"Okay." This time Alex sits on the bed next to Liam. It's harder to tell Liam this than it was to tell Paul. His friendship with Liam isn't only about work. But their relationship started with, and has always involved, the people they are paid to be. Even if that's not in the ways the internet seems to think. But Liam gave him good advice last night, and he deserves to know this.

"You're scaring me a little," Liam says when Alex doesn't say anything after that. "Did you and Paul like break up since yesterday, or is this something totally else?"

Alex laughs darkly. "Something else. I'm quitting."

"Quitting what?"

"The show."

"What?"

"*Fourth Estate.*"

Liam blinks. "Okay. That I really don't understand."

"I'm going to stop working on the show," Alex says slowly.

"Don't be a dick," Liam says, a little sharply. "Also, you know that all that shit about being poly and everything doesn't mean you have to freak out and go and like quit all of your other things so you're not, right? Because we can go up to Poly 201 if we have to, but I thought you were at least not hearing the very opposite of what I was saying."

Alex chuckles. "Lee, I promise, this has nothing to do with that conversation. As much as I do appreciate it. I decided a while ago. I want to try some new things."

"Okaaay," Liam says slowly. "Is this because Paul's jealous of me?"

"No. It's got nothing to do with you. A little to do with Paul, though not how either of you think."

"How, then?"

"I told him he had to stop playing things safe to be with me, which is sort of how we got into this mess. But I also can't wait on his comfort to have my career. I'm good at this, and I loved *Paradise*. I don't want to be some kid who just got lucky any more than I want to be stuck in this year of vacation-free shooting. It was a nasty, nasty thing the network did to Victor."

"Yeah, but he's not quitting."

"No, but he's planning, and I need to be too."

"But the guy in my head is in love with the guy in your head."

Alex makes an incoherent noise and flops backwards on the bed. This is impossible on so many levels. Liam gets to his heart in the crappiest, most inconvenient ways.

"No?" Liam asks.

"I might be breaking up with Paul. Zach is not breaking up with James." Alex is immensely relieved Victor is the one who gets to tell Liam what happens with Zach. He also feels immensely shitty that he's about to, in essence, lie. Because he's pretty sure *death* ranks above *breakup* on the list of terrible reasons to no longer be in a relationship, even a fictional one.

"But your guy is gonna be gone."

"Nope." Alex taps a finger against his sternum. "My guy comes with me."

"I don't know what that means."

"It means that you and I are beautifully fucked up, Liam. And where I'm working doesn't change that."

"I'm going to miss you," Liam says. He sounds profoundly sad.

"Idiot." Alex lifts his head to look at him. "I'm still right here."

"But on the other side of the house."

"No." Alex works to keep several conflicting emotions in check. Liam can be exhausting. "That's a shitty metaphor. I'm still talking to you and we are not broken. You know that."

Liam takes a deep breath. "I'm really glad Victor's coming tomorrow."

"Yeah," Alex says, chagrined. "Me too."

◆

Back in his room Alex flops down onto his bed. He's tired and feeling a little terrible for unleashing that news on Liam. He loves Liam, in a purely platonic way, but it's still exhausting.

He texts Paul.

How is everything going?

The reply comes faster tonight, before he even gets his clothes off to go to bed.

Increasingly convinced Victor is inhuman.

Alex chuckles to himself. *I could have told you that from day one.* It's easier to complain about Victor than stop to actually think about him. If he did, Alex knows he'd have to deal with things about himself he wouldn't like.

I'm not convinced you're human, Paul replies. Alex sighs If only Paul would realize that there's nothing about him, or them, that's abnormal, Alex's life would be so much easier.

I'll take that as a compliment. Sleeping now.

Todd says hi, Paul sends. It's that, that sends Alex curling up under the covers, phone clenched in his hand and desperately homesick.

17

Things are better in the light of day. Once he gets himself out of bed, Alex looks forward to going to set and getting to work. Liam is unusually quiet. Alex is pretty sure that's less about his news than because Victor is expected later that morning. Of course, there may be overlap there, but mostly all Alex can see is someone excited about *boyfriend* and *hotel* on someone else's dime. Even if Liam has consistently refuted Alex's descriptors of the situation every time he's offered up another little of piece of it for his understanding.

Alex finds their relationship strange because it's not the sort of thing that would ever fit into his life. He can't even, really, see the appeal of it. But whatever it is, Alex gets that it tugs at them in the same way as that strange, sad night he and Liam spent together at his parents' place in New York two winters ago. He knows that Liam and Victor are lucky to be able to make a feeling like that work.

He also knows, after last night's conversation with Liam, that maybe his own deal with Liam — at least in Liam's head — isn't even that different. And as long as they never, ever have to talk about it (because direct communication only goes so far), Alex is good with that.

◆

When Victor arrives, he's all business. Not that he isn't to most people's eyes always. But sometimes there's a softness around his mouth and a weariness to his eyes that Alex recognizes as his having time for the more personal concerns of his friends and colleagues. This is not one of those times. Alex suspects Victor is trying to power through the jet lag he claims not to get. Whether or not other people see it, they all stand up straighter for him. Beside him, Liam is practically vibrating out of his set chair.

Victor spends the shoot day mostly silent, ensconced in a fortress of chairs and folding tables and too many digital screens. Alex has no idea if he's watching the rushes straight from camera thanks to the miracle of digital, or if he's working on something else entirely and being ominous for his own amusement. Ultimately, Alex is oddly grateful for his presence. Everything runs just a little bit tighter — and Liam seems just a little bit more solidly attached to this world — when he's around.

At lunch, Victor pulls Alex aside, fingers sharp in the crook of his elbow. "You tell him?"

"What, not how," Alex says.

"And how was that?" Victor asks.

Alex is surprised by the question, having assumed that Liam called Victor after Alex returned to his own room. "We're fine."

"I'm not planning on telling him the rest any time soon."

"That's a shit thing to do," Alex says.

Victor shrugs, amused. "You're an actor; you should have fewer qualms about lying."

Alex throws his hands up in the air at that, because *what the actual fuck.* Victor's only response is to stroll away laughing, which is oddly delightful. Alex spends the rest of the day tapping his tongue against the back of his teeth and wondering if he and Victor are somehow becoming friends.

♦

Back in his room, Alex only considers it briefly before he picks up his phone and dials Paul. It's been a long day and he's tired, even more so after Liam's strangeness and Victor to deal with, but it's been over two days now and a text isn't enough. Paul can beat himself up all he wants for it, but Alex knows Paul's not the only one who's obsessed in all of this.

To his surprise, relief, and not a little bit of fear, because Alex isn't even sure exactly what he wants to say, Paul actually answers.

"Alex," Paul says. He sounds tired, which Alex doesn't know how to read absent further clues. He wonders, though he does not want to ask, whether Paul is still at the office. Is he home yet? Having another sleepover with Carly?

Alex curls up under the covers and presses the phone to his ear. "You picked up."

"I did say maybe."

"It was the kind of maybe that sounded like a no".

"It didn't stop you," Paul says.

"No," Alex says. "You knew it wouldn't."

"Probably."

Alex rolls over onto his back and stares at the ceiling in the dark. "I told him," he says. If they're going to have a conversation at all, he wants to keep ripping Band-Aids off, no matter how much they end up hurting.

"Oh," Paul says. "Liam?"

"Yeah."

"You never told me how Zach leaves the show," Paul points out.

"You're changing the subject. And you're assuming I know."

"I know you. And Victor. And it seemed preferable to yelling."

"Paul, I am not naked in his room right now," Alex says a little testily. "As evidenced by me calling you. I don't even think Liam is in his room right now, although I would like not to dwell on that."

Paul snorts. "I think you're joking?"

Alex makes a face at the ceiling and wishes a little that Paul were here, so he could kick at him under the covers. "I don't know how to say this in words that you're actually going to understand, because I've been trying for years and no go, but Liam isn't the person I call in the middle of the night when everything is shit."

"Does that matter?" Paul asks. Alex is surprised at how plaintive it is.

"It actually does," he says softly.

"I watched the episode, you know," Paul tells Alex, a little sheepishly.

"Which?"

"The one with the Zach and James sex."

Alex frowns at the phone in annoyed disbelief. "Well, that was stupid."

"Yeah. Probably," Paul concedes. "The thought of you and Liam together was bad enough. The actual visual was terrible and also hot in ways I am not equipped to deal with."

"What did you do?" Alex asks.

"I think I threw something."

Alex snorts. "Did you break anything?"

"No. Bent a few script pages, but whatever."

"Paul."

"Yeah?"

"You are fucked up."

Paul laughs. "Yeah. I am."

Alex runs a hand through his hair and debates telling Paul all the ways in which he and Liam were not like Zach and James, but he doesn't owe him that, and the outcome won't be good anyway.

"I'm not setting conditions, although I can see how I might. And I'm not making decisions yet. But I think that's a thing we're going to have to talk about, when I get back, if…." he trails off.

"Yeah," Paul agrees though he sounds far from certain. "If."

"Are you making decisions?" Alex asks.

"Hundreds of them," Paul says. "Every day."

Alex isn't sure if Paul's changing the topic or not.

18

The next day, Liam is as quiet and steady as Alex has ever seen him. Alex's first thought is how obvious it is that Liam's gotten laid, or whatever it counts as when Victor doesn't do sex, until he remembers that Liam gets laid all the time. In fact, Liam probably only doesn't get laid when he and Alex are hanging out. Alex sighs and supposes he's glad Victor is a good influence on someone.

The day is long. While he doesn't have to do much heavy lifting as a performer, the hurry up and wait seems more egregious than usual. No matter how often the production assistants keep asking the pedestrians to keep moving, someone keeps winding up in the back of a shot, gawking. As much as Alex wants to hide in his trailer with the A.C. blasting, if everyone else is outside sweating their asses off, he's determined to be too. The person on set being paid the most should always suffer as much as the person being paid the least. He'd learned that on *Paradise Square* and he's tried to keep to it.

After work, Victor tells him that they're all going out tonight. Alex grits his teeth at how it's not a question. He winds up grabbing sushi with Liam, Raphael, and Natalie before she swans off to a lounge event and the rest of them are due to meet Victor.

"Some launch for some fucking artisanal booze," Liam says of Natalie's destination without any particular malice. As if an event designed to brand a random product with Washington D.C.'s power isn't an entirely ridiculous prospect.

Raphael catches Alex's eye and gives him a look. Alex has to stifle a laugh because Raphael works hard not to be as judgmental as the rest of them, but he is so totally judging. It makes Alex like him more.

"Is there anyone you don't like on some level?" Alex asks Liam. It's not the first time he's thought of it, but it is the first time he's' felt impelled to say it out loud.

"Nope." Liam snags Alex's pickled ginger which his chopsticks.

"I feel like I'm chaperoning you two," Raphael says.

"You're not that old," is Liam's quick reply.

Alex cackles as the conversation segues into Raphael's new baby and his extensive smartphone documentation of its first few months of life. As Liam passes the phone to Alex, he remembers his first brunch with Paul and how lost everyone else's seemingly adult lives had made him feel. Now there is this, as normal as anything in his life.

After they pay — Raphael muttering and throwing in for Natalie, because she forgot and it's not the money but the principle of the thing — Liam leads them to their next destination.

"Are you sure you know where you're going?" Alex asks. The noise and the crowd and the nightlife are clearly three blocks to the left, but Liam is monologuing at them about the Masons. Of course — because Alex and the universe have a timing issue with each other — they arrive at their destination within thirty seconds of Alex's question, Liam opening the door and ushering him in just to be snide. Then he tries to figure out what the fuck he's supposed to think about Liam's or Victor's or whoever's idea this was taste in bars.

The place is a mostly empty dive with a mix of red walls and wood paneling that evoke the 1970s in an alternate hell universe. That Victor and Ellen are sitting at a narrow table in the corner sipping drinks and smirking at them only cements the picture.

"Fuck the artisanal booze," Raphael says from over Alex's shoulder. "Now I know why Natalie didn't join us."

Alex lets Liam slide in next to Victor, and then yanks a chair away from another table and sits down on that instead. Liam pouts, but Ellen laughs and nods her approval in a way that suggests that Victor has told her about their little affair. Alex wants to be annoyed, but it's not Ellen's fault. She's always been kind to him without being patronizing.

"Where's Natalie?" Victor asks.

"Artisanal booze launch party," Raph says dryly.

"She's trying to get in the *Washingtonian* again," Liam adds.

Victor smiles lazily. "And why aren't you trying to get in the *Washingtonian*, Liam?"

Liam gives a shrug and a little preening smile in response. Alex realizes, with some dim horror and an odd fondness, that Victor is actually flirting. The sight of Victor pursuing something and being coquettish about it is flat out bizarre.

Apparently Raph comes to the same conclusion. "Gentlemen, we're in public and your charm is showing," he says mildly.

Liam looks unabashed; Victor, amused.

Alex wonders exactly how terrible this night is going to be.

Raphael pulls his chair in closer to the table. "So now that we've all been summoned…."

"We drink," Victor says matter-of-factly.

Alex and Raphael exchange a glance because that cannot possibly be the entire punchline. Alex levers himself out of his chair.

"Alex, sit," Victor says. "Liam will fetch drinks."

Liam slides out of his chair like this is both perfectly reasonable and a request, when it's clearly neither. He takes two steps toward the bar before turning back to the table and squinting like he's just figured out this situation is fucked up.

"What's everyone drinking?" he asks.

Alex sinks back into his seat and almost groans at how guileless he is. As much as the thing with Victor is not his business, there are times when he feels like it should be. Liam may not need his protection, but as far as Alex can tell he sure could use it.

Liam leans, not on the back of Victor's chair, but on Victor himself, hands pressed down onto his shoulders as he waits for everyone to figure out what they're having. When they're not prompt enough Liam announces that everyone will be getting tequila shots if they don't give him a proper order right now. Alex thinks that's fair. It's not like he's volunteered a plan either.

Victor chuckles under his hands and Liam, to Alex's shock, bends down and kisses his hair.

Alex blinks theatrically. He slowly glances toward Raphael in hopes that a lack of sudden movement will prevent things from getting worse. Raph's eyes slide to him with the same nervous caution and a complete lack of stealth. A second and a half later they both burst into uncontrollable laughter.

◆

Victor ignores them because they are being children and tilts his head back to deal with Liam, for whom sweet and inappropriate are always the same word. What he expects to see is Liam, distracted, amused, and his ill-advised moment of public affection already forgotten such that Victor's required glare will be worthless.

But Liam's looking at him with a soft smile and the too-bright eyes reserved only for him, Carly, and the camera. For a moment the whole room pulls away from them; the noise recedes and the red of the bar goes just a little bit gray before everything snaps back into place.

"You shouldn't do things like that," Victor manages, but he knows he's off-balance and looks it.

Liam shrugs. "Tequila it is," he says and walks away.

Victor straightens up to see Alex and Raphael studiously ignoring him while cackling at each other. An amused Ellen snaps her fingers way too close to his face.

"Careful," he says to her. "I bite."

"Not me, you don't."

♦

If there is any actual purpose to the gathering it remains a mystery to Alex. Liam not only fetches several rounds of truly terrible tequila but manages to flit his way around their seating arrangements all night. At point he jokingly landing in Ellen's lap and at another he drapes himself over Alex's back. Sitting still seems beyond him.

Alex talks to Raph for a good part of the evening, eventually moving from platitudes about his wife and baby to perfectly serious *how do you do it?* questions. The answers would be less heartbreaking if Raphael didn't assume he and Paul were already talking kids. The advice, while good ("Sometimes it's hard and there's nothing you can do about it. You have to decide if you're okay with riding it out when it's like that") makes Alex despair more than a little. He's starting to learn that any problems they fix now, they're going to have to keep fixing over and over and over.

He drinks too much. They all do for a school night. But Victor seems relaxed as Liam kneads his thigh under the table. Ellen tips her head back, watching the room.

"We're the worst sort of interlopers," she says. "Fucking asshole fabulous hipsters who think it's cool to be slumming."

"We're a local shoot; we patronize local businesses," Victor says to her, a finger not quite pointing in her face, something resembling anger dulled by the rounds of tequila. "And you don't get to talk to me about slumming. You're too white and you're too rich."

"You have the biggest house," she points out.

"Yes, darling," he drawls. Alex wishes Paul were here to see Victor actually going in for the kill in the slow motion of alcohol. "Because I'm the best, because I've had to be."

"Burrrrrnnnn," Raph says and reaches across the table to high-five Victor, who responds lazily.

♦

They're all trashed by the time they leave, which is one of the benefits to not being in L.A. and not having to drive. With five of them, two cabs is the obvious solution. But what should either be Victor and Ellen sharing a cab since they arrived together or Victor and Liam sharing a cab because that situation is now more obvious than ever, somehow becomes Ellen and Raphael sharing a cab because Liam is insistent that he should travel with Victor *and* Alex. Everyone is sober enough to realize this plan makes no sense, but too drunk to argue about it.

Liam decides to squeeze the three of them into the backseat. Alex somehow ends up between him and Victor. He leans forward and makes small talk with their driver so Victor and Liam can talk and hold hands — literally behind his back. The situation is fucking ridiculous and only gets worse when they get to the hotel.

Alex and Liam stumble out of the cab while Victor pays. Alex does his best to dodge Liam's arm and get to the goddamn elevator before he and Victor catch up with him. All he wants to do is get up to his room without having to deal with them being low-filter about whatever they are together. He jabs at the button in the elevator bank a few times as he fishes his phone out of his pocket and calls Paul.

Of course, Paul answers, the elevator doors open, and Liam and Victor follow him in before they can close.

"I'm in the elevator," Alex says in lieu of a greeting. "Also I am very drunk."

"Why are you calling me from an elevator?" Paul asks, sounding startled and without all their usual discomfort of late.

"Because I am in an elevator with Victor and Liam and they are also very drunk."

"Alex, calm down, it's not like we're going to go fuck," Victor says probably loud enough for Paul to hear as the doors close.

Paul laughs. "What's going on?"

Liam makes a noise of protest at Victor's side.

"Shhhh, little one," Victor says to Liam. "The way you mean, yes, the way he means, no."

"I DIDN'T MEAN ANYTHING," Alex says far too loudly, before muttering "We're so drunk," into the phone. "And they're putting words in my mouth."

"We could —"

"Liam, whatever you're going to say, do not say it," Alex snaps through his laughter as the elevator finally arrives at his and Liam's floor and the doors ding open. Victor and Liam are lovely together in a way Alex doesn't know how to handle. If he looks at them too long he's not sure he'll be able to look away.

Alex bolts out ahead of them. He doesn't wait to see whether they're going to Liam's room or on to another floor for Victor's. He tries to tell himself he doesn't want to know.

"Okay, safe now," he tells Paul as he gets his door open. It takes a couple of tries with the keycard, because *drunk*. "They're awful!"

"They're in love," Paul says simply. Which makes Alex feel like an asshole. There's not enough happiness in the world to go around grudging it of the people who manage to find it. But *still*.

"Shhhhhh," Alex says. Better not to talk about any of that. "Be quiet with me. Two minutes,"

Paul laughs again. Alex closes his eyes and lets himself enjoy the sound of it and how none of their tension has crept in yet over the absurd.

"Oh, God," he says as a terrible thought occurs to him. "I bet they're talking about us."

"We're talking about them," Paul points out.

Alex moans again in lieu of finding words for his feelings on the entire subject. Then they actually do go quiet, and there's only the soft sound of Paul's breath on the other end of the line.

◆

Victor and Liam fumble their way into Liam's room loudly. Normally Victor would worry about noise or decorum, but this time he can't bring himself to. He crowds Liam against the wall, grabs his face, and makes him wait for the kiss he knows is coming. Liam won't drop his eyes unless Victor asks him, which he's always found fascinating. The sustained eye contact leaves them stuck there for a moment that is unreasonably long.

Victor steps back without giving Liam what he wants. When his hand leaves Liam's face, he brushes his fingers over Liam's lips.

"Get undressed," he says but then ignores Liam as he opens the overpriced spring water the hotel provides. He should be a lot more sober than he is for this. No matter how much he trusts himself, Liam trusts him more.

He leans against the wall watching Liam as he sips at the water. "Are you okay to do this?" he asks.

"In what world am I going to say no?" Liam says.

"In one that scares me less."

"I'm *fine*."

Victor is not impressed with Liam's petulance, but scolding him is so rarely effective. They're on the same side even if they never see the world from the same angle. Victor says nothing until Liam pulls off his jeans and kicks them to the side of the room.

"Fold your clothes. You can be a slob when I'm not here," Victor snaps, although there's not much heat to it. He wants another few seconds to clear his head. Hopefully Liam will understand.

Liam chuckles and does as he's told. Victor says thank you, because manners count.

"Are you going to come here, or do you want to watch?" Liam says, climbing onto the bed and settling back on his heels in a kneel.

"I don't think you'd be very happy if I only wanted to watch right now."

Liam shrugs. "You're here. I'm happy," he says, simple and serious.

Victor doesn't realize the breath has punched out of him until he hears himself on the inhale in response.

"How do you do this to me?" Victor murmurs. He crosses to the bed, grabs Liam by the jaw again, and leads him up onto his knees. "How do you do this to everyone?"

"I really don't," Liam says.

Victor kisses him.

♦

Alex eventually toes off his shoes and curls up with his head on the pillow, staring out the window at the lights of the city. He can feel the mood with Paul settle, and his whole body relaxes when Paul asks "How's D.C.?" in a tone that means he's interested in the answer.

"The first night was a little rough," Alex admits. "I hate the weather. But it's getting better."

"The weather?"

"No. The rest of it."

"You sound happy." Paul sounds surprised.

Alex considers that: The long days, the work, Victor and Liam, all the strangenesses and longings of this city. "I am."

"Is it because you're not with me?" Paul asks. He doesn't sound desperate, but asking clearly hurts.

"No," Alex says.

"Alex," Paul says fondly, but his voice is pleading, too. "More words?"

The mood is subdued now. "I'm not happy because you're not here. But now that I'm not worrying about us every moment of the day, I remembered how not to be miserable all the time."

"I'm sorry I make you miserable."

Alex tamps down his annoyance. Paul keeps finding the strangest and worst ways to take responsibility for this mess. Still, Alex wants to be both honest and kind. "You don't. Your choices and our collective crazy do. Which is why I know the separation is good, but, Paul, I want to be happy *with* you."

"I want to be happy with you, too."

"I know. But it's going to be harder than either of us thought."

◆

Victor refuses to get on the bed with him. That's not new, but the way he insists on standing and keeping Liam on his knees, neck stretching up to kiss him, is. Liam's still tipsy enough that Victor suspects he's only upright because he wants Victor — and to make Victor happy — more than he wants to lie down. He whimpers every time Victor pulls out of the kiss and then hovers just millimeters from his lips.

Victor makes a shushing sound, meant to soothe more than silence. It only makes Liam get louder. Victor laughs.

"Please touch me," Liam begs.

"I am touching you." Victor tightens his grip on Liam's face.

"Please —"

Victor is always tempted to say no. The things Liam wants, that they are both agreed he can have from him, aren't necessarily things that interest Victor. Liam makes him stretch, when he's not making him desperately want to retreat from a world that isn't, particularly, made for him.

The fact that Liam is very pretty when he's denied, when Victor can actually get him to cry, is another thing entirely. It amuses Victor to no end that what makes them incompatible, also provides the path for how they do work.

"What do you want, Liam? If you could have anything, what would you want?"

Liam closes his eyes, and Victor knows he's pushed a little too far and struck a little too deep. He loosens his grip on Liam's jaw, slides his hand over his cheek to cup the back of his head, and pulls him against him.

Liam sags in relief at the contact, his face pressed against the soft cotton of Victor's shirt.

"I've got you; it's okay," Victor says, just a little bit on autopilot because Liam or the alcohol or this much touch has him off balance. He frowns to himself at how unsurprised their audience on the other side of the wall would be to discover that most skin-to-skin contact makes him feel as if his nerves have turned to glass.

Liam makes the most delicious sound when Victor grabs his cock.

◆

"I can hear them," Alex moans, pulling a pillow up over his ear with the phone held to it.

"Hear who?"

"Liam's room is next to mine. Who do you think? Please talk to me to distract me."

Paul chuckles. "Do you know when you get in yet?"

Alex loosens his grip on the pillow a little. "Working on it. We'll wrap here Friday, and Margaret and Vanessa are trying to arrange some stuff for me in New York. So probably another week or so?"

"Define stuff." Paul sounds more tense than he has all night.

"I'm gonna talk to some people about some movies," Alex says enthusiastically. He doesn't like New York much more than he likes D.C., but he does like the work.

"In New York?"

"In a lot of places. The whole world doesn't shoot in our backyard, Paul."

"I just... to what extent is this about us?"

"To the extent that this is my job and these are always going to be the business conversations I am having. And if and when there is something to talk about, we'll talk about it. That means with opportunities and with us," Alex says. The statement is harsher and more practical than he wants, but it needs to be said.

Silence stretches on until Alex feels tense with it. Did he say the wrong thing and break everything tonight?

Before he can ask, Paul says, "I'm nodding at you."

"Oh. Good. Margaret's going to set up some media stuff too so…I'll let you know, as soon as I have the ticket."

"Is Liam going?"

"What?"

"Liam. New York."

"He and Victor are headed back to L.A. Saturday, and sometimes you make me want to lie to you."

"Don't do that," Paul says.

"Then believe me when I say that's never happening again."

"Were you in love with him?"

"Paul," Alex says sharply, because *what the fuck?*

"Well?"

Alex closes his eyes. This is starting to get ugly. He's drunk, and he's tired, and as unreasonable as Paul is being, Alex misses him. "You've been in love with lots of people. Why do I only get one?"

"That sounds like a yes."

"I love Lee," Alex tells him. He still doesn't know how to categorize or define what he and Liam were and gave up even trying to a long time ago. "But I'm not in love with him. Not the way you mean, even if I maybe used to think something different."

"This is why you and Liam scare me," Paul says.

"*Why?*"

"Because I don't understand it, and it seems huge."

"Maybe it is, but it's not about you," Alex still feels protective of that time in his life, terrible as most of it was. Liam is the only person he's been with besides Paul that's meant anything. Hard as it is for Paul to hear, Alex isn't willing to deny that. Liam means something to him and always will.

♦

Paul finally wanders away from his desk and sits down on his bed, across the house from Alex's empty room. Todd scratches mournfully at the closed door.

"Tell me why it's not happening again," he says even though he suspects he shouldn't. He wants an answer that makes sense to him. Alex and Liam never have.

Alex takes a breath. "He can't be what I want. I can't be what he needs. And I am tired of you taking out your guilt on me. It's doing neither of us any good, so can we please stop?"

"What do you want?" Paul asks. He knows Alex is telling him many things, some of which he thinks he may never be capable of understanding. He wishes he understood Alex and the way he uses words better. Although this time it may be the issues — and not how they're communicating them — that are causing so much grief.

"I want everything," Alex says. "I want you, when I'm yours. Even when I'm not. And even if you and I were over I wouldn't, with Liam, because we're a lot of things but we're not *that*. Neither of us can be that."

"The last time," Paul says too sharply, but only because he's scared, "things were bad with us, you went to Liam. You came back different."

"Paul," Alex says softly. "I came back to you."

"I don't even know what I want to hear," Paul admits, far too aware of their empty house, and the room upstairs he hasn't been in since the night Alex left.

"Then can we just go back to being quiet together?" Alex asks. "That was good."

"Okay. Yeah, okay."

Alex is quiet so long that Paul thinks he's fallen asleep. He wonders if he should hang up and go back upstairs to finish up what he was working on, or maybe even just crawl into bed himself, when Alex says with a rustle that must be him getting undressed, "I'm still happy."

"That's a good thing?" Paul asks.

"Yeah," Alex says. "It really is."

♦

After Liam comes, he is so desperately beautiful as Victor helps lower him to the bed that he can barely stand it. Especially because if he's going to stay — and he's definitely going to stay — he really needs to go back to his room for his laptop first. But abandoning Liam like this strikes him as both cruel and irresponsible.

"I'm going to go upstairs for a minute," he says when he's gotten Liam cleaned up and under the covers.

Of course, that makes Liam more alert, but not in a good way.

"I'll stay the night," he says, "assuming you'll have me. But I do need my computer first."

Liam huffs out a little laugh and closes his eyes again.

"I'll be right back, I promise."

Liam nods, thinking hard about it. Victor knows he doesn't make promises lightly, even in the most casual of conversations. Something — even if he has no idea what — is changing in the long, shifting thread of their relationship.

Victor thinks Liam is asleep by the time he returns. But once he sits up against that headboard, laptop open and typing, Liam turns over in his bed and asks, "Why did you do that?"

"What?" Victor asks, jarred out of his writing. It's one thing to feel his relationship with Liam shifting; it's another to address Liam's very fair questions when he's still working out the answers himself. After what happened tonight in the bar and on Liam's bed, there are far more questions than Victor is used to or comfortable with

He's relieved when Liam says, "In the elevator. With Alex."

"He was talking to Paul," Victor tells him. "I wanted him to laugh."

"Do you think it worked?"

"I think we'll find out."

19

The next day, the weather breaks in a spectacular thunderstorm that probably should shut down filming for an hour. But to Alex's surprise, Victor decides that Zach and James having a soaked and hilarious conversation is exactly what they need. Which is awesome and also uncomfortable. Alex is glad when they wrap for the day.

Liam offers to take a walk with him around the city, but Alex shakes his head. He wants to be inside, where it's dry and there aren't any other people. They go to Liam's room. Alex doesn't know where Victor is tonight — and doesn't particularly want to ask — but he does hesitate for a second as he chooses which bed to sit on. He knows he's being foolish and immature, but Liam blurs the lines around everything: Sex, intimacy, public life. Alex is irrationally worried that if he's not careful, he'll be pulled into the orbit of his affair with Victor.

"What's up with the sweater?" Liam asks when Alex curls up small on the bed with his head tipped against the headboard.

"We got drenched today. Still cold."

"Dude, it's like eighty out." Liam reaches out a hand to pet at Alex's arm.

Alex shrugs. "It's Paul's."

Liam snatches his hand back. "That's adorable."

"Don't tease."

"I'm not."

"Okay." Alex is baffled at Liam's sudden caution. Every time he thinks he's used to all of Liam's oddities, a new one crops up.

They talk for hours, first about Paul and then about Carly, before the meat of the conversation turns to Victor. About whom Liam is, apparently, as confused as everyone else, though for different reasons. Liam winds closer to an actual definition of whatever deal he and Victor have than he ever has before. What Alex gathers, eventually, is that deal is changing. Alex isn't sure how something that's been going on for six years can suddenly get more serious in the face of a marriage to someone else, but what went down in the bar last night was something new.

As Alex listens to Liam, drifting for some of it because he's exhausted and Liam is exhausting, what is clear is how desperately Liam *wants*. Alex is reminded, more than a little, of the way he was toward Liam in his room in New York that terrible winter he and Paul weren't together. Considering the object of Liam's focus is Victor, Alex can't imagine things aren't going to work out far worse. Sure, Liam and Victor have been together six years, but it's Victor. Trusting Victor with anyone's heart seems ill-advised. There's something rough to him, violent and proud like Alex's Indiana childhood. He's left with no good advice to offer and no courage to warn Liam of what he suspects are impending wounds.

◆

Eventually Alex, looking worn out and exhausted by work and life, falls asleep. Liam thinks about calling Carly but also doesn't want to disturb

Alex. Tonight is not a Victor night. Even when they can, they don't spend every night together. Victor is an insomniac and is always doing something — tonight, it's dealing with script rewrites — but also, their relationship is historically structured on negative space.

While Liam's impulse is to curl up next to Alex and enjoy the company, he hasn't asked him to. Liam is happy to give Alex his default request for space. The question is how. He could wake him, or he could crash on the other bed and risk getting hollered at in the morning for staying over uninvited. Liam bites his lip at the two bad choices and decides on a third. They'll switch places! He slips Alex's wallet out of his back pocket to find his room key. On his way out the door Liam stops by the side of the bed and touches Alex's hair, brushing a loose piece back off of his forehead. His friend doesn't even stir.

◆

Gemma's at work, sorting through headshots, when the extension at her desk rings. It never rings, and she's not sure she should answer it. She may have all the power in the world sorting these faces into piles of *aspirational* and *character* — beautiful and ugly — but she's barely more than an intern. Everyone knows she's in casting because she can't get cast. There's no reason for her extension to be ringing.

She only picks it up because the actual intern — the nephew of one of the CSAs — snaps at her to. Whatever she's expecting, Carly isn't on the list.

They've always gotten along, but it's not like they're in each other's cell phones. If Gemma's being honest, she's always felt a little awkward around Carly, because she's real and her fiancé is *Liam Campbell*. Gemma's mostly over it, but not entirely. After all, he's still really cute and annoyingly charming, and Alex, her best friend and former roommate who is now a TV star, fucked him.

Gemma doesn't get more comfortable when Carly starts talking. She's worried about Paul, and she wants Gemma's insight.

Which means she wants Gemma's information. Gemma has to cut her off. "Can I call you back on my cell phone? Because you are asking me for gossip about people known to this office, and I should kind of do this in the parking lot."

"Does that mean you have something to tell me?" Carly asks.

"Not really?" Gemma says. Alex is her friend, and as much as that's become Paul and Alex, it's not like Paul's confessing his deepest-darkests to her. She also doesn't want to betray Alex's confidence. "But I do care, and if this is a conversation you think we need to be having, I want to have it. But not in the middle of a casting office."

"I thought you guys just did background."

"Yeah, well," Gemma says. "Everybody wants a leg up. And if we're conspiring, you should at least be willing to give me your damn cell phone number."

"Sold." Carly laughs. They're okay.

Paul, however, is not okay. And both Carly and Gemma are concerned. When Carly suggests they stage something of an intervention, she's ashamed to admit she's a little bit excited. It sounds important, and dramatic, and maybe it can really help. She offers to bring sandwiches. Carly suggests she bring Darcy instead.

The idea is one more symptom of Gemma's life that touches, but does not intersect with, fame. She feels both proud and very small that she is a node, and possibly only a node, connecting Carly to Darcy. She agrees, even if she doesn't entirely understand how Paul's very young discovery is going to improve the situation.

♦

Somewhere in the course of the next day, the internet goes gets unduly excited. Which is not unusual, but this time it's over a blind item that's been posted on some trashy gossip website. Which states that a certain TV star was seen sneaking out of the hotel room of a certain other TV star while filming in a certain city on location.

"You snuck out of your own hotel room." Alex is baffled and darkly amused as they wait for the cameras to reset in between takes. He's a little pissed, too, that the internet tries to intrude into his private life, but this is uniquely ridiculous. "And into mine so you *wouldn't* be sharing a room with me. You spent two nights with Victor and this is what gets printed?"

Liam shrugs. "Victor wouldn't send in a blind about himself."

Alex stares at Liam. "I don't actually know if you're joking."

Liam gives Alex Victor's cryptic smile, and walks away. Alex buries his head in his hands.

When Alex talks to Paul that night he expects him to be pissed. Paul has always followed Alex's presence on the internet and Liam doesn't seem likely to become less of a sore point anytime soon.

Instead, Paul is also darkly amused. "I know I said I was afraid of you and Liam, but I didn't think things were so bad you'd actually run to him with Victor there."

Alex doesn't know how to take this shift in tone. He's unused to light and a lack of subtext.

"They're really, really, not. Believe me," Alex says. He's not sure he'd ever run to anyone in a situation where he and Paul were still together. He's starting to wonder, as his time in D.C. comes to a close, if Paul is different.

♦

The last day of shooting, they're back at the Tidal Basin with Zach and James. Everything they've been filming all week has been happy, which is good. Alex knows that Victor isn't doing foreshadowing because that's not how death works, but he is clearly not averse to full circles.

And maybe, Alex thinks, as they line up a shot for a kiss that's easy and light, that's because life comes with its own circles.

20

It's raining in New York when Alex lands. Which is a blessing, because it gives him an excuse to wear a hat despite the season. Everyone on the streets is too miserable and harried to give him a second glance. He decides to walk down Broadway and into Soho, on streets he's supposed to care about because he can afford to shop on them. He only feels any affection for them because some of the streets still have cobbles and haven't come that far from the old shadow New York that's been informing his choices since he shot *Paradise*. Alex doesn't like New York, the city. But he'll take New York the memory, and New York the ghost, and New York and all the strange witchery of everything that went down between him and Liam.

When he gets back to his room in the early evening, he calls Gemma and begs her to get on a plane. He's lonely, and who else can he call? Liam's working. So is Paul.

"I have work."

"I'll pay for the ticket."

"You're being gross, and I have work, and like, a life. It's Saturday!"

"Do you have a date?" he asks.

"That's not your business."

"Since when do you have boundaries?" Alex asks.

"Since when aren't you happy spending all your time alone?"

"I feel trapped in my room and sort of pathetic," he admits.

"You know people in New York," she offers.

"Biblically," he says dryly. "Talk to me?" The request doesn't make him feel any less pathetic, but she's his oldest friend and has stuck with him through stranger things than this.

Given all of that, she sounds strangely nervous when she says, "Okay, but you're freaking me out."

They talk for an hour about little things. Alex can't tell her that he's leaving *Fourth* yet, and if he can't entirely avoid talking about Paul, he can at least deflect most of her questions.

"Sorry I asked you to come out here," Alex says when Gemma says she has to go.

"You're not," Gemma says bluntly. "But it's okay. It was good to talk to you."

They hang up. Alex thinks about calling Paul but ends up texting instead. He's not sure it's going to make him feel any less lonely or uneasy, but he wants to keep that thread of contact open.

I still hate New York, he sends.

Paul takes a while to reply. *Tell me something I don't know*, he finally sends when he does.

Alex prickles a little. Though Paul may well have meant a dozen other things than that Alex is boring him and he resents the interruption.

It's raining, Alex tries. *Was a little easier to take a walk. I should have my schedule sorted by Monday afternoon.*

Okay, Paul texts back.

This is one of those trial separation days, isn't it? Alex replies when he fails at not feeling needy and pissed off.

Yup.

Alex stares at his phone for a second. *All right. Have fun with that I guess.* He's not sure if he's sincere or angry. Then he turns off his phone so he doesn't have to find out.

◆

Paul knows this evening may not be exactly pleasant, because Carly has been kicking his ass since forever. But they have enough history of enough different types that he always feels a little bit happy as he gets himself together to go over to her place. She is, after all, always happy to see him, and while he owes her everything in a broad context, day-to-day they're not responsible to each other. Right now, that's pretty close to the best feeling in the world. Plus, he doesn't have to shave for her.

His trepidation rises, however, when he parks in the lot of Carly's building and sees two familiar cars already there.

"All right, what are you pulling?" Paul asks, when Carly opens the door with a broad smile.

"You can think of it as an intervention or you can think of it as a girl's night in. Your choice."

"You are a terrible friend." This is not how Paul wanted to spend the night. With Carly it would have been one thing, but there is nothing about his mess of a life that needs witnesses.

"Nope, this is why I'm the best. And when did you decide to turn into mountain man?" She taps his cheek.

Paul's a little offended. "It's been four days."

"Well, you look hot even if this smells like more of your bad ideas." She finally pulls him properly into the house and pushes him into the living room.

Darcy and Gemma are sitting on a loveseat eating bonbons.

"I am not gay enough for this," Paul declares.

Darcy frowns at him very seriously. "You are being an asshole."

"I'm gonna be more of one in a second," he offers.

"Noooooo," she says. "Come here and have candy and talk to us about your pain."

"In case you haven't noticed," Gemma chimes in, "we're more pathetic than you are in that we're here, so make it good."

"I see your hospitality is appreciated," Paul says to Carly.

"I will get booze, and we will make you talk," she warns.

"I don't know what to tell you. Not that any of it's your business."

Carly rolls her eyes and nudges him toward a chair. "I don't think you expect that to work."

Paul sits. "Who have you been talking to?" he asks.

"Who do you think?" Carly says. "You are both freaking Liam out. And one of the many things we will be talking about tonight is how you need to stop being an asshole about him."

"I have done everything in my power to keep that away from him," Paul says. "I'm fairly clear that it's my issue, although not unreasonably, I don't think."

"I don't care," Carly says. Her voice is calm, precise and the angriest he's heard her in years. "You are being unfair to him. You are being unfair to Alex. You're certainly being unfair to me, who has been stuck trying to keep this happy family together for *years*. I'm sorry he and Alex have complicated feelings about each other, but you know what? You and I have complicated feelings about each other, and your shitty behavior about it in someone who is not you is a real slap in the face."

Paul is torn between addressing her very engaging anger and asking why the fuck they have an audience. Especially if they're doing *this* as opposed to platitudes about how awesome he and Alex are together. "The situation is different."

"How? And I swear to God if you say the word *marriage*, I will slap you. Liam and I are not you and Alex. But we are all in each other's lives, and nobody is going anywhere. Unless you don't cut this bullshit out. Do you get that you will lose him over this?"

"Explain to me how I'm not supposed to be jealous of Liam if I could lose Alex over him?"

"'Cause Alex doesn't belong to you?" Darcy pipes up from the sofa. "And you know, like, you don't have to worry about Liam. Liam's so responsible he sucks. Like, he fucks everyone and wouldn't fuck me because I didn't know why I wanted to do it other than he's cute. Carly, your boyfriend *sucks*. And was all freaked out that I'm a virgin."

"Fiancé, Darcy," Carly says mildly as Gemma's whips her head around to stare at Darcy.

Paul says, "I didn't need to know any of that."

"Alex feels what he feels. You should respect the significance of his choices," Carly says before stalking off into her kitchen.

"So this is going to suck," Paul says.

"For you." Gemma shrugs.

Carly comes back with alcohol, and if drinks don't break the mood they at least moderates it. Paul still finds it bizarre to sit here with his best friend, Alex's best friend, and Darcy. That Carly is telling him, albeit with more words, things Alex has been telling him for months also sucks.

"He keeps saying no," he tells Carly when she finally lets him say *marriage* again.

"Why do you keep asking?"

"Because I'm in love with him and want to be with him? Jesus, Carly, why are you marrying Liam?"

"Because it's a thing we both want and we work by finding new ways to work, all the time."

"We're not working," Paul says despairingly.

"I know you're not. And one of the reasons why is that you are not listening to him and are not making choices he can understand. Hell, you're not making choices I understand."

"I just want to know why I moved out of that house so you could take over my side of it? That was not the point," Gemma asks. "Like, how did you go from not being able to take your hands off each other to this?"

"I need another drink before I talk about that," Paul says.

"Shots." Darcy bounces up off the couch and heads for the kitchen. "Definitely shots."

"Should you let her alone in there?" Paul asks.

"I think I can trust her not to run with scissors or poison you," Carly says.

"That might not be the worst thing at this point," Paul says.

Carly frowns. "You of all people should not be making jokes about that."

Paul lifts a shoulder. "Where's the gallows humor tonight?"

Gemma becomes fascinated with a throw pillow, but is obviously listening.

"You scared Alex," Carly tells him.

"When?"

"I got an email from him right before he left for D.C. After you had your 'trial separation' conversation. And nothing you've been doing this last week is making me think he's wrong to be worried. I have not kept you alive this long to lose you over this mess. Besides, Alex will kill me if I let you kill yourself, so let's be adults and talk about the options you're going to take, okay?"

"I'm not suicidal."

"You are depressed."

"Why are we discussing this in front of Darcy?" Paul asks as she reenters the room, carrying a bottle of gin and juggling shot glasses.

"Because leadership comes from the leads," she says, handing them around.

"Thank you, musical theater summer camp wisdom," Paul snipes.

"Don't be a dick," she says. "I'm trying to help. And I'm not going to, like, go tell or anything."

"Okay, so, borrowing from my boyfriend," Carly says. "One, you need to take care of yourself in a context other than whether it will it fix things with Alex. Two, to actually fix things with Alex, you need to step up and do the work, not just react to his own attempts, which, believe me, I know are a mixed bag. Three, please fucking go back to therapy because this is not my job."

"Three sort of sounds like one," Paul points out.

"Have you heard Liam make a list?"

Paul snorts.

"And don't tell me you're actually happy right now. I don't care how awesome your show is. You're not Victor. You have what you have wanted forever, and you are miserable. That's not about you or your work ethic; that is your brain lying to you. You deserve better. And now we're going to do shots, and then you're going to tell us why you and Alex stopped living together despite technically still being in the same house."

Somehow, that's even harder to talk about than the rest of it. It takes Paul several false starts and more than a few confessions that don't quite get to the heart of the matter. Which isn't just his terrible schedule and the burden of disappointing Alex, who is now more or less used to getting everything he wants from everyone.

"Wait, wait, wait," Carly says. "So you're having issues about being faintly kinky and stopped fucking Alex because you didn't trust his *yes*?"

"Yes?" Paul says meekly.

"This is very educational," Darcy tells her drink seriously.

"This is a really shitty intervention," Paul says.

Gemma kicks Darcy in response, which doesn't really resolve the issue.

"And why the hell are you here?" he asks Darcy.

"Way to be a friend, boss."

"*Anyway,*" Carly says. "Alex does not say yes to things he does not want. He, in fact, is saying no to you quite a lot, which is part of why you're pissed at him. Until and unless you can trust and respect him saying yes, he is never going to be a partner to you."

"You saw what I did to his back," Paul says. "I've done worse since then."

"Yeah. And he was as proud of that as he knew how to be without being a tacky, bragging asshole. Why are you so dense?"

"I slit my wrists because it was a marginally better option than stabbing my father. What the fuck am I going to do to him, if he lets me?"

Darcy goes a little pale. Paul doesn't ever bother to cover his scars, but this is the first time he's ever talked about them in front of her.

Carly frowns. "Okay, *wow*, you are mixing up about eight different issues in your head. You are depressed and have anger issues, and you have a young, sexy boyfriend who loves you and trusts you and likes when you mark him up. Which is, let me say, not as kinky as you probably think it is. These two things are also completely separate."

"I hurt him."

"Not the way you're afraid of. Except for the part where you're breaking his heart because you're not trusting him because you've got your kink and your history confused."

"He said he's not allowed to say no," Paul protests, still baffled by it.

"Oh my God," Gemma says. "Is that what this is about?" She sits up abruptly.

"What do you mean?"

"I told him that. When Victor offered him Zach. Like, *years* ago. He didn't know if he wanted to take it, and I flipped out at him. And then he started saying it all the time, because of how much time he spends being a human doll for hair and makeup and fans and everything. That's never been about you, Paul. It's about being famous."

21

Alex emails Paul his flight information the night before he leaves New York. All he gets back is *Have a safe trip*. The trial part of their separation may be just about over and actual, permanent separation imminent. The last few days in New York have been fine and make him hopeful about what's next for his career. But he still hates photo shoots, and he has no idea what he's flying back into. Which makes it harder to leave New York than it would be under any other circumstances.

He spends the flight back to L.A. with his headphones on, staring out the window when he can't sleep, and thinking about how much he hates flying. Six hours where he's utterly helpless to do anything make him wild with impatience.

At the gate, Alex texts Paul to say he's landed. He has no idea if he'll care, and he doubts he'll be at the house by the time Alex gets there anyway. But it seems like the worst kind of luck to break that particular ritual now.

The last thing he expects, as he makes way out of the terminal through all the drivers with signs for their pickups, is to see Paul. He's holding a sign with the stupid fake name Alex uses for stuff like this, unexpectedly unshaven and looking faintly hopeful.

Alex's first response is to be annoyed, because *public* and *ambush* and *emotions in front of people* and no real idea of what the intent even is. But it's still Paul and home and a gesture that's stupid and romantic and absolutely perfect. He manages about three more steps before he drops his bags and flings himself into Paul's arms.

Paul catches him around the waist, and for a long moment it's just him and his familiar body. Alex melts into him.

"I know we're a mess," Paul eventually says quietly. "I know we don't know what's going to happen. But I wanted to do something ridiculous for you."

Alex nods. He can't speak. He isn't remotely willing to let go.

"People are looking," Paul says softly into Alex's hair.

"I don't care."

Paul holds him tighter. "I've missed you. Fixing this terrifies me. But I want to try."

Alex nods again into Paul's shoulder. "I'm scared when I let go of you it's going to go back to being awkward and messed up."

"It probably is," Paul pulls back and catches Alex's face in his hands. "But it won't be as awkward and fucked up as having the rest of this conversation in the middle of LAX."

◆

Paul sets Alex's bags down in the entryway and continues on into the living room. Todd jumps down from the couch and trots over to Alex for a pet. Alex picks him up because he wants to keep holding on to things right now, even though since Todd is a cat this particular activity won't last long.

"I think he missed you too," Paul says as Todd nuzzles into Alex's hand for an ear scratch.

"We haven't been giving him the quality time he deserves," Alex admits, as Todd jumps down again only to wind between his legs. One of the side effects of he and Paul sleeping in separate rooms has been both of them avoiding the shared areas of the house.

"Yeah." Paul takes a seat on one of the couches as Alex takes the other.

"So," Alex finally says when Paul doesn't add anything else. As strange and as happy as their reunion has been, Paul started this by being at the airport. Alex is determined to make him go first. "Conversation?"

Paul nods. "I don't like how this sounds, but I think the space, the last ten days, anyway, has been good. At least for me. And my extravagant gesture aside, I don't think we have any business sharing a bed with each other right now."

"It has been good," Alex agrees carefully. "All I want to do is crawl into bed with you and I know that's not going to solve anything, which is weird, because I feel like that's how we used to solve everything."

Paul leans forward, his expression earnest. "I think it solved less than we thought it did. Or that it stopped solving things when it started to be a problem itself."

Alex glances around the room like he's going to find an explanation for Paul's words floating somewhere in space. "When did it start to be a problem itself?" He can practically feel the conversation turning to Liam again. Which is something he's more than run out of patience for.

"While you were gone Carly, Gemma, and Darcy launched an intervention."

Alex's eyes go wide. "That sounds scary and entirely like something they would do. I also can't tell how much humor is present in that word choice." He wants it to be less potentially relevant to Paul's state of being than he's inclined to think.

"Not much," Paul admits. He looks at his hands instead of at Alex. "I think everyone initially thought it would be funnier than it was. Can you let me talk for a bit?"

Alex restrains himself from pointing out that he's been trying to get Paul to acknowledge him as something other than a burden or distraction and just talk to him for a long time now. If Paul is finally going to speak, he does not want to do things that will make him stop. He nods.

"We talked about some things. And Carly pointed out to me that I may have gotten some shit about sex messed up in my head with the shit I did when I was a kid. Stuff I still haven't really stopped doing now and that has never meant anything good for anyone. Particularly for me, but the people around me too."

"I don't know what that means."

Paul scratches the back of his neck as he looks up at the ceiling. "Why is this so hard? I'm an adult. I've fucked lots of people."

Alex smirks, not unkindly, but doesn't say anything.

"So here's the thing. As you know, I have some fucked up anger issues — "

"You've barely ever yelled at me," Alex says. "You tell me the things you want to do instead of doing them."

"Yeah," Paul says. "Because my wrists and my dad and that lost summer and yeah. Anger's really scary for me. It should be. And then you show up and are like.... God, I think about when I met you as compared to now. Did you even know this is how you'd like to fuck?"

"What?" Alex says. He's a little defensive and a lot surprised. "That I like to get fucked?"

"No. That you like when I scratch you, when I mark you. And that when I'm too fucked up about all the other shit going on in my life to give you the attention you deserve, your first line of action it to goad me into hurting you?"

Alex blinks several times as he processes that. About half of what Paul has said — as dreadful and agonizing as it is — makes sense. The other half feels like such a misread of everything, Alex doesn't know where to start.

"Is this where I can talk now?"

Paul nods.

"Okay, first of all. No, I didn't know what I liked when I started this with you. You know that. You were there. Maybe I just like what I like. I don't want to blame things in my life for that. And if you like what you like, that doesn't have to be about shit that's happened to you either. Or about the ways in which you're fucked up. I mean, I hear what you're saying, I'm glad you're saying it, but my main answer is *no*. I don't want my desires written off like that or the way we fuck written off like that."

"I do hurt you, though."

"It's not like that." Alex says.

"Then what's it like?"

"It's like being awake because I spend ninety percent of my life sleepwalking because of my schedule and the things my job forces me to ignore. It's like climbing and knowing sometimes I will tear my body apart to do something amazing. Are you trying to hurt me when we fuck?"

"No. At least — no. I'm trying to make you pay attention. And fall apart."

"Do you enjoy it?"

"Yes. That's the problem."

Alex shakes his head slowly. "This actually seems pretty perfect as far as compatibility goes? Like — whatever you're afraid of is in your head. You're not hurting me the way you're scared of. If you were, I would say no."

"I'm trying to tell you where I am right now, Alex, not fix it all in a day."

"Okay, but do you want to fix it?"

"I know I've said as much today."

"You have, but when you're telling me you aren't willing to believe me when I say yes, I don't feel listened to. And I definitely don't feel whatever magical safer I'm supposed to feel if we weren't sexually compatible this way, so…."

"So it's going to take time."

"And you're going to sort this out on your own while you don't touch me?"

"I don't know! I'm just trying to tell you what's going on."

"Okay, well, what else is going on? Because seriously, Paul, if this is the whole thing, I might strangle you."

"Don't make light."

"Someone has to," Alex mutters.

Paul chuckles. "Carly said the same thing."

"Look, I've never said you have bad taste."

"No, I really don't," Paul says fondly, gazing at Alex. "I'm sorry I've been a dick about Liam."

"You've said before."

Paul rocks back at that a little bit. "I know you chose me —"

"It's never been a competition," Alex interrupts firmly. He's trying not to sound as exasperated as he feels.

"You're here, despite how fucked up we are right now, because you want to be. And I know I should respect that — and respect your friendship with him the way you respect mine with Carly. I'm sorry. And I'm working on it."

"She threatened to never speak to you again, didn't she?"

"Actually, she threatened to slap me."

Alex laughs. Carly truly is awesome.

"And then she told me to go back to therapy, because clearly I am way more fucked up than any of you can really deal with."

"That's probably good choices." It's about fucking time.

"I haven't called anyone yet. And I still think you should go too."

"That's not unfair," Alex says. "But your well-being regarding activities you have total control over choosing to participate in shouldn't be determined by my willingness to negotiate."

"Is there a no in there somewhere?"

"I'm not saying I don't have issues." Alex doesn't get as sarcastic as he wants. That would be the opposite of helpful right now. "I'm saying your tendency towards codependence is not helping you here."

"How do you even know what that word means?"

"I live in L.A. Look at our friends."

"Go back to telling me about your issues," Paul says with a smile.

Alex smiles back at him. He's amazed that this is what passes for flirtatiousness in the current state of their lives. "I goad you into sex. That doesn't mean I don't like it," he says just to make that absolutely clear. "But I push you at least as much as you push me and not in a good way. I need to learn how to ask for things from you. I'm still learning how to talk."

"You've gotten better," Paul offers.

"Not as much as you think I have. You worry about hurting me, and I worry about all the ways in which you own me, which isn't, I get, something you necessarily signed up for."

"You own me too, you know."

Alex tips his head to the side. "Okay. That's good. I think. What do we do now other than retreat to our corners and let our jobs work us to death?"

"I think we keep having these conversations. And we think about therapy. And I kiss you good night, because not fucking is fine, but God, I've wanted to since the airport."

Alex slumps against the back of the couch. "Do you think that's all over the internet by now?" he asks, chagrined.

"I don't think I care," Paul says. "But if you wanted to go look at complete strangers telling us how in love we are while we're trying to figure out if we should split up, gotta say, I'm not going to stop you."

Alex pats the empty space next to him. "Come kiss me, then."

Paul almost trips over the corner of the coffee table in his haste to get to him. Alex laughs in delight. The kiss is chaste for only half a second before they tug at each other's hair desperately. Alex shivers at the delicious scratch of Paul's scruff; Paul groans and grabs the back of Alex's head to keep their faces pressed together. But when they go from vertical to horizontal on the couch they stop, Alex curling in on himself to press his head to Paul's chest.

"This is hard," he says. He doesn't mean the stopping; he means everything.

Paul curls a hand gently around the back of Alex's neck. "I know, but this is nice too."

♦

Going forward is complicated and both harder and easier than either of them expect. Neither of their jobs get less demanding as the summer drags on. Paul is still working too much. But they're not making their work the central item in the mess that is their relationship, which means they're not instantly at silent war the second they are both in the house at the same time.

Sleeping apart continues to be hard, even if it's less fraught now that it's part of their attempt at finding a solution and not the problem itself. On Paul's birthday, in early August, it feels cruel to just text him happy wishes in the morning. He'd rather go out together or welcome Paul home that evening with a celebratory blowjob.

Aside from the sex, Alex misses the easy connection of skin on skin in a shared bed. Some days he wonders how much of a solution separate rooms can really be.

Alex has a conversation with Margaret. Sitting down with her to talk about the pictures from LAX and why they happened is a unique kind of terrible. He tells her to come up with a plan to deal with a breakup that he hopes they'll never need. He also asks her to tell him about it once she's got it figured out. There are days he needs all the reasons he can get to stay with Paul, even if some of them are convenience.

He starts therapy, but only to passive-aggressively goad Paul into the same. When that doesn't work, they have their first shouting match since his return from the East Coast. They're both surprised when somehow they get through it without it being the end.

Margaret and Vanessa help Alex to keep looking at his options beyond *Fourth*. Alex isn't sure if the projects that would keep him away for months are the best option, given the good his trip did them, or the worst.

Talking to Paul about those projects when Alex isn't sure they're going to be together by the time any of them start is hard. What's worse is that he knows that taking one of them could be the thing that splits them up for sure.

When he goes up to Paul's office one night and taps on the wall at the top of the stairs, Paul looks annoyed when he first glances up. Then the annoyance turns to fear. Alex takes the smallest amount of vindication in that.

"Can we talk?" Alex asks.

"This doesn't sound good," Paul says.

Alex aches at how serious Paul sounds. "It's okay," Alex says. "At least, I don't think it's bad. Not unless you want it to be. But it's important. Can we?" He tips his head away from the room.

◆

They go downstairs because Alex says he wants neutral territory for this. But once they reach the living room Alex sits on the opposite end of the couch with both feet on the floor and his back carefully straight. Paul's anxiety ratchets up.

"I've been looking at some movies," Alex says.

Paul nods and braces himself.

Alex goes on. "There are a few options that might be good, but there's one I really want. When I was in New York I sat down with the director and did some chemistry reads. Nothing's set in stone yet, and nothing's going to be certain for maybe a long time, but I really want this. I think they want me. It just depends on whether they think the audience wants me too."

"Of course they do." Paul is still worried about where this conversation is going, but he lives daily with the consequences of just how much America wants Alex.

Alex looks surprised. "Sweet. But you know it's not that simple."

"No. But you're amazing."

"Do you want to flatter me, or do you want to hear what I'm trying to tell you?" Alex's tone is playful, but there's a note of warning there too.

Paul shakes his head. "Sorry. You were saying?"

Alex crosses his legs in a gesture Paul recognizes more from seeing Alex on TV than from their living room. Alex being this deliberate about things makes him even more nervous. But, given their current situation, it's probably fair.

"They've changed the name of the project like three times, but it's about street kids in Richmond — which is apparently a shitty, shitty city, by the way. What the hell is wrong with the South?"

"Researching again?"

Alex shrugs. "I have to do something when I'm home alone. Not that it really needs much background reading to figure out, Mr. Crickets."

"There were about three different things in that statement that were terrible," Paul doesn't know what to think about any of them.

"Were there?" Alex says evenly. "Anyway. Supporting role. Street kid who's a little too old to be called a kid. And a lot dangerous for it. Crime, drugs, prostitution," Alex shrugs. "Sounds like a challenge. It's definitely something new, and I want it."

"Okay," Paul says. So far none of this has been bad information. Serious, certainly, and worthy of discussion because this is Alex's career and Paul loves him, but he's sure there's another shoe waiting to drop. "What's the schedule like?"

"If everything goes as planned — that's a big if — it'll be shooting in Toronto, this winter."

"That's a long way from home," Paul says carefully.

"Closer than New York. In a way."

"For how long?"

Alex bites his lip. "Three months."

"Oh my God, Alex." Paul sits back heavily.

"I know," Alex says. "This is why I want us to talk about this."

"Is 'this' what I think it is?" Paul asks warily.

"I can't read your mind so I don't know what 'this' is. No, I'm not breaking up with you. But if we're going to talk about our futures, this — or something like it — is going to be a part of it."

"It feels like you're running away."

"This isn't about us, Paul."

"Up and leaving for three months?" Paul knows he should be calmer lest he piss Alex off again, but now that it's come to this he's scared.

"I am not *up and leaving.* I am talking about my career options with you because you are my partner and, fucked up as things are right now, this is a discussion I need you to be a part of."

"Are you coming back?"

"*Paul,*" Alex says. He sounds as weary as he does exasperated. "I don't even know if this movie is going to happen, much less if we're still going to be together when I leave for it. Don't go paranoid on me. Especially when you're the one living in your office."

Paul frowns. "I know we're still learning how to do logistics. But you travelling has always been hard. I need to be sure this isn't you giving me a limited renewal instead of a cancellation."

Alex, to Paul's surprise, laughs. "I can't believe you just turned our relationship issues into a *Fourth* joke."

"Yeah, well. You make me all sorts of crazy."

Alex smiles and tips his head against the back of the couch. "So can this be okay?"

"Frankly, you disappearing for three months scares me."

"I'm not yours to keep here." The smile is still there around Alex's eyes, but his voice is sharp. "I know you have reasons to be scared. I'm scared, too. And I know this kind of separation would be hard even if we were solid right now. But you're assuming the worst and sometimes it feels like my loyalty is one more way you're trying to own me. That's not doing either of us any good."

Paul looks away. "I know. But, Jesus, Alex. Three months."

"Believe me. I know."

22

They keep having conversations — about their relationship and their future and the shape of it all — in the rare moments they're both home and awake. Alex finally works his way around to telling Paul how Zach is leaving *Fourth*. Somehow that turns into a conversation about how long they're actually going to do this repair work and how to decide when it's time to pull the plug on the whole thing. They don't reach any conclusions, but it's another conversation they're going to need to keep having. At least until the day that Alex wakes up and decides he wants the relationship to be over much the way he randomly decided he wanted Zach to be dead.

"Please try to remember that was so I could keep him," he says, but Paul doesn't seem interested in getting it. Alex is grateful he's not interested in fighting about it either.

The prospect of shooting Zach's death is exhilarating. It's also going to be exhausting. As they start to swing into Zach's final arc Alex gets informed that Zach has decided red is far too conspicuous for another foray into Iran.

◆

"They're going to dye my hair," Alex tells Paul one night in the middle of August. Paul's sitting at the kitchen table, working, and Alex has just gotten home.

"Ah?" Paul saves the file he's working on and closes it and then his laptop. He doesn't think Alex is angry, exactly, but he's definitely not thrilled. "Why?"

"Because I decided Zach was going to die and Victor decided to fuck with me."

"Why did Victor say they're going to dye your hair?" Not that Paul would be surprised if 'Because I say so' had been Victor's reason.

"Because Zach is going to Iran and needs to blend in."

"That seems like a valid writing choice," Paul says. He tries to imagine Alex with brown hair. It's a strange picture, but not an unappealing one.

"I'm going to be spending a month as a brunet." Now Alex sounds pissed. He slumps into a chair across from Paul. "Not just Zach. *Me*. Victor decided that, and the team agreed on it, so that's what happens. I don't get a choice."

It's not the first time Alex has been annoyed about something regarding *Fourth* and the constraints Zach puts on his appearance, but it's the first time he's ever explained to Paul why. It certainly makes what Gemma told him about Alex and his *no*s make a lot more sense and be a lot easier for him to believe.

♦

They're going to use temporary color to shoot the scene where James helps Zach with his hair the night before Zach leaves for Iran. Because not only is Liam clumsy with fiddly things like combs and tubes of color, hair dye is a nightmare and is going to get *everywhere*. ("You've got enough freckles," Ellen tells Alex at the table read. "We don't need you to be blotchy, too.") After, he'll have to go to a salon to get his hair permanently dyed. And then he'll have to wait for it to grow back out before he gets to look like himself again — unless he wants to shave his head.

There may be something a little kind, though, about making Zach look less like Zach, and less like Alex, as far as Liam is concerned. The less he looks like Alex, the less losing him will hurt — hopefully. Alex doesn't know what, if anything, Victor has told him. Since he hasn't gotten a worried phone call from Liam about it yet, he assumes he hasn't told him anything. With the end approaching, it makes Alex nervous. If Victor's waiting to tell Liam, the reason can't be good.

A home hair-coloring session involves messy dye and a bathtub which also involves being shirtless, another reason Alex chooses to be annoyed at this whole thing. The day of the hair shoot, someone from makeup walks them through the process. Ellen obnoxiously thanks Alex for not getting himself marked up. He snaps back; it's mostly good fun but she has no way of knowing the issue bruises are in his life right now. Aside from the occasional kiss, Paul isn't touching him. In his more pessimistic moments, Alex is afraid that's as much an excuse for Paul not to hurt him as it is a part of their agreements.

The set is closed to reduce the chance of leaks. Victor is there, not directing, just observing. Alex tries not to feel like his eyes are always boring into the back of his head.

Right before they're about to start shooting, Victor crooks his fingers to Liam. Liam leans half out of the frame to him, and he cups a hand at Liam's ear and whispers something. Alex can't hear what, but he watches as Liam preens from the intimacy before going ashen. Victor has to push Liam back onto both of his feet and into the scene.

After the second take, with James being falsely cheerful, Liam won't look him in the eye. Alex realizes Victor didn't say, "We're killing off Zach" but more likely, "Zach's going to die."

◆

When Alex bangs through the door that night, he's furious. He's sure the scene turned out fantastically, but that doesn't matter. Liam had spent the rest the day not looking at Alex, and, more disconcertingly, not speaking to him. He'd dropped things, more than once, and his hands shook the whole time he'd had them in Alex's hair.

"Victor is a manipulative asshole!" Alex calls up the stairs at Paul's loft. Thank God he's home.

Paul takes his headphones off and leans his arms on the railing. "I thought you got okay with the dye thing? Oh. Hey. Brown hair."

"*Yes*," Alex snaps. "Are you busy?"

"I was starting to think about dinner," Paul offers.

"Come down here and think."

They sit together on the couch in the living room. Alex tells him about the day and how Victor had chosen to spring the news on Liam in the most cruel way possible. Based on what Alex is hearing from Liam, Liam and Victor's relationship continues to shift. Still, Alex doesn't think something this terrible should be part of that.

Paul settles himself more comfortably into the couch. "You don't know what he said," he reasons.

Alex shakes his head. "I know Lee. I've never seen him like that. All I hear from you is about how it's your job to take care of your people — sometimes to the very detriment of you and I — and Victor did *that*."

"You sound afraid," Paul says.

"He's his lover!" Alex exclaims. Even Victor, who doesn't do human relationships the way anyone else does, surely should take better care of Liam than *that*.

"Then they'll sort it out between them."

Alex opens his mouth and then closes it. "Really?" he says, suddenly blackly amused. After all, he and Paul are lovers. Which has not meant they're capable of working out anything between them.

When Paul meets his eyes, they both crack up. The reasons are terrible, but it feels good, and they keep setting each other off.

"I'm going to kiss you now," Paul says right before he does. He pulls back, wrinkles his nose, and informs Alex he smells like hair dye.

23

The next day, Alex gets his hair properly, permanently done. He's still pissed about it, but most of his emotions are focused elsewhere. He's more worried about what Victor is doing to Liam, and what Victor is going to do to Alex before this is over. Because it's definitely going to be over now. Zach is coming to an end, and Alex hardly recognizes himself in the mirror. He'll get used to it eventually, just like everything else in life.

A week later he and Liam have the last scene they're ever going to do together as Zach and James. Liam is quiet and small in a way he never is, tucked into his chair in a corner of the set with his feet up on the seat. Alex walks over to him and gets close enough into his bubble that Liam eventually has to look up at him.

"Hey," Alex asks. "Are you okay?"

Liam blinks. "Why are you the one asking me that? Zach's the one that's...." He trails off.

"I'm fine, Lee." Alex reaches out to rub Liam's shoulder. "I'm tough, remember? Not the twink."

Liam smiles at that.

"Nothing changes because I'm not here with you every day." Alex grabs Liam's hand and kisses his palm. There will always be a thousand secret codes between them. Alex used to hate that, but the more complicated his life gets, the more he appreciates language in any of its forms.

When Liam suddenly beams, even as he still looks like he's about to cry, Alex knows he's done the right thing.

That night when he gets home, Paul asks him how he wants to handle the *Winsome* premiere. It's a testament to how long their relationship has been seriously broken that Alex hasn't even realized it's barely more than a week away.

"What do you want to do?" Alex asks him. *Winsome* is Paul's show and he is still Paul's partner. Paul has so often played this part for him.

"I want you to be there," Paul says simply.

◆

One evening a few days before Paul's premiere, Alex calls Gemma.

"And here I thought you'd left me for another woman," Gemma teases when she picks up.

"What?"

"*Darcy*," Gemma hisses.

Alex doesn't know if she's joking or if he wants to find out. "Hey, I'm the one who wanted you to come to New York. You said no."

"Yeah," Gemma sighs. "I know."

Glad as Gemma seems to be to hear from him — Alex knows that things have been bad and that he's been distant — she's aghast at his suggestion that they go to the gun range.

"I taught Darcy," Alex wheedles.

"You sure know how to make a girl feel special," Gemma grouses. "Why are you so hot on the whole weapons thing anyway?"

"Because you hate climbing, and I want to aggravate America."

"You know, you can just tweet that you're going to the range. No one would know the difference. You don't have to go every time."

"Yeah, but this way I get to shoot things too. Come on, I need stress relief. It'll be awesome." Alex may be famous now, but he's not above wheedling, especially with Gemma.

"Fine."

♦

"This is marginally more boring than bowling," Gemma states flatly when they take a break. "And way more sketchy."

"That's because you're from the wrong part of America," Alex tells her mildly. As much as this activity is one he's become provocative about, he does believe there's room for it to be treated with the neutrality of any sport.

"Yes, thank God."

Alex does his best not to irritate Gemma further. All he wants is a day out of the house doing something he's good at to blow off steam. Also a chance to talk over his and Paul's precarious position with someone who has always badgered him for more information than he usually wants to give.

But when he starts telling Gemma about the Richmond movie and his fear that their relationship can't stand a three-month separation, she stops him.

"Okay, I know Paul and you are having a hard time right now. But Alex, seriously? You are famous and successful and are complaining to me that you and your also famous and successful boyfriend are having potential logistics problems because you're too fucking good at your jobs."

Alex blinks. Gemma hasn't said things like that to him in ages. And he's well aware he deserves it.

"I am the same age as you, and my career has gone nowhere. That's fine, not everybody gets the dream. *Whatever.* But sometimes it is really fucking hard."

"I thought you liked your job," Alex says carefully. He knows he behaves badly toward Gemma sometimes, largely because he's still not used to thinking about other people; so much of surviving Paragon had meant pretending other people didn't exist. But that means he doesn't know how to fix the gulf between them. Gemma hasn't talked about her jealousy in a long time, but that doesn't mean it's gone away.

"I am amazing at my job. And one day I will do very big and very amazing things. Just not on the path I thought I was going to be on. You get to say 'fuck you' to the world with a tweet." She taps Alex's hip where his phone is sticking out of his pocket. "Some of us have to do a lot more."

◆

"Would it be super weird if I invited your mom to the wedding?" Carly asks Paul. It's Saturday night, Alex is still working, and Paul is at Carly's for a movie night. If he's going to make a serious effort with Alex, Paul knows he must be a person who exists outside of work.

Paul looks up from where he's digging in her cupboards. "When was the last time you talked to my mom?"

"Last week. Don't look so scared; we weren't talking about you."

"How often do you call her?" Paul asks, surprised. His mom and Carly had gotten on well when he and Carly had been dating, but he'd had no reason to think they'd spoken in years.

"Often enough. So, is it weird?"

Paul chuckles and finally manages to find the chips at the back of the shelf. "Probably. But if this is your way of asking me if I mind, no. Even though I'm kind of freaked you guys have been talking forever and I had no idea."

"Your mom is amazing and not everything is about you." Carly crosses off an item from a list on her refrigerator titled *Wedding Shit to Do*.

"So how are the wedding plans going?"

Carly tosses the pen down on the counter. "They're pissing me off. Liam's way too busy to help, which is fine, because putting him in charge of logistical decisions is a bad idea anyway. But this shooting schedule gives us no time."

"What about a house? Are you guys still going to move in together?"

"Don't ask," Carly says. "Tell me about your problems instead."

Paul laughs as he grabs a bowl for the chips and heads into Carly's bedroom, where they've got *Shark Attack 4* set up already.

Part of being a person who exists involves keeping up his friendships. Like by having movie nights with Carly. Another part of that involves talking to his best friend about something that's not his troubled relationship. While mutated sharks wreak havoc on New York, Paul tells Carly about the effort he's making to delegate at work, because he has a good team who is brilliantly capable and it is not his job to be everywhere at once.

She nods approvingly.

"My days are still fourteen hours long," Paul tells her. "But they're starting to look different."

"And Alex?" Carly asks.

Paul shakes his head. "He's fine. I don't know if untangling my shit at work is going to make anything better for us, but I need to do it."

Carly throws a chip at him. "It's about fucking time."

24

Paul has been nervous about the premiere for ages. When the big day finally arrives he can hardly eat for nerves. While he's attended big industry events with Alex and been in the spotlight with things like upfronts, the premiere is a sort of focused attention he's never had in this way before. No one's red carpet performances tonight will make or break the show, but every bit counts. Paul desperately wants things to go well.

Unsteady as things still are between them, he's incredibly glad to have Alex next to him for this. Paul grabs his hand as the car pulls up in front of the venue. Alex squeezes back, his eyes bright.

Stepping out of the car and onto the carpet is like stepping into another world. Flashes go off around them, and Paul has to keep himself from blinking too much. He's never been on this side of the camera before, not like this.

"How do you do it?" Paul asks Alex. He's passed 'nervous' and gone on to 'practically petrified.'

Alex shakes his head. "Practice."

◆

Although Alex has lots of familiarity with the stop-and-pose nonsense of the red carpet, the experience is completely different at Paul's side. They're separated often in the controlled chaos outside the theater. Alex is asked over and over again about his new hair —"that would be telling" — and whether he's proud of his man. To Alex's knowledge, Paul has never been asked if he's proud of *his* man, but then Paul has never been important enough to ask until now. If they're still together the next time Alex has a premiere, he plans on keeping score.

When he won't give away any spoilers for *Fourth*, the spare, tanned people that pass for journalists in L.A. ask him about his future plans. *Any movies coming up? Will he guest on Paul's show? Could marriage be in the works?*

Alex smiles benignly. "We're talking about our futures a lot right now." He's unsure if he's very clever or very cruel.

Any time he can get back to Paul's side, he tucks himself close in a way he's never allowed himself to in public before. Paul gives him a worried, doting glance or two and soldiers on either like Alex is a given or, possibly, like he isn't even there.

When they walk into the theatre, Paul puts his hand on Alex's back. Alex lets himself lean into it. Their eyes catch briefly. In that moment, the entire evening is a shared victory.

♦

Victor skips the carpet at the premiere because this is Paul's night, not his. But at the afterparty, he seeks Paul out as soon as he can. He does it not just because Paul craves approval in a way Victor's not even sure his business partner realizes. He does it because Paul has created a very good thing and should be aware of the quality of the work.

He finds Paul in a corner with his arm around Alex. What shocks Victor isn't the way Alex is curled into Paul's side, looking small and vulnerable. What's jarring is how happy Alex looks there.

As Victor watches, Paul smiles and says something in Alex's ear, who grins and tips his head onto Paul's shoulder. They're gorgeous, and the sight is all the more delightful to Victor because he had no idea that this is who they are when no one is watching.

Finally, he understands why Liam and Alex were beautiful and could not work, with both of them too much in love with being under someone else's sway. Alex and Paul, on the other hand, are also beautiful, but so very challenging. Alex does not go gently into any form of submission, Victor knows from work. Until this moment, Victor had never realized this was a place Alex could take pleasure in. Whether Paul knows how to handle it.... He has to assume not.

"Good work," Victor tells Paul when he can finally bring himself to interrupt them. "I'm proud of you." He expects Alex to disentangle himself from Paul, or at least lift his head from his shoulder. But he doesn't, instead looking up at Victor with a dazed blink that makes his eyelashes flutter the way they had when he'd been lying in a hospital bed. The image is more gorgeous than Victor could have hoped. "I'm proud of you both," he adds.

◆

They stay at the afterparty only long enough for Paul to graciously thank everyone. Alex is willing to tough the night out as long as Paul wants, and says so, but Paul beams and shakes his head.

"I just want to go home with you."

"Okay," Alex says. This night has been good and now it feels scary in the best possible way.

The car ride is pure, delightful torture. Neither of them says anything, but there's a charge between them. Like lightning ready to strike.

Once Paul parks the car they both scramble to get out and inside. They make it as far as the foyer before Paul pushes Alex up against the wall, kissing him hard. Alex whimpers and lets himself be pushed, fisting his hands in Paul's hair.

"I realize this is a total cliché." Paul strokes his hands up and down Alex's sides.

"I don't know, night of your greatest triumph is working out pretty well for me." Alex strains forward to keep kissing Paul. Paul hasn't touched him like this in months and he *wants*. "Upstairs?"

Paul nods but starts unbuttoning Alex's shirt instead.

"What are you doing?" Alex asks breathlessly. Paul's hands on him feel so good he can barely keep his eyes open.

"What does it look like I'm doing?"

Alex digs his fingers into Paul's jacket and pushes him away. Paul looks devastated for a moment. "*Upstairs*," Alex repeats and saunters toward the stairs.

Paul races after him.

◆

Paul hesitates in the doorway. Alex pauses too, standing in the middle of the bedroom, his hair messy and weirdly dark from the dye, his shirt half unbuttoned. He thinks about everything he should be saying, about agreements and space and what this means for what comes after, but all he can see is Paul looking at him.

"Paul," Alex says softly.

"Yeah?"

"Take me to bed."

Paul is gentle with him at first. But Alex is impatient. This, right now, is a real thing he can have. Even if they fall apart with finality tomorrow, they love each other, and they've earned this. The problem, it seems, is earning it day in and day out.

"Can't wait," Alex breathes against Paul's ear. He has to curl around him to do it, as Paul is intent on dragging his bottom lip across Alex's ribcage and up his side.

"Shhhhhhhh."

"No shhhhhh." He yanks Paul up to him by the hair. "We haven't had this in months. Let's go."

"No bells and whistles?" Paul asks with a chuckle and a ridiculous grin.

Alex lines their cocks up and wraps his hand around them as best he can. He smiles wickedly when Paul gasps. "Not even remotely."

◆

After, they're lazy and giggly, unwilling to go to sleep and wake up remembering that this was a respite, not a resolution. Eventually Paul makes the mistake of checking the internet from his phone to see if there's any buzz from the premiere.

There surely is, but stuff about the show the network will track for him. He's more interested, with his current limited bandwidth and relative happiness, on whether the internet thinks the whole unshaven thing is working for him. He's pretty sure Alex thinks it's cute, and he is not remotely above using Alex's curiosity and love of sensation play to keep him interested while they do the real work.

The internet response is less good than it could be. Not because of the beard, but because Paul has the bad luck to stumble almost immediately on someone offering in-depth commentary on whether Alex's smile reaches his eyes in the photos and interviews. Paul knows he should laugh when someone defends their analysis with the declaration that their dad studied sociology in college and knows about body language, but it's a testament to how terrified he is of losing Alex that he's not amused at all.

"What are you looking at?" Alex mumbles from where he's draped across Paul's chest.

"You telling the world we're spending a lot of time discussing our future lately," Paul says as neutrally as he can. He's not angry, just sad.

"I didn't know what else to do."

"It was very clever."

"I thought so."

"The internet's discussing whether you seem happy."

Alex opens an eye so he can give Paul a condescending look. "The internet is discussing no such thing," he says. "Obsessive people are saying irrational things because Liam."

Paul sighs. "I know I sort of count as irrational right now, but, so you know, I don't actually think he's the love of your life and you're just slumming with me."

"Well, that's good," Alex says, amused. "Because that would be crazy above and beyond our actual mental health issues."

"As opposed to in line with our mental health issues," Paul offers.

"Yes. Please don't be more crazy, because I would like to keep you."

Paul squeezes him just a little bit tighter. "Me too. Also, God, Alex, if we can't solve this, it's going to be so public."

Alex pushes himself off Paul's chest and sits up. "Okay, no. Our relationship belongs to us, no matter what happens. And none of that," he grabs the phone out of Paul's hand, "matters. I know tomorrow you're going back to sleeping on the other side of the house, and we're going to keep trying to figure out whether or not we're doomed. If you want to consult the internet on that, that's your business, but I want to throttle you and a legion of sixteen-year-old strangers right now, and guess what? *The smile is still reaching my eyes.*"

"You've talked to Margaret about it, haven't you?" Paul says.

"Having a plan we don't need is better than not having a plan we do," Alex says.

"But today was good," Paul says.

"Today was good," Alex confirms, as he settles back down. "I truly am proud of you."

25

When Paul comes home a week after the premiere to find Alex sitting in the corner of the couch again waiting for him, all signals point to this being the end. Though he realizes he thinks that every time he comes home to Alex waiting for him.

"Hi," he says carefully. He watches as Alex gets up to come stand in front of him. He looks uncertain but not solemn, and Paul tries to take that as a good sign.

"Go out to dinner with me?" Alex asks.

Paul stares at him, trying to calibrate. "What?"

Alex sighs. "Small words, Paul. I. Am. Asking. You. Out. On. A. Date."

"A date?" Paul repeats.

Alex nods. "Yes."

"You mean that thing people do where they make obligatory awkward conversation before sex happens?"

Alex laughs. "You are such an asshole, can we please go out to dinner?"

"Now?" Paul asks.

"Oh my God, it's a good thing I'm still in love with you," Alex mutters. "No. This is where you check your calendar and tell me when you might like to go out with me or ramble on about how you really need to wash your hair instead. I'm going up to my room. When you figure out how to say yes, you have a phone."

"Yes," Paul blurts before Alex can even turn for the stairs.

Alex grins. "Good."

◆

Planning a date turns out to be one of the things Alex's life has not prepared him for.

"Where did you guys used to go?" Gemma asks him when he calls asking for help choosing a place.

"We didn't," Alex says. "It needs to be something new anyway. Also, I have no idea what's appropriate."

"Yeah, because there's a book for that," Gemma says. "'I'm famous and my famous boyfriend and I are about to have a very public divorce unless I can find a super cute place to take him to dinner because I had a bright idea I didn't think through all the way.'"

"Like letting my best friend move into said boyfriend's house for almost no rent," Alex shoots back.

They bicker happily for another ten minutes. When Alex finally hangs up he has a list of recommendations that aren't about sweeping Paul off his feet but about offering to be in the world with him. Gemma's exhortations in regards to his wardrobe choices, however, he ignores.

◆

"Hey, no hat?" Paul asks when Alex comes downstairs on their agreed-upon date night.

"Living dangerously," Alex grins. "Also, brown hair!"

Alex drives. When Paul asks where they're going Alex refuses to tell him, with a look that's both smug and shy. He's ridiculously adorable.

Santa Monica is the eventual destination. "How have we never been out here together?" Paul asks after Alex parks and they're walking the pier.

Alex shrugs. Paul finds it bizarre to see him walking out in public without his hat, even if he does still have his sunglasses on.

"We got busy," Alex finally says.

"I'm sorry," Paul offers.

Alex shakes his head. "Not what I meant. We were just doing other things. Both of us."

Paul can't tell whether Alex is trying to talk about them and their mess on neutral territory or whether he's trying very hard not to. He brings things up, offers leading statements, but then retreats again whenever Paul cautiously engages. On their first date, when Paul had made them dinner at his old house, they'd hardly been able to stop talking long enough to get to the sex. The awkward pauses and hesitations in the conversation now feel like bad signs.

They get food and Alex leads them to a bench where they can sit with their backs to the pier and look out at the ocean. They get a glance or two from passers-by, but Paul only cares about things like that to the extent that they annoy or upset Alex. And Alex seems, with regards to the rest of the world at least, unusually relaxed.

At one point, as Paul is thinking about asking Alex what the hell he is up to, Alex looks at him, intent and curious over his sunglasses.

"What?" Paul asks.

Alex doesn't say anything. Instead he reaches out and folds his fingers through Paul's where his hand is resting on his thigh. He smiles coyly and holds Paul's hand as he turns his head to look back out at the water.

Once the sun starts to go down, Paul offers to drive them home. Alex, after an evaluative look, hands him his keys.

There, Alex kisses him in the kitchen, grabbing onto his shoulders and dragging him down into it. Paul staggers for balance and catches himself with his arms around Alex's waist.

Eventually Alex pulls away, but he can't stop touching Paul's shoulders, his chest, his sides. "This really sucks," he says a little breathlessly.

Paul nods.

"I want to," Alex says. There's the hint of a whine in his voice, and every part of Paul aches to touch him.

"God, me too."

Alex shakes his head minutely. "Good night," he says with that coy smile again. This time it's a little wistful. He kisses Paul one more time, long and deep, and then he's up the stairs to his room and gone.

26

Paul is just falling asleep one night when Alex knocks on his door.

"Hey," Alex says when he opens it. He's got his hat on and his bag slung over his shoulder. He looks far too awake for the hour. "I'm going out. I promise it's not what it looks like, but I didn't want you to worry."

"Where the hell are you going?" Paul's more baffled than concerned, even if 'secret midnight tryst' does fall somewhere near the top of the likely list of explanations.

"Effects for Zach being dead."

"It's two in the morning."

Alex shrugs. "Victor's being sneaky."

Paul shoves a hand through his hair. Victor's done a lot of strange things in the time Paul has worked for and with him, but this is near the top. "Jesus. As a showrunner, I feel so sane right now."

Alex laughs. "See you," he says and heads down the stairs.

◆

Effects shoots are always fun, and there's something particularly magical about this one in the dead of night in an otherwise abandoned set on the lot. The subject matter is fairly grisly, and there are gross effects Alex will have to wash out of his hair later. Getting shot in the head is a messy way to die. But it's a challenge, and it's fun. Tonight, at least, it's the kind of acting he loves best.

Filming the scene that segues into that effects shot is another matter entirely. It's being shot, not on the lot, but at Victor's house. Alex loved dying in *Paradise Square*, but he knows when he throws his bag together a few days later to film Zach's death he is in for a much, much different sort of day.

So much of Michael's death in *Paradise* was about quiet in the midst of chaos and Alex finally understanding the very minute control *The Fourth Estate*'s reviewers keep saying he has over his body. But Zach's demise is simply about terror and regret. It's not pretty, and it's not noble. It's just a waste; not all heroes die brave. Alex knows the fans will be enraged. A rather significant part of him is happy to think that they can go fuck themselves.

Alex taught himself how to act *by accident* so something as brutal as this didn't happen to him American-style in the shitty, shitty place he grew up in. But as hard as it's going to be, and as much as he's going to have to go to what-if places that don't feel as far away as he would like, he's looking forward to playing the scenes. Margaret has hinted that this may be award territory. He knows he's not supposed to let himself consider it.

He gets in his car. All he can think about is how the fuck he's going to survive twelve hours in Victor's basement. Victor's probably threatened the families of the skeleton crew to ensure secrecy. Absolutely no one is supposed to know Zach is going to die.

♦

When he gets to Victor's house, Alex realizes this day is going to be much, much worse than he imagined. Victor's going to shoot it himself on a hand-held high-def camera. The footage that James eventually sees for the first time when he shows it on air will be as unproduced as it's possible to be and have audiences accept it.

"Look, even rebels and terrorists know how to color correct these days," Victor says with a casual wave of his hand.

When the makeup artist starts working on his makeup — bruises and cuts and worse — Alex asks if she really needs the mirror.

"You don't want to see?" she asks. Normally Alex loves this stuff. After all, this was the side of the camera, the production of illusion, he had always meant to be on.

He shakes his head. "Not this time." Zach wouldn't have a mirror in those circumstances, but he'd still know he wasn't pretty anymore and that he was breaking James' heart, as if not being clever and lucky enough were some sort of betrayal. Liam won't take it much better.

With Liam no doubt preoccupied with imagining the worst for their shadow selves, no wonder he's been peculiar. Carly had even sent an email last week asking if Alex knew anything yet about how Zach was going to die. *This*, she'd written, clearly irritated, *is what we talk about every morning. Can you make it stop?*

Alex had written back *No.*

You're a liar, Carly had replied with a smiley face Alex is sure she didn't mean.

Liam's barely been in touch since the last scene they shot together, and Alex has no idea what that's about — anger or fear or trying to stay away from the mess with Paul. Hell, maybe Victor told him not to taunt the dead. The thought is grim, but Liam's pleasure at following directions from their evil overlord has become more than obvious. Increasingly, Alex suspects Victor is completely not interested in using that power only for good.

"Does Victor not have good lighting down here or is he trying to set the mood?" Alex grumbles at the too-bright work light the makeup artist has shined on his face.

She shrugs and frowns.

"There's nothing we find unreasonable, is there?" Alex asks.

"Just our wild success," she says drily.

He smiles, but it feels wrong on his face already.

He finds it harder to not look when she does his arms, especially when she starts on the rope burns on his wrists.

"Is this really necessary?" Alex asks Victor, who's hovering with his own personal professional-grade camera already in hand. The marks aren't like Paul's, but looking at himself through Victor's eyes, they're all Alex can see. Alex is unsettled, to say the least. He feels a twinge of real fear for what's about to happen to him at Victor's hands.

Most of the basement is finished. But toward the back are bare concrete walls that have been hung with the same backdrop they used in the studio. There's a chair pushed into the corner with loops of rope knotted but left loose on each side of it. Too-bright work lights flood the space. It feels like the setup for a horror movie. Which, Alex supposes, it is.

All the safety precautions he's used to for every shoot he's been on with any physical content are notably absent. As much as they've historically annoyed him, for the first time he understands their purpose. Without them, you get this — a rogue shoot in someone's basement with no boundaries that seem any type of good or useful.

Alex laughs when he registers the complete absurdity of Victor steering him into a chair and then kneeling behind him to loop the coils of rope over his wrists before pulling them tight behind his back. But this is not any sort of funny.

Alex has been clear from the pages for this scene that this was going to be a mostly improv-based scenario that will likely be edited down to just a few moments interspersed throughout the episode. Still, he does not expect the first thing Victor says to him when he turns on the camera to be, "Tell me about Paul."

"What?" Alex is shocked and aggrieved and there are people here — lights and sound and makeup. Even the most spare crew is never tiny. Whatever fucked up exercise this is, Alex has no interest in saying anything remotely personal in front of people. And *especially* not in front of Victor.

"Tell me about Paul," Victor repeats.

"He's fine," Alex says shortly.

"Don't lie. He's not."

"It's not your business." Alex grits his teeth. He's furious at Victor for bringing his and Paul's personal shit into a performance.

"When was the last time you told him you loved him?"

"What the actual fuck?"

"There are things you really don't want me to ask," Victor says darkly. "And since I'm going to, you might as well get comfortable with the easy stuff."

"I don't remember," Alex snaps. He knows, given Zach's present circumstances, that he's supposed to feel regret that, regarding James, it's never even happened. That Alex actually does feel regret makes it worse. But Victor's actions are also a violation of him and Paul and it's awful.

Alex expects another intrusive question about his relationship, but what Victor says next is, "Tell me about Liam."

"You're scaring the shit out of him with this," Alex snaps. He's been pissed at Victor for that facet of this particular stunt for weeks, and now he's too blackly angry to care who's watching.

"I know," Victor says, inhumanly calm.

"Carly's pissed I won't tell him how Zach dies."

"She'll be okay."

"Liam might not be."

"Liam will be fine."

"*You don't know that.*"

"You're right, I don't. You two always surprise me."

Alex teeters between rage and fear. Victor pokes around his edges, looking for the thing that will knock him off the edge.

"Tell me about James."

Victor keeps asking questions, and they remain all over the place — in character, out of character, alternatingly vague and precise. Alex feels unbalanced. Acting, certainly, feels impossible. He knows that the solution to this exercise is to surrender, to say whatever he needs to get through to the end.

As soon as he does, this whole thing will be easier, but giving Victor the satisfaction is unappealing. That sensation of falling under has only ever been something good and lovely and private for him. He doesn't want to use it in these circumstances, and he certainly doesn't think Victor deserves it from him. At some point the entire thing has stops being an acting challenge and has clearly become torture.

They go for hours. At one point, the makeup artist leaves the room, probably just to make a personal call, but Alex can't help but think that this is simply no longer something she wishes to witness. Victor is cruel; Alex feels crazed and, eventually, not even there. He loses whole chunks of time to the sheer emotional exhaustion of it. He also loses track of the number of times Victor actually makes Zach die. Hanging still in the chair after the gun to his head goes off is easy; the three seconds before that moment are horrific every single time.

◆

"Okay," Victor finally says. "We're done."

Alex doesn't respond for a long moment. Victor wonders if he realizes he's still crying.

"Shhh," Victor murmurs. He kneels down next to the chair, pulling his utility knife out of his pocket to cut the ropes himself. "You're okay now."

Alex shakes his head once and otherwise stares ahead glassily. His hands are white and cold to the touch from the lost circulation. Victor holds them until the blood starts flowing again. Alex looks like he wants to pull away, but doesn't have the strength or brain to manage it. After what he's done to him — and Victor knows that he's violated more than most people's sense of personal ethics here — he damn well needs to make sure Alex is okay.

When Alex finally looks like he can stand, Victor pulls him up to his feet and hugs him until he stops shaking, or at least stops shaking so violently. Alex isn't Liam. The things that will break him are different and so are the things that can put him back together.

While the rest of the crew starts cleaning up, Victor pulls a P.A. aside and tells him quietly to go upstairs and get orange juice from the fridge. Then he walks Alex over to the makeup chair and starts taking off the makeup himself.

♦

"Victor," Alex says. His voice is scratchy, and he clears his throat. Now that his awareness is filtering back in, all he wants to do is be out of there. And to not have fucking Victor in his face. "I can do that. Or the makeup artist."

"Shhh," Victor says. "I'll be out of your space as soon as I can."

"You could be out of it right now," Alex says sharply.

"No. I know you hate being here, but this needs to come off. I can't let you drive until you're at least a little okay."

Alex acquiesces, in part because he doesn't have the bandwidth to do anything else. But at least Victor knows Alex hates him and that he's been left a mess by Victor's actions.

It takes a long time. Alex just wants to be left alone with his own thoughts, but Victor is quiet in his work and doesn't ask or say anything. So Alex breathes and gets himself back under control. The orange juice helps, too.

Eventually, Victor spins the chair around so Alex can see himself in the mirror. There's no bruises, no blood, just Alex's own too-pale face.

"See?" Victor says, squeezing Alex's shoulders. "You're fine. Now go home and let Paul take care of you."

Alex doesn't know what to say to that so he doesn't say anything. It's early evening on a weekday and there is no way Paul is not at work for hours at least. But Victor hands him back his bag and his keys and waves him out the front door. Alex doesn't have to be told twice to leave.

The drive home is a blur, and when he finally pulls into the driveway he takes a moment to sit with his forehead resting on the steering wheel. When he lifts it again he finally registers that Paul's car is there too. That makes no sense.

He unlocks the front door to find Paul on the couch, glasses on and tapping away at his laptop. He's surprised, considering how much both of them still tend to avoid the common areas of the house.

"How was it?" Paul asks.

Alex shakes his head and drops his bag to the floor.

"What do you need?" Paul sits up and shifts his laptop to the side.

Alex sits beside him and curls in close. "Talk."

Paul stammers as he wraps his arms around Alex.

"Anything," Alex clarifies with the words he can find. "Not my job. Not Victor. Not Liam. Not Iranian politics. Not Chechen separatists. Weather. Weather would be good."

Paul chuckles and squeezes Alex just a bit tighter. Paul obviously thinks he's being a little absurd as he obeys and actually talks about the weather. But the sound of his voice is soothing enough that Alex can close his eyes and not think about terrible things. Hearing that it was sunny and the world continued to turn while Zach was dying and he wasn't is oddly helpful. When Paul starts humorously ascribing emotions and motives to the sun and the clouds and that not-quite-perfect ocean breeze, Alex feels indulged and loved in a way he hasn't in a while.

"Why are you home?" Alex asks after a while.

Paul takes a breath. "Victor called a few days ago and suggested it might be the decent thing to do."

"So you did it," Alex says sullenly.

"He also told me not to tell you. And you seem pretty glad I'm here, so…."

"Sleep with me tonight?" Alex asks.

"I want to say yes, but tell me why," Paul says carefully.

"Not for sex. Just be with me. If I wake up in the night I want to know I'm not dead."

♦

They eat dinner together. Takeout, because Alex is not in a state for the kitchen and Paul doesn't seem to want to leave his side. As Paul gets him situated on the couch with chopsticks and asks if he wants the TV on — Alex shakes his head — Alex suddenly realizes that this is the end of his terrible scheduling. At least for now.

"It's really over," he says. It seems impossible that filming for *Fourth* is well and truly done.

Paul settles down next to him, keeping their shoulders pressed together. "It is. Cashew chicken or the one with the broccoli?"

Alex cracks the first hint of a smile. Nothing about this night is normal, but it's still good to be here with Paul. "Broccoli."

Upstairs, Alex curls up on Paul as soon as they're both in bed.

"If I don't quit acting because of this, nothing will ever make me quit acting." The terror of the day, in Paul's warm arms, is hardening into a resolve.

"Why?" Paul wraps an arm around his shoulder again.

"Because it wasn't acting. Remember that when you watch it."

Paul rubs Alex's arm. "That sounds cruel."

"Victor's a sadist. This may work for Liam, but it does not work for me."

"So that's an insight into the thing with you and Liam. That I didn't have before. And that I'm still not sure I wanted." Paul sounds surprised.

"I've been trying to tell you that. You do get it, right?" Alex says.

"I'm going with no?"

"Paul." He grabs Paul's hand and holds it. He needs him to pay particular attention to this. "I give up control to you because I trust you. I *like* when you push me. I love when you mark me. None of that makes me feel anything bad. I never have to sit alone in a room staring at a wall for hours after doing things with you in order to feel human again."

"You go quiet, though."

Alex lets out an exasperated sigh. When will Paul ever believe him? "That's different. Incredibly different."

"How?"

"When you hurt me, you're taking pleasure from my pleasure. When Victor hurts me, he's taking pleasure from my pain."

Paul takes time to process that. "Victor has way too much control over all of our lives."

"Write down the date and time you said that," Alex says.

27

Without *Fourth* to keep him busy, Paul worries aloud that Alex will go back to the restless boredom of the summer shooting hiatus. But the end of shooting means that Alex gets to focus on what comes next without anything else to worry about, and that's what he's wanted all along. He spends a lot of time with Margaret, looking at different projects and talking through what he wants the shape of the next year to look like.

It would be easier to do that if he knew what shape he and Paul were going to be in next year, but Alex has always made decisions with variables unknown. This variable just hurts a little more than most.

In one of their meetings, Margaret asks what Alex thinks about paintball.

"Excuse me?" The question seems apropos of nothing.

"Your *Fourth* character is about to die violently via a gunshot wound on network TV. Meanwhile the bullshit with guns keeps cropping up, thanks to your insistence on sharing with America the one hobby that pisses all of America off —"

"I am awesome," Alex interjects.

" — And you're looking at roles that involve yet more people with guns," Margaret continues with a heavy sigh. "Considering the state of the American film industry, I can't really blame you. But to keep things under control, and fun instead of terrible, running around with play guns might take a bit of the edge off."

"There is nothing about this that is not ridiculous," Alex says.

"Yeah, but you'd get to play paintball."

◆

Carly, of all people, is the one who ends up talking Alex into it. They're on the phone one night when Alex calls her because Paul is still at work, Liam isn't picking up, and Alex is feeling lonely. She's also the one who suggests making it a date.

"I'm dubious," Alex says.

"You're the one who climbs rocks for fun. And shoots. This should be right up your alley."

"Not as a media stunt!"

"Then think of it as a bonding activity. Paul needs a hobby. And some stress relief. When was the last time you two fucked?"

"I appreciate that it's you asking me the intrusive questions about our sex life for once, but I'm not going to answer that," Alex tells her.

"I'll get a group together. You just get him there."

"Will Liam be there?" Alex asks. If this madness is going to happen, he wants to know exactly what kind of madness to expect.

Carly sighs. "Guns? Not on your life, baby boy."

◆

Alex asks Paul out for the game via text because their schedules aren't lining up at all. There's also something fun about being flirty and coy. Paul finally sends back *Alleexxxx I have to go work now.* Alex replies with *;)* and lets the question rest until Paul finally gets back around to asking for a date and time.

Carly's organizational skills are practically occult; in order to manage her and Liam's lives, they have to be. By some miracle she manages to get their friends together on a Saturday afternoon in late September. It's a big group, with people from the brunch posse, Alex's crew buddies, and a handful of Paul's work people. Alex feels a little green as he contemplates Gemma chatting with Brian like an old friend.

◆

To Paul's surprise he and Alex end up on the same team — because Alex insists on it. Paul expects to lose track of him quickly, but he sticks by Paul's side. Twenty minutes in, Paul realizes, chagrined, that's not because Alex wants to be an epic team of awesome. Alex is covering him, because Paul *sucks*. It's embarrassing, but it's also sweet.

Alex loves the whole exercise. Paul, to his own surprise, does too. He's hardly done anything but work on set or at home for months. He hasn't had time even to go running. Tearing around a field while getting to shoot friends with paint is the perfect sort of outlet.

Paul feels guilty about going after any of the girls right up until Darcy shoots him in the chest. She runs away giggling while he frantically tries to wipe the splattered paint off his goggle lenses. So much for benevolent sexism. Maybe Alex is right, and Paul needs to start taking people at their word when they say they are up for some rough and tumble. Alex certainly has no compunction about it. Looking amused, he shoots Darcy between the shoulder blades. Paul is momentarily horrified until he hears her laugh even harder.

Everyone gets hot and sweaty and covered in paint. "I like the rainbow hair," Paul tells Alex, pushing dark hair that's just starting to show red at the roots off his forehead for him.

"I have a thing for headshots."

"That's gruesome."

"Only a little." Alex shrugs. "It's weird that we're doing this while we look like other people."

At first Paul thinks he means the paint. As the day goes on it gets harder to tell people apart at a distance as they get splotched with different colors. But as they're cleaning up for the drive home — Paul wants to get the paint out of his beard because neon green is not a good look for him — Alex meets his eyes in the mirror of the shitty park bathroom and smiles in the way that makes his eyes crinkle. It's then that Paul realizes Alex means his hair, Paul's scruff, and the current messy state of their relationship.

Alex starts taking off his clothes the second he walks in the door. "I'm taking a shower. I feel disgusting," he says.

The statement and the stripping aren't flirtation or invitation, Paul realizes, just comfort and familiarity. He's still happy that they can shower simultaneously without having to do so together. He feels gross too, and they've had a good day; he has no intention of pushing his luck.

The comfort and familiarity thing must be going around, because by the time Paul pads downstairs in sweats and a T-shirt after his own shower, Alex is in the kitchen, shirtless, frowning into the fridge as he considers a snack. Alex may be a good shot, but he's also clearly a good target. His arms and torso are covered in bruises from too many shots fired at excessively close range.

"Do they hurt?" Paul asks, lightly brushing his fingers over Alex's back. He's bruised too, but not as much and not as badly. Alex's paleness makes all marks look more alarming.

"I've had worse," Alex says with a shrug, closing the refrigerator door, and turning under Paul's scrutiny.

"I hate that," Paul says.

"Whatever," Alex says amiably.

◆

touching. Alex is happy to lean back against the refrigerator and arch his back just a little. Paul isn't even really doing anything and it feels amazing. One of the side effects of the current mess their relationship is in is that Alex is touch-starved and horny all the time. Now that he isn't working fourteen-hour days five or more days a week, he's awake enough to notice.

He watches Paul's fingers. It's easier than looking at his face and being too hopeful. Or asking for things and getting told no for reasons that are, at least relatively, sound.

It takes less than thirty seconds of both of them breathing too loudly in the silent kitchen for Paul's fingers to pause at the bruise on Alex's hipbone and press his fingers into it.

Alex hisses and tips his head back against the refrigerator.

"Sorry," Paul says but makes no effort to stop touching him.

"Don't be," Alex says.

Paul's fingers are almost a tickle as they move up his side and down his arm. He edges closer, and Alex can feel the heat radiating off him. He's scared to move lest he startle Paul off.

Paul runs his hand down Alex's arm, palm curved and fitting tight to the muscle. When he gets to Alex's wrist, he grips too tight, just for a moment. Then he tickles his fingers up for a moment and pressing his thumb into another bruise.

Alex moans.

"You're so beautiful," Paul whispers.

"Keep touching me," Alex says hoarsely, the words barely formed.

Paul obeys. Everything is light and fleeting except for the way he presses into Alex's bruises, making him moan. They're both trembling from holding back.

"Upstairs?" Alex finally breathes.

Paul nods.

They don't race. It's not frantic. In the room Alex now thinks of as his own, they don't turn on the light. The room is shadowed, having lost its direct sunlight while they were still out running around the field.

"We should probably talk about this," Paul says as he slides out of his clothes.

"What?" Alex says lightly. "We've gone on a few dates, and now we're going to bed."

"We'll talk about it later, then," Paul says, unable to take his eyes off of Alex as he kicks his jeans aside.

"Yes. Exactly." Alex climbs onto the bed.

Paul follows and resumes mapping his bruises. He's not teasing, the way he so often is. He's thorough and reverent and soothing. It makes Alex's breath catch and his cock fill. At one point, Paul gets himself so turned around on the bed he winds up kissing Alex's ankle and then sucking on his toes one after the other.

Alex moans loudly. "Why the hell haven't you done this before?"

Paul laughs with his mouth full. Alex retaliates by getting his hands on to Paul's ass and dragging him back so he can pull his cock into his mouth.

"Holy shit."

Alex pulls off for a second to say, "You should probably take this as a hint."

Paul laughs and then gasps. "This is gonna be way more challenging than you think."

Alex makes an unintelligible sound around Paul's cock.

Paul's not wrong. Alex is shocked both by how good it feels to get sucked off while he has a cock in his mouth too and just how difficult it is to concentrate on anything enough to get off. It's a perfect sort of misery. So much of sex with Paul is.

"Oh my God." Alex pulls off with a gasp and starts jerking Paul with his hand; that at least he can sort of concentrate on. Paul is grateful, based on the sounds he makes and his renewed efforts with his mouth. Alex knows Paul well enough to know when he's close. He urges him on with the small sounds of his own pleasure as his balls pull up tight.

Even so, Paul's orgasm catches them both off guard. Alex follows almost immediately, the orgasm wrenching out of him as Paul's thumb remains buried in the bruise at his hip.

Alex wants to talk as they both roll onto their backs and lay there head to foot, panting at the ceiling. But he feels too wrecked and too startled to make words.

"Why is that so hot?" he eventually gasps.

Paul puts a hand on Alex's thigh and squeezes. "Sorry about that," he says as Alex wipes his fingers across his now very messy face.

"Whatever," he pants. "Just discovered a thing."

"Oh, really?" Paul says.

Alex nods vigorously. "Uh-huh."

Paul makes a smug sound.

"Oh, shut up and get us a towel." Alex shoves at him ineffectually.

"Bratty," Paul says. It's fond, though, and he squeezes Alex's ankle gently before he heads to the bathroom.

◆

Alex lets Paul clean both of them up, declaring that it's his mess anyway. Paul does it willingly. He's happy to keep touching Alex, even when he's merely running a warm washcloth over his skin. When Paul tosses aside the towel and pulls the blanket up over them, Alex rolls onto his side and presses his forehead to Paul's.

"We should probably talk," Paul says.

"I don't want to stop doing this," Alex says. His voice is quiet, and he sounds almost afraid.

Paul finds Alex's hand and holds it tightly. "No. Me neither."

"The dating is good, though."

"The dating is very good. So is the sex."

Alex snorts gently. "Understatement. We're not moving back in together, though."

"No."

It's scary to lie there with Alex in the bed that used to be theirs and work out the terms of their new arrangement. As they're clarifying when sex is okay — in terms of dates, yes; booty calls and expectations, no — Paul realizes that their trial separation is over. They're living in the same house, but not together. They're boyfriends, but Alex wanting to go on dates isn't him being cute. They're back to a phase of their relationship they never had to begin with because Paul was inappropriately obsessive and Alex was in over his head. They aren't partners anymore.

When he says as much to Alex, he nods a little shakily. "I know."

"What we do to each other is amazing," Paul says, tracing a constellation of bruises on Alex's shoulder with his free hand. "But that makes it harder for us in some ways. Not because I've got my head messed up about my kinky," he says when Alex makes a noise of protest. "We're just way too good at doing this and never talking. Case in point."

"We're talking now," Alex points out.

"Because we're being very good."

"Yeah. We should keep doing that."

"We really, really should."

As they breathe together, Alex's eyes dart over Paul's face, dark and compelling.

When Paul asks what he's looking for, Alex says, "Why does this feel so scary?"

Paul's heart aches. He's feeling it too, laying here so perfectly with Alex. It's terrifying. "We forgot how good we were."

"God, you're so much to lose." Alex tightens his hand around Paul's. His voice is rough.

Paul wraps his free arm around Alex's side, pulling him close. "You too," he says into his hair.

Alex tucks his head under Paul's chin and clings.

28

As the *Fourth* shoot for James' terrible scene — broadcasting Zach's last footage and execution live — approaches, Liam is increasingly unreliable about being in touch. Alex, meanwhile is increasingly worried. Not only about Liam's capacity for dealing with the episode as written, but about the very massive and intentional gaps that exist between what they did at the table read and what Victor has actually been shooting. Alex almost wonders if Victor is trying to get the show killed early. Certainly, he's about to piss off a lot of people, none of whom have ever liked him and all of whom control the money and the network's schedule.

Alex badgers until he finally gets Liam to agree to meet for lunch the first week of October.

Something is off right from the start. Liam isn't meeting Alex's eyes, and his usual vibrancy and energy isn't quite right. He's fidgety, easily distracted, and seems to lose the thread of the conversation every other sentence.

"Are you okay?" Alex asks after Liam manages to drop his fork a second time.

Liam nods.

"Lee…."

"I'm fine." Liam nudges Alex's foot under the table. "Happy birthday, by the way. I missed having a party for you on set. Did you and Paul do anything cool?"

"No, he had deadlines. It's fine, I climbed rocks," Alex adds when Liam frowns. Frankly he doesn't give a shit about not celebrating the day, especially compared to the rest of everything he's trying to sort out in his life. "Thank you, though."

Close as they are, neither of them is part of the other's day-in and day-out support group. Liam has Carly and Victor and whoever else makes up his strange life to take care of him; he is not Alex's to worry about like this.

But with the day of the shoot getting closer, Alex thinks about his own terrible last day of filming. At least Liam's will be on the lot and not in Victor's fucking basement. But Victor is still Victor. Alex does not understand his relationship with Liam any more than he understands how Liam's brain works. More than that, Alex knows what Victor is capable of. He's not sure whether that means Victor will hurt Liam less or much, much more.

◆

"Lee," Alex says when Liam finally picks up the phone a few days later. It's late afternoon, Paul is at work, and Alex is on the couch with Todd stretched out next to him. "I know what you're shooting. And I know you have people who will take care of you. And I don't know why you're like this, but some of this is my fault and some of it is about me. What do you need from me?"

Liam takes a breath that Alex can hear all the way down the line. And then he tells Alex what he needs. This is how they have always worked and Alex is glad they still do, despite what Liam's request turns out to be. Paul's probably going to freak out. Alex has to figure out if that's a reasonable response before he's confronted with it.

Considering the size of his contact list, Alex has remarkably few people he can call to ask. This surely qualifies as high on Margaret's Do Not Tell Me These Things list. Carly, as much as they have some sort of simpatico going on, is both too biased and too much of a hobbyist when it comes to interpersonal strategy to be a choice that isn't going to blow up in his face. While Gemma may be his best friend, mostly she just wants to see him and Liam fuck. Which, if he thinks about it objectively, he can't really blame her for, but it's not useful and is fairly horrifying.

Which narrows it down to Victor, who is both untrustworthy and, as far as Alex is concerned, entirely responsible for this impending clusterfuck, and Darcy, who probably talks to Paul more than Alex does these days. Alex sighs. He's never thought she would be the lesser of so many evils but the gossip she shares isn't likely to make any sense to anyone else. And she might be somewhat familiar with whatever's going on in Paul's head these days.

Darcy, predictably, is incredibly excited when Alex tells her he needs advice.

"Let me get this out, okay?" he says before she can derail the conversation to unhelpful places.

"Now you're kind of freaking me out," Darcy says. "You never call to ask me anything. And you sound like somebody died."

"Yeah, okay, the person giving the advice is not the one who gets to freak out. Is it weird if someone you used to date asks you to stay over at their place — not for sex! — like, 'cause they're really sad about something? Is that a thing boyfriends get to freak out about?"

"Why do you ask?" she says coyly.

"Because I need to know, Darcy. Come on, why would that be hypothetical?"

"Well. Yeah. That's definitely weird. And he's totally trying to get in your pants."

"He's not."

"Yeah…no. I thought you were smart. All the magazines say what a smart actor you are."

"Stop mocking."

"Then don't call me asking questions so you can decide my answers are bad. That's really rude. Just talk to Paul about it. Since he's your actual boyfriend."

Alex sighs. "Thank you, Darcy. For your maturity and complete lack of help. I owe you forever."

"Cool! When are we doing guns again? I miss you."

Alex pulls his phone away from his ear and stares at it.

♦

"Do you have time to talk?" Alex asks.

Paul looks up at Alex where he's standing at the top of the stairs to the loft. He has things he needs to be doing, but Alex looks serious and this is one of the things Paul is working on. Twenty minutes talking to his boyfriend is not going to kill him. Or his show.

"I talked to Liam today," Alex says.

Paul tries not to have any sort of visible reaction to that, particularly not one Alex would find egregious. "How is he?"

"We talked about the shoot coming up. I asked him what he needed from me. He's been upset, and that's on me."

"It's not your fault —"

"It is, actually." Alex shrugs. "But it's mostly Victor's, because God knows what he's going to do to Lee. He asked if I would stay over with him the night before and go into the studio with him on the day."

"I realize you're expecting me to be jealous and uncomfortable, which we'll get to in a moment, but is he five?"

"Paul. Don't be mean. Liam is a lot of things, but he doesn't exaggerate and he isn't sneaky. I asked what he needed, this is what he said, and after what Victor did to me, I believe him."

"Are you asking me for permission?" Paul says even if he doesn't for a moment think Alex actually is.

"Not really. I'd still like us to have a clear conversation about the consequences, though."

"You were a mess when you got home," Paul admits.

Alex nods.

Paul looks at Alex for a long moment. "I wish to hell there was a way for me to say no that didn't make me an asshole."

"There really isn't."

"And it has to be you," Paul says.

"Yes."

"Can we talk about boundaries?" Paul is desperate to hang on to what little control he has in the face of all the things Alex may or may not be willing to do for Liam.

"If you mean agreements, yes."

"You can't sleep with him," Paul says quickly.

"I've told you I won't," Alex says. He doesn't snap, but his voice is firm.

"If you do —"

"Paul. I will not fuck Liam. That is a thing that is true and a thing that is as much about my relationship with Lee as it is about my relationship with you. Don't assume I'm a liar, don't assume I can't control myself, and *don't* threaten me."

"Don't make out with him either," Paul says weakly. He feels like he has to keep saying something, even if none of it seems likely to help.

"I don't ask you not to make out with Carly."

"I don't make out with Carly!"

"My point," Alex says. "Or not to sleep in the same bed with her —"

"I can't think about that. Is that what he asked for?"

"Paul. Stop. I have no idea. My point is that someone I feel responsible to and have made promises to has asked me to step up. I feel responsible to and have made promises to you, too. I know I'm pretty, but I'm not so pretty I can't keep two ideas in my head at the same time."

"This makes me uncomfortable," Paul says.

"I know it does. I'm a little uncomfortable too, but can you get to okay with it?"

"What would happen if I said no?" How bad, exactly, would it be?

"Then we'd keep talking."

♦

Alex has never liked Liam's house. It's massive, ugly, and decorated in the worst sort of pretentious interior design. He's spent nights here before — he and Paul both have, crashed out together in one of the extra rooms when they've been hanging out with Liam, Carly, and a couple of bottles of wine. More often, they all get together at Carly's place, which Alex prefers anyway. Her more modest apartment is one of the most normalizing things in his life. What Alex has never figured out about Liam's place is *why*. It doesn't suit him at all.

"Have you ever actually read any of these books?" he asks as Liam ushers him into the den or the great room or *whatever*. He slumps down into one of the leather chairs.

Liam shrugs. "Some of them."

"Really?" Alex asks skeptically.

"Sometimes I get bored," Liam says blandly. "Do you want a drink?"

"I don't know. Is the point of this distraction or what?"

"I don't know," Liam echoes back at him.

"Did Victor tell you about our shoot?" Alex asks, pulling up his legs to sit cross-legged on one of Liam's ugly and excessive chairs.

"He said you were great." Alex isn't sure if the pride in his voice is Liam's own or unintentional mimicry of Victor's dark enthusiasm.

"Thanks, but did he tell you what we did?" Alex never knows how much information Liam gets from Victor and usually assumes it's a lot. This situation, however, is unique. He wants to prepare Liam for what might be coming as much as he wants to not say anything that's going to set him off right now.

Liam shakes his head. "No. I keep asking, but no. Not in detail, anyway."

"Does that feel okay for you or not?" Alex asks bluntly.

"If I needed to know, Victor would tell me."

"Okay. That's positively creepy," Alex says before realizing he's being rude.

Liam shrugs.

"It was really hard," Alex tells him. "And kind of awful. I'm here right now as much because of that as because you asked."

Liam nods. "James's stuff will be different, though."

"Okay," Alex says even though he does not at all have Liam's faith in Victor's benevolence. "Then why are you so worried about tomorrow?"

"I told you I don't really do death well." Liam's face is drawn tight, and he's staring somewhere past Alex's knees. "And Zach is going to die."

Alex thinks about pointing out that, from his own perspective, Zach is already dead. He's sure it won't be helpful.

"Hey, can I see your pages?" he asks. It might give them something to talk about that's rooted in the reality of their jobs, as well as give him half a hint of how cruel Victor's about to be.

"Is it fucked up that this feels wrong?" Liam asks as he gets up to fetch them.

"I'm done," Alex says. "I'm certainly not about to leak your details about my grand departure."

"It's not that," Liam says as he rifles through a stack of papers. "It's an actorly thing. Or, no, not even that." He flicks his hand sharply, the way he does when words aren't coming as easily as he wants and he's frustrated.

"A my-guy-and-your-thing?" Alex asks as Liam looks at the pages in his hand for a moment before he holds them out to him.

Liam nods as Alex takes them. "Yeah. Like, you're *dead*. It doesn't seem right you get to find out what happens to the rest of us after."

"Are they making you do press around this when it airs?" Alex asks, skimming over Liam's script, which has been marked up in color-coded highlighters that convey information in no way Alex understands.

Liam shrugs. "Probably."

"Okay, can I ask that you work on your specificity? Because *I'm not dead.*"

Liam nods earnestly. "Yeah. Totally. Sorry. It's just hard."

"No shit."

Eventually Liam puts the pages away, at which point he apparently rediscovers the power of locomotion. Now he won't stop walking. Or talking. Which is probably good. It's also exhausting to keep up with.

"Okay. Drink now?" Alex tips his head back in the chair to follow Liam as he paces around the room.

"Sure." Liam diverts from his path around the room to head for his obnoxious bar set-up. "Hey, how's Paul?"

"In a general relationship sense, or a me spending the night at your house sense?"

"Two."

Alex shrugs. "He wasn't thrilled. But he and Darcy went out to dinner tonight, so at least he's not sitting home and brooding."

"Dude, do you need me to talk to him? I didn't mean to cause more problems between you guys or whatever."

"It's fine, Lee," Alex says. As far as he is concerned, Liam trying to have another conversation with Paul about him is something that needs to happen never.

"Are you two going to be okay?"

"I don't know." When Liam is silent for long enough Alex feels obligated to fill the space he adds, "Things are a lot better, but…."

"But what?"

"But we've got some bad cases of crazy and love might not be enough?" Alex abruptly realizes he doesn't want to say more.

"I don't understand that," Liam says.

"I know," Alex says. "Sometimes I don't either."

◆

"Okay, sleeping arrangements," Liam says once they've worked their way through a drink and another strange conversation that jumps non-linearly between Paul and Victor and Carly.

"Yes?" Alex says cautiously.

"Sleep with me?"

"I'm going to assume you mean that in the logistical sense and not the euphemistic one."

Liam laughs. "How about in whatever way you feel comfortable with?"

Alex rolls his eyes fondly. It's pretty clear Liam doesn't actually think that's going to get him laid. Though he's leaving the option open.

"Okay." Alex pushes himself upright in the chair. "Ground rules."

Liam makes a *go on* gesture.

"One," Alex starts.

Liam looks pleased to be getting a list.

"No sex. Two, no making out. Three, PJs stay on."

Liam nods. "Is cuddling okay?"

"Cuddling, yes. Groping, no."

"I sort of feel like you're assuming the worst about me here," Liam complains. "Also, the no making out thing sucks."

Alex makes a mental note that complaining is a shitty way to respect someone's boundaries. "Liam. My relationship can't handle any gray areas right now. I am here because I have promises to both you and Paul to honor. But I am also saying these things because I have promises to both you and Paul to honor."

Liam smiles a little proudly. "You're really good at this communication thing."

"Thank you?"

Liam grabs Alex's bag for him before leading the way upstairs. The gesture is sweet, but it's also a little unnerving.

"Not actually a girl, you know," Alex says dryly.

"I know. I'm being polite. Although, by the way, you should be less snide about women."

"I'll add it to the list."

They pass a few rooms Alex has been in before. At the end of the hallway, Liam shoulders open the last door and flicks on the light switch. Alex follows him in.

"This is completely not what I expected."

On some level, however, the room is exactly what Alex expected. But the small bedroom doesn't go with the rest of the house at all. It's far more like Liam's room in his parents' house in New York.

Liam shrugs.

"No, seriously, what is the deal with your weird house?"

"I moved out here, I had some money from all the work I did as a kid, and I had to prove to the world I had actually graduated from Nickelodeon, I bought a house and hired an interior designer and did some press that was shot here and whatever. Old school, classic Hollywood bachelor. It was supposed to make me look sophisticated."

"It makes you look ridiculous," Alex says.

"The colors are soothing."

Alex waves that off as he stares at Liam's bed. "How do you have so much sex and only have a full?"

"Most people don't get to see the real bedroom," Liam says.

"There's a fake bedroom?" Alex is incredulous.

"Hookups, whores, orgies, photoshoots," Liam says casually.

"I can't tell if you're joking."

"Yeah," he says. "Neither can I."

♦

"I can't believe you have glow-in-the-dark stars here, too."

Alex can feel, if not see, Liam shrug in the dark. They're not actually tangled up with each other yet, although he knows Liam's habits and knows they will be. For now though, the proximity makes everything tense in a way that feels good and possibly a little bit dangerous.

"Carly gave them to me," Liam says. "She thinks they're cute."

"Have you guys found a house yet?"

"No, still looking."

"Sucks," Alex says. He keeps his hope that Carly will be in charge of decorating this time to himself.

"It's fine. We're both busy. The schedule doesn't offer a lot of downtime."

"I noticed."

"I get why you wanted to leave," Liam says. "Mostly because you're you and I know how you do shit even if I don't always get how your brain works. But what I don't get is why you wanted to leave like this."

"I wanted to make it big," Alex says, thoughtful. He rolls onto his side and scoots closer to Liam to have it over and done with. He misses sharing a bed most nights, and even if this is a small and dangerous pleasure, it isn't one that has been explicitly declared off-limits. On some level, he suspects it probably should have been, but Carly and Paul crawl all over each other with absurd familiarity when they have their trashy movie nights. Intellectually he can't quite see how this should be different. "Also, I wanted to keep Zach." Experimentally, he puts a hand on Liam's waist.

"That doesn't make any sense," Liam says irritably. He grabs Alex's hand and tugs so that they are well and truly cuddling.

"If Zach just leaves, he could be doing anything. Everybody would get to make up their own idea of what he's up to. This way, I know where he is. Nobody else gets to own him." If fame means Alex can't own himself, then he can damn well own the character that made his life this way.

"That's fucked up."

Alex shrugs. On the nightstand, his phone buzzes. He cranes his arm awkwardly to reach it because Liam has him in a death-grip and isn't letting go.

"Who is it?" Liam asks.

"How many people do you think I have that text me this late?"

"Is it Paul? It's totally Paul. Let me see!"

"What? No!" Alex holds the phone at arm's length to try to read the message, while Liam drops his hand to make a grab for it. "Oh my God, you're five, stop!"

Thinking of you, the text says with a smiley. Given their texts while he was in D.C., Alex doesn't know whether to be exasperated or find it adorable.

"Awwww," Liam coos. "That's so cute!"

"That is Paul feeling uncomfortable and not knowing what to say," Alex says as he shoves his shoulder into Liam to get enough space to text back. *Liam's being annoying about how cute we are.*

"I'm not annoying," Liam says.

"Yeah, no, you totally are." Alex doesn't look at him, staring at his phone instead as he waits for it to chime again.

Got back from dinner with Darcy a while ago. How's it going?

"Okay, that's slightly awkward," Liam observes over his shoulder.

"Ignoring you," Alex tells him. He texts back, *Good. How's your night?*

Little weird, little lonely, mostly bored.

Glad to hear it ;) Alex types back.

"I hope you tell him how fucking in love with him you are all the time."

"Liam," Alex chides. Everything is such a mess of tentative and redefined commitment right now.

Liam stares at him. "Oh my God, you don't."

"Lee," Alex says more sharply.

"Why *not?*" Liam gives up on the phone and sits up.

"It's just not how we communicate," Alex says.

"Text him," Liam says.

"No."

"Yes."

"*Seriously?*" Alex says, annoyed. Liam catches him completely off guard by lunging for the phone and toppling Alex, who yelps, backwards and half off the bed in the process. High school wrestling seems a painfully long way away and possibly more like the unfortunate beginning of a porn movie than ever. He sighs and tosses Liam the phone.

"Yay!" Liam catches it. "*This is Liam,*" he recites, thumbing over the screen. "*Alex loves you.*"

"You dick," Alex makes a grab for the phone, but Liam punches send first.

"What? You do! Don't give me bullshit about *how you tend to communicate*, I've heard him say it to you *tons* of times."

"Yes, well, Paul's Paul, and I'm me."

"I hope this is on the list of things you're working on," Liam says sullenly.

I'm terrified of both of you right now, Paul texts back. *But in a much better way than I could be.*

29

Alex wakes up in the morning to find Liam thoroughly wrapped around him, their legs tangled and Liam's arm hooked around Alex's side. Alex moves gently as he can to brush Liam's curls out of his own eyes. Liam's face scrunches up but then smooths, and he rolls a little closer to Alex before his breathing evens out again. Being here with Liam is lovely, but it's also a little melancholy. It feels like a terribly solemn privilege to be able to hold him like this when their relationship is so not about them being lovers.

As sweet and sad as this is, though, certain rules of human biology are always in play. Liam is a restless sleeper and if either of them moves wrong things are going to get very awkward very quickly. Given what Liam's asked of him for today, what Alex has promised Paul, and his own need for sanity, that's something Alex would rather avoid.

When he slides out of bed, Liam frowns in his sleep and rolls into his spot, pulling Alex's pillow into his arms. Liam remains nothing quite like what all of America thinks he is. But all these years on, Alex can't quite believe how truthful his beauty and sweetness actually are.

He pads around quietly, takes a shower, gets dressed, and then sits in the chair-and-a-half by the bed, one sole up on the seat. He texts Paul to let him know he made it through the night unscathed and tells him he'll see him at home later. After a day like this, Alex knows he's going to be craving Paul's presence. He hugs his knees as he goes back and forth between glancing at Liam's incomprehensibly marked-up pages and Liam himself.

Alex is glad Liam's call isn't until late morning. He's also worried about what Victor is going to spring on him once he gets to work. The whole situation is such an amazingly clear argument for why people shouldn't fuck the boss, he has to stifle a laugh.

When Liam finally opens his eyes, he looks confused and then worried until his gaze lands on Alex.

"I thought you'd left," he says, his voice rough from sleep.

"Nope, right here." Alex goes to sit on the side of the bed. When he does, Liam grabs his hand and holds on tight.

"Promise me you won't go anywhere?" Liam's face is drawn, and Alex can feel how tensely he's holding his muscles. Whatever trust in Victor he has, he's also clearly afraid for today. It makes Alex's heart ache.

"For as long as I can," he says, as horrible as it is. But things happen in the world no one can control. That, of course, is what the material they're shooting right now is about. No matter how much Liam may need or want reassurance, this seems like a particularly inauspicious time to ignore that particular truth.

They drive to set separately but park next to each other. On the walk inside Alex knows, because he is familiar with the energy of Paul doing the same thing, that Liam is exerting effort not to hold his hand. He gives up on it as soon as they're inside.

Alex rubs his thumb over the back of Liam's hand. Liam's shoulders relax slightly. "Right here," he says quietly. "I'm always going to be right here."

Liam nods a little frantically.

Victor interrupts them on the way to hair and makeup. He gives their linked hands a feral smile. "And what are you doing here?" he asks Alex.

"Moral support," Alex says.

Liam swings their hands a little.

"No, I don't think so."

"What?" For all of Alex's — and Liam's — worries about today, the idea that Alex wouldn't be allowed to be present for this had not occurred to either of them. Alex really should have anticipated this, though, because Victor is Victor.

"I said no. Alex, you're not coming on set today. Liam, you're late, run along."

Liam stands there looking stunned.

"Go on," Alex says softly, squeezing his hand. "It's just work, and you're going to kill it." As angry as he is at Victor for forbidding this, yelling at him in front of Liam is not going to do any good right now.

Liam goes a little gray but nods. Another moment passes before he disentangles their hands and gives Alex a sad look.

"You know where to find me," Alex tells him.

Liam nods, stepping into Alex's space like he really can't bear to leave just yet. "Bye," he says sadly and kisses Alex dryly on the mouth.

Alex gives him as brave a smile as he can before Liam turns and walks away. As he goes, he shoves his hands in his pockets in a manner that's incredibly characteristic of James.

Victor folds his arms over his chest and watches with Alex until Liam turns a corner and disappears from sight.

"Was that really necessary?" Alex asks.

Victor shrugs. "James is going to lose Zach. Liam doesn't get a safety net."

"That's cruel."

"That's storytelling. You didn't get a safety net either."

"I'm not your lover. And I'm not as fragile as Liam."

"And you are being as unwise as you are being imprecise." Victor's voice is calm, but Alex can tell he's hit something soft.

"Liam isn't going to tell you when you push him too far," Alex says.

"That's not your concern."

Alex stares at him in disbelief. "Yes, it is."

"What makes you think that?"

"Liam has been my concern since I got shoved into a scene with him and our lives got magic."

"You're revising history. He's not your responsibility, Alex. He's mine," Victor says dangerously.

"You're not going to take care of him," Alex snaps. At this point he is past caring how Victor and Liam work. Nothing he is seeing right now aligns with anything he knows Liam actually needs.

"I always take care of my people," Victor says sharply.

"Like you did with me?"

"I pushed you. You were incredible. You are also standing in front of me right now. You are fine, so stop being dramatic and let Liam do his job."

Alex realizes he's shaking. He doesn't feel fine. Not after the ordeal in Victor's basement and certainly not standing here on the lot having what feels like a fight over Liam's soul.

Victor goes on. "Today, Liam is going to give one of the best performances of his life. After this, he's going to be able to do anything he wants."

"Because you took me away from him." Dimly, Alex is aware their raised voices have started to draw bystanders and that he is probably being unreasonable. Someone yelling at Victor is not rare, but Alex doesn't remotely care enough to reign himself in.

"Yes."

"I can't believe you."

"Why?" Victor turns so that he's even more in Alex's space. He's not as tall as Alex is, and probably not as strong, but his presence has always been bigger than the physical space he takes up. Right now, every part of that presence is radiating menace.

"You're not even human! Liam is not a thing for you to play with." Alex is far too angry to care about the danger.

"Everyone here is a thing to play with. They knew that when they signed up for this and so did you. You're just the only one who doesn't like it."

"I promised him I'd be here today. You made me a liar."

Victor sneers. "Then don't promise things you can't control, little boy."

Alex reacts without thinking about it; he is far too furious for words. He shoves at Victor. Victor doesn't react, just watches him, fascinated, like Alex is merely another toy in his box doing something new and interesting.

His weight is far too well planted for Alex to move him, which enrages Alex more. Before Alex can get his fist back to really take a swing there's an arm hooked around his chest. Raphael is holding him back.

"Hey, hey, hey, steady there," he murmurs in Alex's ear. Alex wants to fight him off because *Victor is still standing right there,* lips pursed triumphantly. But Raphael's got a good grip and Alex doesn't want to hurt him. After struggling for a few seconds he forces his body to relax.

"I'm fine, it's fine," he snaps at Raph. He'll owe him an apology later, but that can wait. When Raph lets go of him Alex thinks of punching Victor anyway, but the moment is gone. Alex shakes his head and stalks away toward the doors. "Go to hell," he shouts over his shoulder at Victor.

Victor just stands there, watching him go.

30

Alex drives to the nearest climbing route he can remember. Waiting in the studio parking lot for Liam to be done with the day is impractical and also impossible. He'd stormed off after shoving Victor (maybe he'll regret that later, though he doubts it), and he can't just sit in his car and sulk. Going back to the house to stew alone all day is likewise unbearable. He has his bag and his climbing shoes in the trunk; he'll be fine. He has hours and restless energy to burn.

While Alex is tying knots and getting his harness situated, his phone rings. He's in no mood to talk to anyone, but given all the facets of his life he can't afford to ignore it.

It's his agent, Vanessa. Alex listens in shocked disbelief as she gives him the good news: The Richmond movie wants him. Nothing is certain yet, of course, because of scheduling issues and money negotiations, but if Alex wants it to happen, it's probably going to happen and very, very quickly at that. It is, Vanessa says, time for him to figure out what his demands are so he doesn't look as damn overeager as she knows he is.

Alex is dazed and angry and tried to punch Victor two hours ago. He can barely get the words together to assure her he will get back to her with some random, arbitrary points of negotiation as soon as possible.

When he hangs up, Alex regards the cliff above him carefully. He wants this movie badly. Having it so close but not absolutely certain makes him feel restless and hungry. He also has no idea how Paul will react to the news. With this on top of everything else that's happened this morning, Alex knows he's a mess.

The route is not one of his favorites. It's hard in an ugly, complicated way that Alex doesn't enjoy. There's no elegance to it; it's simply difficult. That's the sort of challenge he wants right now, though. Something to occupy his body and enough of his mind that he doesn't keep running over all of the way that he hates Victor. Or how he's afraid for Liam, for himself, for Paul, and for everything the future threatens and promises.

He's glad he got out of *The Fourth Estate* when he did. And on his own terms.

Alex climbs recklessly for a while before he slows down and tries to take things deliberately. He tries to shove everything out of his mind that isn't his body and the rock in front of him, but it doesn't work.

When he slips, it's a little thing, a thing that's happened a hundred times before. Alex hardly reacts except to brace himself for the inevitable and slightly unpleasant snag of the harness and probable collision with the rock.

But the rope doesn't catch him. He keeps falling. After the mental fog he's been in all day, one thought is all that comes through with devastating clarity: *So this is how I'll die.*

He scrapes against the cliff face until his backup rope brings him up short thirty feet down, slamming him against the rock. His shoulder blooms with pain.

It takes a moment before he can even draw in a breath or process that he's not dead yet. Once he's able to take in his situation Alex is terrified to move, lest that start him down again.

Alex makes himself breathe, fights off the instinct to panic, and checks his ropes the way he was taught. There's a knot that isn't tied right. He examines it very carefully as his stinging shoulder starts to throb. There's no way to fix the rope in the air, and he's still fifty feet above the ground. Any slip from here, physical or mental, and he's done for.

He closes his eyes and takes a deep breath. And then, very slowly and very carefully, he starts the climb back down.

◆

Paul is grateful for the text he'd gotten from Alex this morning. For the most part he feels okay with Alex and the choices he's made about the people in his strange and tangled life. It may still make Paul nuts, but he's working on that.

But as the day goes on without more word from him, Paul starts to worry. He had expected at least an update when Alex had gotten to the lot. At lunch Paul texts him with *How is it going?* He tries not to be a jealous asshole when he doesn't get a reply. Alex would react poorly to that.

Paul's on his own set watching Darcy in her gas station convenience shop preparing for a night of work, both legal and illegal. If Melissa, the high school graduate, is going to start a business wrangling prostitutes, it's going to be a full customer-service experience. She's got a gun under the counter next to the case of poppers she ordered off the internet, has stolen nearly all the condoms the store stocks, and has some joints and single-serve party bottles of truly terrible liquor too.

In a break between shots as the camera resets for a turnaround, Darcy skips over to Paul with her phone in an outstretched hand. She waggles it in his face insistently until he takes it.

"Look what we did!" she says.

"What did we do?" he asks warily. His eyes try to focus on the tiny text on the poorly designed website.

"You're my new squeeze," she coos and tries to sit on his lap.

Paul laughs and shoves her off. "Lemme read."

It's a blind item that's incredibly not vague in its insinuations and is most definitely about his and Darcy's dinner out last night. Paul suspects he should be pissed about the rumor-mongering, but really it's just funny. If nothing else, the headache of it is a welcome distraction from worrying about whatever the hell Alex is up to right now.

"Did you call this in?" Paul asks her. The description of her blonde bounciness and as a long-time pro only new to the Hollywood scene is more flattering than this particular website tends to be.

"Mmmmm, I dunno. A girl has to do something in the ladies'."

♦

Zach's death as it will be revealed on screen takes six hours of shooting. The shot isn't complex, thanks to the news studio setting. But they need that much time to get all the coverage on Liam, Natalie, and Raphael. Victor is almost sure the main take he's going to use is Liam's second one. His shock is honest on the first take, but in the second, the way he ticks over from confusion, to horror, to despairing personal control and the well-practiced cadences of TV news is *exactly* what Victor wants.

Liam isn't — can't be — always a detail-oriented actor, but when he is, he's perfection. It's also one hell of a counterbalance to the chaos of the material with Alex. In the editing room, Victor knows he will wonder why he ever yelled at Liam for sleeping with Alex. In the end, public spectacles and minor headaches aside, that's been one of the most useful choices any of his people have ever made.

Raphael and Natalie are as on as they can be. Supporting a scene like this is thankless work, especially when Liam has to ask to step off set briefly on two different occasions. He lies and says that his throat is bothering him, that he just needs some water. Victor clenches his jaw as he watches. He's spent every second he's known Liam marveling at all the things Liam reflexively lies and passes regarding. Even now that he's out, the list has barely gotten any shorter. The list isn't unwise, but it makes Victor ache. There is a difference between privacy and the way that Liam has forced himself to live in the world.

Victor says nothing to be a comfort. Once Liam cracks, he'll break. Everyone's job is just to get to the end of the day. The longer Liam thinks he has to convince everyone that he is more okay than he is, the longer he'll be able to keep it together.

When he has all the coverage he needs, he thanks Liam for his work and dismisses him with a P.A. to walk him back to his trailer.

"Stay put," he says before they go, "I'll be with you in an hour." He wants a hair more reaction material for Raphael and Natalie, just to be sure.

Liam's still outwardly holding it together by the time Victor herds him into his car, but he's fairly non-verbal. Victor has to remind him to put on his seatbelt. His compliance is the only indication Victor gets that he's listening at all.

"Try to relax," Victor says. "We'll be home soon. I called Carly, she'll come over for brunch tomorrow."

◆

When Alex's feet finally touch the ground, he makes himself reel in his ropes, check all of his equipment, and go through the motions of putting everything away properly before he slumps to the ground next to his car and starts shaking. The adrenaline rush is terrifying. Now that he's on the ground and not actually afraid for his life, he's able think about how fucking bad that almost was. Zach seems like a terrible cautionary tale, an awful omen that pales in the face of what nearly just happened.

Alex only remembers how badly he'd hurt his shoulder when he finally climbs into the driver's seat and has to put on his seatbelt. He can't move his arm without being in unbearable pain. In the cup holder, his phone flashes with missed calls and texts. Whatever they are, Alex doesn't remotely have the bandwidth to deal with them. He ignores them and starts driving.

♦

When Liam and Victor get to Victor's house and pull into the drive, Liam fumbles with his seatbelt for a moment and then gets out of the car silently. Victor unlocks the door and watches as Liam heads for his room on autopilot.

"Not this time." He wraps a hand around Liam's bicep. "Let's get you upstairs."

Liam looks confused and doesn't look any less confused when Victor leads him into his bedroom. The first and only time Liam's ever been in here was after the pilot party for *The Fourth Estate*, years ago. He'd clumsily tried to seduce Victor and, on some level and by some definition, succeeded.

Victor has to peel Liam's bag off his shoulder. He'll obviously have to help Liam do anything beyond sit there. He's been in this place with him once or twice before. He accepts Liam's brain and the way he copes with it for what it is. But it's still terrifying when Liam loses his ability to communicate verbally. Ever since Liam explained it to him, the question always becomes whether this is the new normal, whether Liam can really dodge his nature forever.

Victor finds himself kneeling at Liam's feet and taking his shoes and socks off. "I can't take care of you the way you like if I don't know what's going on with you and can't tell if you're consenting," Victor says.

Liam squeezes his eyes shut and gestures in a way that seems to go with, or in fact be, a sentence he can't actually utter right now.

Victor rests his chin on Liam's thigh. "I can be infinitely patient with you," Victor says even if it's probably not as practically true as he would like.

"I know," Liam says after several minutes.

An hour, maybe two, passes before Liam seems present enough in his extremities and surfaces to take off his clothes and crawl into bed. Victor stays on the floor watching him as he cocoons himself in the blankets and stares at him, eyes bright and wet and saying things Victor can't be sure he can allow himself to hear.

"I need to know that you're able to consent right now," Victor says but feels like an asshole for it. Liam isn't impaired, he's just not doing communication in a way Victor can totally read. Which is only confirmed by Liam's annoyed sigh and the way he pulls at Victor's hands until one palm rests over his chest.

"I'm sorry about the story," Victor says.

Liam shrugs.

"I'm sorry we're such terribly different animals." The way Liam loves has always scared him.

Liam presses his eyes shut again and shakes his head. Victor can read *Pain* and *please don't be in pain because of me* clear enough without Liam actually using words.

There are no words in any language Victor has for the way in which he loves Liam, which in the past meant he didn't have to consider whether he loves him at all. But today, when everything in the world seems fragile because of a story he made up, that's harder than usual. It occurs to him that, with an entirely different set of capacities, Alex may very well love Liam in a terribly similar way.

Victor says as much, even though it might not mean anything to Liam right now and may not even make sense at all. Liam gives him a half smile, beatific and sad. Victor runs his palm over Liam's face, fascinated by how, at times, his body is the only language he has.

"Touch," Liam says. The word is too small for all the things they do. Still, it's enough for Victor to kiss him and feel Liam flutter open.

"Do you want me to touch you?" Victor asks. "Do you want me to hurt you?"

Liam nods to the first question and manages to croak out a yes to the second. This, Victor thinks darkly, is what Alex will never understand about them.

◆

Alex's car isn't in the garage when Paul gets home, and the house is concerningly dark. After a circuit of the downstairs Paul checks Alex's room. Maybe he had an even stranger day than anticipated and got home by some means other than his own vehicle. But the bedroom is empty.

Paul calls Carly.

"Why isn't Alex home yet?" he asks when she picks up.

"Why the hell are you home, and how should I know?"

"Because my starlet — who I am apparently fucking, by the way — told me to go home because all I was doing was annoying people. And because my boyfriend spent last night with *your* boyfriend and I haven't heard from him since seven this morning."

"Awwww. And you're not even poly. Good job there, Paul."

"Carly."

"I have no idea where Alex is, but Victor called and said they finished shooting. Maybe he's on his way home. But, Paul, when Victor calls from set to tell me about the state Liam is in and that he *will be* okay, your boyfriend is not at the top of my worry list."

"Point taken," Paul says after a shocked pause. "I have no idea what else to say."

"Thank you."

"If you hear anything, will you let me know?"

◆

Liam trembles in Victor's bed. He's on his side, because his muscles can't support him any other way right now. His hands are tied in front of him, thick cotton rope braided ornately over and between his wrists, binding them tighter than any cuffs ever could. Liam's bound hands hold the dildo he can't stop sucking on; there's another one vibrating in his ass. Victor has been bringing him right to the edge and pulling him back from it all day, just in radically different ways. Tears track down his face at the realization.

Something must show in his eyes, because Victor says "Welcome back," and then gives him a smile that's slightly evil.

Liam laughs wetly, although it's muffled by the busyness of his mouth. When he comes, it's brutal, drawn out, and overwhelming. After, Victor pulls his hands and the toy away from his mouth to kiss him.

"I absolutely cherish you," he says.

Liam hums happily and closes his eyes, glad he's no longer expected, at least for a little while, to say anything even with them. He frowns when Victor doesn't quietly unbraid the ropes as Liam is used to. Instead he pulls out a knife and saws through each segment of the design. Eventually he pries Liam's hands from each other, links of rope falling around them.

That surgery done and the toys put aside, Victor cleans him up, gets undressed, and crawls into bed with him. Liam knows this means Victor will likely sleep poorly if he sleeps at all. Liam knows the humid scrape of flesh is one of those things Victor generally tries not to think about, but apparently Liam's well-being is far more important than Victor's own comfort right now.

Liam has never even seen him naked before. He turns in Victor's arms, presses his forehead to the man's sternum, and sobs.

◆

"Where the hell have you been?" Paul demands when Alex finally walks in the door. He's been waiting in sight of the door and front windows with steadily increasing levels of anxiety all evening

Alex gives Paul a look that's angry in a way he never is for the camera. "Victor banned me from set, so I went climbing and am very lucky not to be dead right now. I also tried to punch him. My shoulder really hurts. And I'm probably going to get that movie."

Paul is dumbstruck. "I don't know where to start with that."

"Neither do I. Um." Alex drops his climbing bag by the door and rolls his shoulder gingerly. "Can you help me with this? I think I'm bleeding, I can't see it."

"What did you do?" Paul is instantly at his side, hand carefully at his waist as Alex cranes his head to look over his shoulder. His T-shirt is torn through, and there is most definitely blood.

"I fell," Alex says. "Help, please?"

If Alex can manage this much irritability, he's probably okay. Still, Paul follows Alex into the first floor bathroom with a distinct sense of doom.

The blood has dried enough that the shirt sticks to the wound. Alex grits his teeth while Paul dabs at it with a wet paper towel until it loosens enough to peel away. Paul's trying to be gentle, but it still hurts.

"Talk to me," Paul says. Alex hisses as he pulls another bit of the torn cotton away. Paul winces sympathetically. "Oh my God, I'm sorry."

Alex shakes his head. "It's fine."

"What happened with Liam?" Paul asks. He wants answers as much as he wants to distract Alex from the pain. "And what's going on with your movie?"

While Paul works at his shoulder, Alex tells him about the strange overnight. Paul's sure he's not getting the full story, but he's also sure he's not supposed to ask. Alex will tell him what he feels safe telling him, and Paul will have to be okay with that.

There are, however, some things he can ask about. "Okay," Paul says as he tosses a bloody paper towel in the trash and rips off another. "Do I want to ask about what happened on the rocks or what happened with Victor next? Or about how you're going to leave for three months?"

"You're patching me up from a fall down a cliff and you're still acting like I'm abandoning you for a job? Nothing is set in stone, and I'm not leaving you for a movie. Ask about Victor," Alex says shortly. "He makes the rocks make sense."

"Okay, then, what happened with Victor?"

"I promised Lee I'd go to set with him today," Alex recites, staring at the wall. "When I got there, Victor told me I couldn't. We got into an argument, because he's a sadistic son of a bitch and is making life hard for Liam on purpose."

"So you tried to punch him?" Paul pauses in peeling away another bit of the shirt. He doesn't know whether to be more horrified or impressed.

"Well, I shoved him first. Which was stupid. Because by the time I took a swing other people felt prepared to step in. I should have just decked him."

"Oh my God, Alex."

"I owe Raphael an apology. Incidentally."

"Please tell me you didn't try to hit him too."

Alex shakes his head. "No. He pulled me off. If it had been someone else, I might have taken a swing at them. I don't know."

"Okay. That's good, at least."

"Maybe," Alex shrugs and then winces. "*Fuck.* Ow. Anyway, I didn't want to come home and stew, so I went climbing. Which was dumb, because I was pissed and distracted and not paying attention. Ow, shit, fuck, okay."

The last is because Paul is finally pulling Alex's shirt over his head. Once it's gone, Paul stares with horror at his shoulder and back, which are scraped almost raw. What skin isn't bloody is black and blue.

"Alex," he says hoarsely. "How bad did you fall?"

"Bad enough to give me that and leave me feeling lucky."

Paul frowns deeply. "There's gravel in here. We should be going to the emergency room. Me and a bottle of hydrogen peroxide are not going to fix this."

"I'm not going to the emergency room," Alex states flatly. "No media attention. No institutional anything."

"Yeah, we'll see. Why didn't you call me?" Paul asks.

"I didn't call you because I was halfway up the side of a cliff on a rope I tied wrong. I didn't exactly have any free hands."

"That's not what I mean," Paul snaps.

Alex takes a deep breath. "I had a good three seconds where I knew I was dead. And then I had to pull myself together when the rope actually fucking caught me and get down in one piece."

Paul has no idea how he can sound so calm.

"Then I focused on putting my gear away, getting in the car, and driving home. With my full attention on every step, because it was the only way I'd be sure I'd get here."

Paul's day waiting for Alex has been more or less terrible. Now, confronted with the reality that Alex almost didn't come home at all, he's truly frightened.

More than that, he's angry. "Nobody knew where you were," Paul says, touching the side of Alex's face to make him look at him. "And then you come home looking like this. What the hell would have happened if you had fallen all the way? How long would it have taken anyone to find you?"

Alex glares. "Today has been hard enough without your pissiness, no matter how justified you think you are. I have had to deal with Liam and Victor and the movie and the fall, and now I just fucking hurt. Also, I didn't fall all the way."

"God, Alex." Paul holds his chin still and checks his eyes for a sign of concussion and also an answer that makes any sort of sense at all. "You want me to take care of you and then you can't even take care of yourself. How the fuck do you expect me to be in this relationship with you?"

Alex's eyes narrow before he jerks away. "This from my suicidal boyfriend."

31

Liam thinks the best thing about fucking Carly in his house, other than the fact that he's fucking Carly at all, is that they can both be as loud as they want without her appalling neighbors pounding on the wall.

She's on top of him, straddling his hips, riding his cock, both hands on her clit. Liam is too dumbstruck by her beauty and how fucking good it feels to be very useful at all beyond holding her waist and helping her bounce up and down while telling her how beautiful she is.

"Fuck you," she gasps with a laugh. "Even when you compliment me it's all about your ego."

He laughs, because she's being ridiculous, but it's also totally true. "I make the best choices," he says.

"No," she manages. "You just said yes to the right girl."

"Yeah?" he says, his hands joining hers as he presses his thumb against her hard.

"Oh God." She half doubles over with the too-much of it. She's just right there and not there yet, *damn him.*

He shoves her hands out of the way. She leans back, tosses her hair out of her face and braces her hands against his thigh. He rubs her in quick little circles while fucking up into her as hard as he can.

He almost wishes her stupid neighbors were pounding on the wall, because knowing that they're jealous and pissed off is awesome. When she comes, it's long and loud. She levers herself forward so she can kiss Liam through it, her tongue fucking into his mouth while he encourages her to keep moving because he is so Goddamn close.

It's all exquisitely over when she leans up just enough to whisper in his ear, "Come already, so you can lick it out of me."

◆

"So tell me how your day was," Carly says, propping her head up on her hand. The last week has been rough. Being back in Liam's bed like this hopefully means things are starting to improve.

Liam shrugs, playing with her hair. He looks more serious now that the sex is over. "I don't know."

Carly frowns.

"Victor's off. I'm off. Alex isn't there," Liam says. Carly can tell there's more there, but he's clearly not ready to articulate it.

"Have you two talked about it any more?" Carly asks for what must be the tenth time since Liam filmed the reveal of Zach's death. Victor had been quiet at brunch the morning after, but Liam was still barely talking. A night like that would have been a lot for anyone. Since then, the little pieces she's gotten from Liam about his and Victor's night together suggests a shifting landscape, but not to what or why. Liam really, really doesn't need any more change right now. Carly's worried about him in a persistent and absolute way that may well involve her calling Victor and chewing him out if she doesn't get some satisfactory answers soon.

"No," Liam says. Carly can't tell if he's being taciturn out of ability or willingness.

"Are you worried about it?"

"Yes."

"Okay," Carly says when he's not more forthcoming. "What is it you're worried about?"

Liam rolls onto his back and gropes for her hand on top of the covers. "Victor's brain and how he's making decisions. What's happening with me and him. It's all —" Liam trails off and makes the flustered gesture he always makes when he's run out of words.

"Baby," Carly chides gently. "He needs to know what you need in order to make decisions."

Liam doesn't say anything.

♦

Days pass before Alex can sleep without waking himself up every time he rolls onto his banged-up side. Paul had stayed with him the first night; pissed as they both had been at each other, having him there had been good until morning came and Paul had insisted Alex see a doctor.

"Not going to the ER," Alex insisted flatly, as Paul dug in Alex's first aid kit for more gauze pads to tape over the wound.

"Alex," Paul had said, as if he were some particularly unreasonable, petulant child. "If this doesn't get properly cleaned it's going to go septic. It doesn't have to be the ER, but you're going somewhere."

Which is how Alex had ended up in Paul's car, hunched forward so his back didn't touch the seat while Paul drove him to urgent care.

"Don't you have work?" Alex had asked sulkily. Paul's missing work for this. Things were difficult enough between them that he didn't want to give Paul one more excuse to blame Alex for being a distraction.

"You almost died. I think I can spare the time," Paul had said way too evenly.

His tone had pissed Alex off as much as anything. "Glad I rank *somewhere* in your list of priorities."

They'd had another argument that night, because when Alex refused to let Paul sleep in his room again Paul had taken that as an excuse to be neurotic and scared about the three-month separation for Alex's movie.

"If you think you can't be in this relationship because I'm reckless, you don't get to use my pain to make yourself feel better," Alex had snapped and stalked off to his room, while Paul had sat, visibly angry and frustrated, in their kitchen staring after him.

Alex is scared too, frankly. Even more than whatever fight they're currently having, he's as afraid as Paul is of such a long separation. Alex lies muzzily in the bed that used to be theirs while Todd scratches mournfully at the door to be let in, thinking about it. No matter what entirely legitimate grievances with each other they might latch onto, if they fall apart it won't be because they didn't love each other hard enough. It will be because the logistics of the lives they lead are simply impossible.

◆

With all of the uncertainty going on with Liam right now, Victor knows that it's particularly important to keep up their weekly date nights. The first time they do dinner and an overnight after *that* night, Liam shows up as usual and the evening also progresses, more or less, also as usual. He's is more verbal that he has been recently, but he's not yet as talkative as usual. Victor is worried.

As they make out on the couch after dinner, Liam is lovely and pliant and at ease. Victor remembers, yet again, that measuring how Liam is by his ability and willingness to speak isn't always the best plan. Sometimes Liam is fine overall but not fine for the world of other people. Even so, Victor reminds himself to be careful. He doesn't want to add to Liam's stress right now. As the evening grows later, and Liam is making the sweetest little sounds into his mouth, Victor still fears the things Liam wants that he in turn very much does not. Inevitably, Victor will make things worse for him.

He braces himself for when it's time to go to bed and Liam asks to go to Victor's room instead of his own. Victor doesn't know what the answer to that request is or should be. The uncertainty feels as alien as it does dangerous.

But when they finally do get up from the couch, Liam leads the way happily to his own room as if this destination is the same matter of course it always has been. There, Victor takes care of him as he usually does; Liam is always so aesthetically pleasing in his need.

After, however, Victor makes Liam shove over, so there's enough room for him to sit up against the headboard and write. Liam curls against him once he opens his laptop and rests his head against Victor's arm.

"I'm not going to type less because your head's there," Victor says.

"S'okay."

"Mmmm, tell me that when I've been bouncing your skull around for two hours," he says as he opens a file.

Liam moves his head back onto his pillow, kissing Victor's arm as he goes.

"I'm still recalibrating," Victor says.

Liam taps his fingers against Victor's side, his shorthand always for having heard when he doesn't otherwise want to speak.

32

"I can't believe you're going back up there," Paul says, flabbergasted and more than a little afraid. Alex is laying out plans for the next route he wants to try, his tablet and a tattered book of local trails open on the kitchen island next to whatever he'd made himself for dinner. "Can you even climb, with your shoulder?" It's been a couple of weeks, but Alex's back can't possibly be better yet.

"It's better than it was. Besides, I know what not to do now. I will never go climbing after I try to punch Victor again," Alex says solemnly.

"Famous last words." Paul tries not to laugh. "At least tell me you aren't going to try this alone."

"Well, actually." Alex looks up from his planning to catch Paul's eye with a gaze that's intense enough to make Paul's breath catch. Alex wanting something is always glorious and terrifying. The recent weeks of renewed tension and anxiety haven't made that less true. "I was hoping you'd come with me."

Carefully, Paul says, "I thought I slowed you down."

"I really don't want to be up there by myself."

♦

Even aside from the horrible inherent in having to play James and his private grief, working without Alex next to him is strange. As much as Liam is friends with the rest of the cast, he misses having Alex around desperately.

He's looking for someone he can sit and be with without having to talk when he barges into Victor's office without knocking, as he usually does.

Victor is there, behind his desk. Next to him, is a man Liam's never seen before in his life. He's sitting way closer to Victor than Liam is used to seeing anyone sit. And he's insanely attractive and has his hand on Victor's thigh.

They both look up at Liam. Neither seems particularly startled to see him. But neither of them says anything, either. The guy gives Victor a look that Liam can't read at all.

Liam has no idea what's going on right now, or what he's feeling, except that someone he doesn't know is in his place next to Victor. He can't get his brain untangled enough to stammer out an apology, so he leaves. He doesn't even mind letting the door slam behind him.

♦

"So that's Hurricane Liam," Nigel says once the door has crashed closed.

Victor groans. Having a friend like Nigel he can rely on for reasonable and useful support when in the midst of a crisis is something for which he is duly grateful. However, he is not sure that the frustratingly multifaceted crisis that he is having over how he and Liam fit together has not just gotten a little bit worse. "That was not the most auspicious first meeting I could have hoped for."

"I can see why he's driving you up a wall."

"Because he's beautiful or because he's exhausting?"

Nigel considers that for a thoughtful moment. "Yes, but I wouldn't blame him if that's what's required to hold your attention."

♦

When they get to the mountain, Alex checks all of their equipment obsessively before making Paul check it too. Then he checks it all again, just to be sure. Paul refrains from saying a word about any of it and is rewarded when Alex kisses him briefly before he grabs the first handhold.

The climb is slow. Paul can tell that Alex, despite his protests to the contrary, is in pain. But if this is what Alex needs to work things out both for himself and between them, Paul is willing to be here for it. There's something to be said for team-building exercises.

When they finally get to the top, Alex teases Paul for not wanting to get too close to the edge. Paul takes a few pictures of the stunning view while Alex sits with his arms around his knees staring out at the distant hills. Paul gets one of him, too, in profile, and is thrilled when Alex suffers him to post it online.

Paul knows that none of this — the climb or the pictures or even Alex's amused smile over his shoulder at him — means they're okay. But he is absolutely going to hoard the good moments while he can. He has no idea how many they have left.

Finally, he takes a breath and says, "Victor called yesterday."

"Is this really a thing you want to tell me before I have to climb rocks again?"

Paul chuckles. "It's fine. Odd, but fine. He wants us to go to dinner with him next week."

"Okayyy." Alex is clearly thrown. "That makes me nervous."

"Yeah, I don't know what's up, but I wanted to let you know."

"So I have time to properly prepare myself?"

Paul shrugs. "More or less."

◆

They discuss the topic in the car on the way home but reach no conclusions. Once they park, Paul goes to grab their stuff out of the trunk, but Alex stops him with a hand on his arm.

"We'll clean up later. Date now."

Paul is surprised. He'd hoped, but had no idea what Alex's plans for the day entailed. He's probably making decisions based on how Paul had comported himself on their outing.

Inside, Alex leads them straight to the couch, apparently not caring today that they're both sweaty and sore and dusty with chalk. They get horizontal quickly, but clothes stay on. Paul runs his hands all over Alex's back and arms while Alex whines into his mouth.

When he gets to Alex's shoulders and tugs because he wants to be as close to Alex as he can get, Alex pulls back with a hiss. "Fuck, *oww*."

"Oh my God, sorry, I forgot." Paul tries to pull back, terrified he's accidentally just ruined the day.

Alex sits up, knees bracketing Paul's hips to keep him in place. He rolls his shoulder with a grimace. "It's okay. I did too."

He doesn't look upset, and the look of concentration on his face as he stretches his arm experimentally is appealing. Paul rubs his thumbs into the skin above Alex's waistband. "So you can say no."

Alex barks a laugh and gives his shoulder one last roll before he falls forward onto Paul again. "Give the man a prize."

33

"Liam, why the fuck would I have any idea who Victor keeps around?" Alex is exasperated. He and Paul are getting ready for whatever dinner clusterfuck Victor invited them to. And now Liam has called him in a panic about somebody visiting Victor on the lot. Alex tries to keep his knowledge of Victor's private life to an absolute minimum, which is usually not difficult except when it comes to Liam's involvement therein. But he hasn't been on the lot in weeks and can't even begin to fathom why Liam sounds so very close to completely unspooling over the issue.

"Victor likes you," Liam whines.

Alex gives a little shudder. He's glad they're on the phone and Liam can't see it. "Yes, but Victor *likes* you. Also, last I checked, you don't do jealousy. What gives?"

"I'm not jealous."

"You are," Carly's voice comes over the line. Alex can hear the sound of Liam zipping up her dress.

"I don't even know what jealousy feels like," Liam says, presumably to both of them.

"Like this," Alex says darkly.

"What's going on?" Paul asks, as Alex puts the phone on speaker and sets it down on the counter so Paul can do his other cufflink.

"If I knew that," Alex says not even bothering to cover the mouthpiece, "I'd be avoiding it better."

"Alex...." Liam whines.

"Not you! It!" Alex says. He's starting to hope Victor is planning to poison them all so he doesn't have to sit through this whole meal.

◆

The restaurant has the same sort of uncomfortable, aggressively modern and understated decor as Victor's house. Alex considers the possibility that Victor doesn't mean to be a creepy unpleasant bastard but just can't help himself.

He dismisses his charitableness as wishful thinking when he and Paul arrive at Victor's table to find everyone else already seated. Alex suspects they were intentionally told a slightly later time when Carly, straight-backed, voice tight, and seated between the only two empty places at the table says, "I didn't choose the seats."

"Clearly," Alex says under his breath.

Victor points to the empty seat between Carly and the mystery man Liam had been ranting about on the phone. "Paul," he says before pointing to the other seat. "Alex can sit next to Liam."

"I've reminded Victor that a lady should always do the seating assignments," Carly says.

Alex has to stifle the urge to laugh. The impulse only gets worse when Paul pulls out his chair for him. As absurd as the gesture is, Alex appreciates it. However rage-inducing the evening may prove to be, Paul at least seems unlikely to blame Alex for it.

"Someone should also remind Victor to do introductions," Paul says good-naturedly. He steps away from Alex's chair and offers his hand to the only unknown quantity at the table.

The unknown looks placidly amused at the entire proceeding but shakes Paul's hand warmly. "Nigel. Pleasure to meet you, Paul," he says.

"Same." Paul prolongs the handshake a moment longer than is strictly necessary. Next to him, Carly looks highly entertained.

After the introductions, Nigel sits back and says, "You'll have to excuse Victor. His plans tend to not take the people involved in them into account."

"We've noticed," Alex says less sarcastically than he could. They're in public and there's a stranger in their midst. But this entire thing is still ridiculous.

"Yes," Carly says. Her tone echoes Nigel's somewhat unfriendly teasing one. "What is this even about?"

They're interrupted by a member of the wait staff placing an amuse-bouche down in front of each of them. Everyone lapses into a tense silence until he's gone again.

"Oh my God, did you order for us?" Alex asks.

"Expand your palate," Victor says dryly to him. He turns to Carly. "And who said it had to be an occasion?"

"I have known you for years. Both the group social outing and the mysterious stranger are entirely new tricks for you." Despite her tone, Carly gives Nigel a charming smile. Alex takes a moment to be impressed at her ability to so keenly focus her wrath.

Victor leans over to Liam, who looks faintly ill. "I have always liked her."

Alex looks to Paul for help interpreting any of it.

Paul gives a tiny shrug. Then he asks Nigel, in a desperate attempt to get this evening on something resembling normal footing, "How do you two know each other?"

Of course the story involves upfronts. Hell begets hell.

Liam, who has been quiet since they've walked in, finally bursts out with, "Yes, but why are you here *now*?"

Alex has never seen him so socially unfluid, not in public. He braces for an explosion, even though he hadn't known until this moment that Liam is capable of one.

Victor and Nigel look at each other and chuckle, apparently unfazed. Either Nigel is as cunning and manipulative as Victor is, or he's just very used to Victor's methods of dealing with people. Alex isn't sure which of those possibilities is less comforting.

"You are all here," Victor says with a fond, if pointed, look at Liam, "Because, whether we like it or not, our lives are a tangled mess and I was raised to believe in family dinners. Mainly, though, Nigel's been badgering me."

"We don't even know you," Liam says.

"I'm trying to rectify that." Victor sounds both apologetic and a little desperate.

"Speaking for me is not rectifying it, Victor," Nigel says softly. Alex gets the impression he's said similar many times before.

Alex looks at Paul nervously. Paul shrugs. As much as he walked into this worrying about what power play Victor might be making, he now realizes he's watching his control over all of them fall apart. The possibility is weirdly awful considering it sometimes seems as if that's more important to Victor than all his public success.

The table drifts into small talk, as if pointed and stilted chatter about things as significant as Carly and Liam's wedding count as such. Then Victor has the temerity to ask when Alex and Paul are planning to get married.

Alex takes a deep breath and then another. He doesn't want to deal with this and he can't hit Victor again. He probably shouldn't have done it the first time. He leans across Carly to Paul. "I'm leaving you to answer that," he says. "Come on, Carly." He grabs her arm. "Time for girl talk in the powder room."

"Please tell me we can go outside and smoke instead," she says as she clatters after him.

"Oh my God, anything, yes."

◆

"I appreciate your concern with our wellbeing," Paul says once Alex is out of earshot. He means it, in the twisted way he's sure Victor doesn't actually intend to be evil when he asks things like that. Alex would probably disagree on the latter point. "But our relationship, and any issues regarding it, are not your business. You're not making things any easier at the moment, either."

"Are things getting any better?" Victor asks. Paul is surprised at how simply the question is phrased.

"Yes, actually. This dinner probably aside."

Victor smiles. "He's very young, Paul."

"No one is more aware of that than us, and it would be unfair to blame our issues on that complication." Paul can't believe they're talking about this in public. "I value what I view as a real friendship between us, Victor, but your good intentions are, as I remind you nearly weekly, generally poisonous."

"Yet you keep making good things come of them. And from the obstacles I put in your way."

Paul takes a moment to process the horrible novelty of Victor admitting that so frankly. Nigel doesn't say anything but is clearly riveted. Liam, however, sullenly continues to pleat his napkin while the other men ignore him.

"I never could get Alex to do a thing he didn't want to," Victor adds. "Bear that in mind while you sort out your future."

"Do you really expect me to take advice from you about him at this point?" Paul asks, disbelieving. He considers the merit of running out after Alex and Carly. But he wants to show Victor he can stay and tough this out.

"Of all of us," Victor says, "Alex and I are most alike. You don't have to take my advice, but you should at least listen."

The thing is, Paul can see how he's right. "Why is every conversation with you so ominous?"

Victor laughs with obvious delight.

◆

Outside, Alex slumps against the wall of the restaurant while Carly fishes in her purse.

"I am going to kill Victor," he says.

"So things aren't better on the marriage question, I take it," Carly says.

"You say that like we're sure we're not breaking up."

"Are you breaking up?" She pulls out a pack of cigarettes and a lighter.

"If I knew, tonight would be a lot less awful. I mean, I'm starting to think we're not, but he's still sleeping on the other side of the house. He's jealous of Liam, afraid of everything he doesn't understand about me, and a workaholic. And that's the short list."

Carly sweeps some of her hair back out of her face. "You know, back when Paul and I were dating, he was afraid of everything he didn't understand about himself. *And* a workaholic. He's making some sort of progress. But I know exactly how infuriating he can be. I also know that he loves to be loved. If you're worried about him staying, that's easy. If you're worried about your willingness to stay, I can only sympathize."

"I just turned twenty-four and I spend all my time worrying about his issues." Alex tips his head back to look up at the sky. Thanks to light pollution, he can't see a single star. "There is so much fucking up I haven't had a chance to do. It's infuriating. I told him this when we first got together, and yet here we are."

"Well, what sort of fucking up are you missing?"

"You mean other than that shithole apartment Gemma and I had?" As terrible as that apartment had been, it was the last normal thing he'd had. He misses it sometimes. Or maybe he just misses the simplicity of his old life, the one between Indiana and stardom.

"Yes."

"He's the only boyfriend I've ever had — the only relationship, aside from Lee, and that's a mess he doesn't want to touch."

"If you need to date around, you need to tell him that."

Alex shakes his head. A poly solution to their problem isn't necessarily wrong, but it's not the one he's after. "Mostly, I want him to feel my pain and not treat us like we're already married, which, by the way, is apparently some game he wants to win so he can stop trying."

"Baby boy, Paul's been acting like you've been married since you started dating."

"Not news. And not actually making me feel better."

"Shhh, listen. Paul is messed up. But being married in his head doesn't mean the door gets shut on anything you want to do or try or be as long as you keep him involved in some way. Which, you know, I couldn't deal with because I like my space, but you're so not me."

"I'm not Victor either," Alex says.

Carly laughs. "Oh, I know."

"Among other things, I'd miss the sex," Alex says.

"You might, but it works for him," Carly says gently. "I take it you and Paul still aren't fucking?"

"*No.* Well — yes. Depending how you define it. But. No. Not how I'd like, at least."

Carly raises an eyebrow. "Informative."

"I can't believe we're having this conversation out here," Alex says, looking up and down the sidewalk, where cars and people are passing, going about their more-normal-than-his lives.

"Would you rather have it back inside?" she asks.

Alex shudders and takes a breath. Anything is better than going back to that table. "It was part of the deal where we're dating but not completely together. Sex is for fun. Not a replacement for relationship work."

"That's obnoxiously mature."

"I think it's helped."

"Good. Is he still all into that an-tici…pation thing?" she asks, leaning over to pop the syllables close to his ear.

"You're bizarre," he says laughing, "but yeah."

"Wait. Have you never seen *The Rocky Horror Picture Show?*"

"Nope."

"Ugh, I was going to suggest a threesome and now I have to take you to the movies? This night is fired."

"Could do both," Alex offers with a shrug. His life can't get any weirder right now.

"You are actually blushing. That is fucking adorable."

"Ginger. We did talk about it, sort of. After Victor's party," Alex says, although he is not sure why. By any reasonable standard he should be changing the topic as fast as possible.

"He dirty talked it, didn't he?"

"Phone sex, but yeah."

Carly laughs. "I'm guessing the verdict was favorable."

"Yeah, and then everything went to hell. Unrelatedly."

"I don't want to dare you into a thing that's going to cause more strife, but hey, adventures with Paul," she says, laughing.

"You are intensely manipulative. Maybe you're the most like Victor," Alex says like it's a prize that must be awarded somewhere.

◆

From where Paul is sitting, he's the first to see Alex and Carly approach the table again. Alex has his hand at the small of her back and a gleam of fun in his eye. He catches Paul's gaze across the table and winks as he slides back into his seat. Whatever they talked about out there, Paul, or at least the rest of the table, should clearly brace for it.

He's not wrong. Conversation resumes — this time, about the far less fraught topic of Nigel's most recent ad campaign — as if no one had stalked off in irritation. Alex and Carly are clearly at play. There's bantering and whispering and hands on each other's thighs. Alex keeps grinning at Paul every time Victor frowns over it. Paul has to look anywhere else so he doesn't burst out laughing right in the midst of it all.

◆

Liam, while unperturbed by him and Carly — he actually smiles at them a few times — remains completely perturbed by everything else. Alex increasingly doesn't blame him. Especially when he makes occasional cutting comments at Paul's reflexive need to be gracious to Nigel. Paul's deference definitely verges on flirtatiousness.

Alex watches, fascinated, when Victor gets sick of disapproving of his and Carly's overly theatrical impression of teenage heterosexuality and bored of chatting with Paul and Nigel. He turns to snap at Liam about his manners instead.

Alex puts a hand on Liam's thigh as if that will protect him. Victor's done a lot of things to Liam recently of which Alex does not approve, but snapping at him in public is a whole new bucket of not okay. Carly reacts next, with a quick, appreciative nod to Alex before leaning back in her chair to try to catch Liam's eye behind Alex's shoulder. As the table descends into awkward silence Nigel and Paul stop talking as well, unable to keep up any facade of normality.

Without saying anything, Liam tosses his creased-through napkin on the table and pushes back his chair.

"Liam, honey." Carly gets up to follow him as he heads for the exit.

"No, I'll get him," Victor says.

Carly bristles. "Victor, I appreciate it, but things have been kind of tense lately and you're not helping."

"They could be so much worse."

"And they could be so much better," Carly hisses. "We have already caused enough of a scene and the public demise of this evening is not going to come down on Liam's head."

"I'll get him," Nigel says, not waiting for anyone's approval. "You lot sort yourselves out."

Alex watches him go but wonders if *he* should be the one to go talk Liam down at this point.

Carly sits again but continues to glare at Victor. "You are seriously making his life hell right now. And mine, actually."

"I am doing my best." Victor's voice is surprisingly gentle and small.

"You're really not."

Victor sighs. "Liam is one of the greatest joys of my life. Until very recently, I knew what I was supposed to do — and feel — about that."

"And, what, that's changed and you took us out to dinner to tell us?"

"Not quite, Carly. Show, don't tell," Victor says with the air of a teacher whose students have finally caught up.

Alex and Paul look at each other, and as much as their glance should probably be about what is happening to their friends at this table, Alex is nearly certain it's not. He offers what smile he can in such strange circumstances, and it's hard to tear his attention away when Paul returns it.

"I am genuinely trying to make life better for Liam," Victor goes on. "Within the landscape of the things that I have the ability and the desire to do for him, but this is very new and very difficult territory for me. I don't want him to be mad at me, Carly. I don't want you mad at me either."

Carly gapes. "I didn't know you were capable of fucking up this badly. Or this publically. He is in so deep with you, and he is terrified of losing all of it."

"Have you ever considered that maybe I am too?" Victor asks. "I am very glad he is marrying you. You can do so much for him. Have, for years."

"Yes, well, I'm amazing," she says with a nervous twitch of her hair. "Just warn us next time about the secret best friends. And don't ever, *ever* let me see you treat him like a child again."

◆

Nigel finds Liam outside the restaurant. He's leaning against a building and fidgeting with something that looks like a keychain. He's clearly angry, which is better than any alternatives Nigel can imagine.

Liam acknowledges Nigel's presence with a nod, but doesn't say anything. Nigel is too annoyed with the course of this evening to wait him out. None of this should be his job.

"Why didn't you yell at him?"

Liam looks up, startled, and shoves the keychain back into his jacket pocket.

"You're clearly as pissed at him as everyone else, and they haven't held back," Nigel says.

Liam opens his mouth to respond but closes it again without saying anything.

Nigel isn't sure if he doesn't have an answer or if he's calculating what he says. Victor makes everyone around him political.

"We're different," Liam says eventually. "Them and me."

"I know," Nigel says gently, because he does know. Liam is the only thing Victor talks about that isn't work. Whether Liam seems different to the rest of the world, or just to Victor hardly matters. In this mess, this young man isn't like anyone else.

Liam folds his hands behind his back and looks up at Nigel while he settles back against the wall next to him. "I don't know who the fuck you are to him, and I don't know why I'm supposed to keep guessing."

"Old friends." Nigel shrugs.

"You used to fuck," Liam bites.

"You don't want what we had. It didn't work and it's not on offer. I am sorry my old friend is being an asshole tonight and I am sorry he's doing it in public. He doesn't know how to do anything else, but Liam, just so we're clear, I can see why he's angry with you." Nigel

"He's as important to me as Carly, and I don't get random surprises about her life," Liam points out.

Nigel, for all that he's known Victor for decades, is not prepared to be having this conversation, on a neon-bright L.A. sidewalk, with the man Victor is, for lack of a more precise term, dating. He wishes Pris had come out with him to L.A. this time. Then at least Nigel could vent about all of this absurdity to her in person. "Yeah, well, you did. But you don't need to take it out on me. I certainly don't take it out on you for being something to him I couldn't."

"Then you don't know what it's like to be afraid of losing someone you don't even get to have."

Nigel sighs. "For a poly guy, you really need to adjust your viewpoint on possession, and if it's all down to sex, you need to step away from this mess. Just because Victor's Machiavellian and the world is hard for you, doesn't mean you're not complicit in the not-so-fun pain you're both experiencing right now."

♦

Alex, along with everyone else, watches nervously as Nigel and Liam return to the table. Neither of them looks particularly cheerful, but Nigel looks less grim than earlier. For the rest of the evening, Liam makes an effort to actually participate. Alex and Carly exchange relieved looks more than once, and Alex smiles as Paul reaches behind Carly's chair to catch his hand.

As they're leaving, Alex can only hope that Victor and Liam have a chance to clear up whatever injury this was supposed to help fix.

When they get into Alex's car, Alex turns the key in the ignition and then stops, both hands on the steering wheel. Very cautiously he turns to look at Paul. The second their eyes meet they both start laughing, nervously at first and then with more and more enthusiasm.

They've just spent an evening watching Liam fall apart, *Victor* fall apart, and a group of famous people behave dubiously in public. He and Paul weren't even the couple with the most issues for once.

"Okay, I know that was terrible," Paul says, "but what the fuck just happened?"

♦

They're still laughing by the time they get on the road, even as it's interspersed with some serious concern about Liam and general confusion about Victor. Alex relentlessly teases Paul about how flustered he was about Nigel. Which Paul supposes is fair.

"The rest of us were like, who is this asshole? And you're, like, rolling over for the pretty," Alex says as they take the turn up into their neighborhood.

Paul realizes Alex is neither jealous nor offended, just really, really amused. "Pretty isn't the word I'd use," he says.

"I've never seen you do that before. It was interesting. And probably a less bad choice than pretty much everyone else's."

Paul shrugs. "He was very compelling. But do you want to tell me what the hell you and Carly were up to?" He looks over at Alex to see him grinning at the road.

"Among other things, we decided payback was in order for the seating arrangements."

"Yeah, it's the other things I'm asking about."

"The short answer is obvious, I hope," Alex says. "The long one is actually all sorts of serious."

"Okay," Paul says. "Are we going to talk about the long one now? Because tonight was good but now I'm nervous."

"Tonight was *terrible*," Alex corrects. "The stuff I have to say isn't, but it's work, and I don't want to do it right now. I'm enjoying your company. Everyone else sucks."

Paul smiles as Alex pulls into the driveway. "I'm enjoying yours too."

"Seems like it's been a while since that's happened," Alex says without accusation.

"I don't think that's true," Paul says just as mildly.

"We haven't done it without a date, or a plan, or some effort."

"Okay, that's true," Paul acknowledges. "It shouldn't be, though."

♦

Once they get inside, Alex stops Paul with a hand on his arm before they get into the living room.

Paul waits eagerly for whatever Alex is going to say next. From the look on his face, it's going to be good.

"I had a good time tonight," Alex says. Paul would laugh at him for being facetious, but Alex is grinning and clearly means it.

"We should do this again?" Paul offers, sliding his hands around Alex's waist.

Alex giggles. "Oh my God, no. Never. Now, shh." He kisses Paul.

Paul deepens the kiss. Alex lets him for a too-short moment, then steps back. He smiles at Paul, shy and proud all at once. For once, Paul's not afraid of having hit some invisible boundary of his.

"I'll see you in the morning," Alex says before disappearing up the stairs.

Paul's shocked at how breathless he is. He's also surprised he doesn't get an invitation up to Alex's room. If there ever was a night they've earned together, it's this one. But if this is how Alex wants to play, he's content to go along with it, even if he waits pitifully for a moment to see if Alex will change his mind.

He doesn't though. Paul eventually wanders up to his own room, nudging a disgruntled Todd out of the way before the cat can sneak in.

◆

Alex is almost asleep when the yowling starts. Todd has never been thrilled about being banned from both bedrooms. He's taken out his frustration with midnight howling and scratching at their doors before. He usually gets tired of it after a few minutes, but tonight seems to be an exception. Every time Alex thinks he's stopped he hears him thunder down the stairs and then up the stairs to Paul's loft, before the yowling begins again and the whole process repeats in reverse.

The situation is absurd — and aggravating. Alex really would like to sleep without a demon running around his house. By the sixth or seventh iteration of the cat steeplechase from hell, he has had enough. He throws off the covers and storms to the door, for his own satisfaction more than any practical effect. It's not like the fucking cat cares.

"Paul!" he yells, while Todd utters a joyous mew and shoots past Alex's feet into the room. When he doesn't get a response, he just yells louder. "PAUL!"

"What?" Paul shouts as he bangs out of his bedroom.

"Your fucking cat is driving me fucking crazy," Alex shouts.

"He's your cat too!"

"It has been a very long, very hard night, and now there is a fucking hellion getting fur on my bed."

"Shouldn't've opened the door!" Paul yells back. He's clearly trying not to laugh.

Alex turns and looks back at Todd, who is happily building himself a nest in the blankets. "Paul's door is open now too," Alex says conversationally. "You could go bother him."

Todd purrs and keeps kneading the bedding. Alex sighs.

"Paul. Marion. Keane," he yells, and clomps halfway down the stairs so he can lean over the railing and see the loft. "Come get your creature out of my bed."

"Alex," Paul says, his voice softening.

"Yes?"

"Did you want to come over?"

"To your room?" Alex asks. He feels as stunned by the unprecedented invitation as he has by a dozen different things tonight, just in a much better way.

♦

Alex hasn't been in the loft bedroom since Paul moved into it. Once he's inside, he leans against the door. "I realize enough may have happened tonight that you've forgotten about me taking that fall on the rocks —"

"I haven't forgotten."

"I'm sorry about what I said." Alex fidgets with the drawstring on his sleep pants. "About the suicide thing," he clarifies.

"Thank you," Paul says. Tonight, apparently, is for discussing all the things no one could possibly want to.

"So," Alex says. "Is this a friendly chat about your cat's bad behavior, or am I spending the night?"

Paul laughs. He shouldn't let it be this easy, but he crooks a finger at Alex anyway. "Come closer and find out."

"I'm getting the impression I should lose the pants," Alex says as he shoves them off.

Paul shrugs. "I dunno, this works pretty well too," he says before grabbing Alex's hips and mouthing at his dick.

♦

After they fuck, they end up on their sides, heads together, while Paul runs a finger over the scrapes and callouses on Alex's hands.

"Do you miss how they were?" Alex says softly. The question is strange to ask. He's never liked looking soft and wound up in this whole life of his because he couldn't stand to be called a twink. Now his hands are more battered than they were from every shit job he had in high school to earn money and get away so it wouldn't matter if someone thought he was soft.

Paul shakes his head, rolling their foreheads together. "I don't like the idea that they hurt, that any of you hurts, but no. They just interest me. You interest me. It's a condition I have."

Alex smiles. From this close he can't focus on Paul's eyes. "You too. But I don't feel like that much of me is hurting right now. I got these doing some pretty amazing things."

"I know; I remember. You scare me to death half the time." Paul strokes a thumb over the back of Alex's knuckles.

"Are you getting used to that? I feel like maybe I need you to get used to that. And I don't mean like movies and interviews and stupid, creepy photo shoots that aren't even of me but, like, whatever it is the world thinks I am. I have so many more adventures and mistakes and drama in front of me. I don't want us to get back together and feel like I can't because you're all looking at me and wondering if you see husband material."

"So I can't ask you to marry me."

"You can't ask me to be a fixed point," Alex clarifies.

"What did you and Carly talk about?" Paul asks, suddenly urgent.

"We talked about that. And about how I need to keep having adventures and fucking up. And about how you're probably more okay with that than I've been willing to realize, as long as I keep you in the loop. Also about how you're a workaholic asshole, but we can't have everything," he adds.

Paul grins. "We can talk about adventures. I didn't know you thought we couldn't."

Alex shrugs. "Not to drag out the skeletons, but the Liam thing does not bring out the best in you. So I extrapolated from the data I had. I also know you're trying, and I can be okay with the Liam thing bugging you, if you can be okay with it too. Because

I'm not willing to change what that friendship is. Mostly because I don't think I can."

"Oh, let's definitely talk about adventures instead," Paul says with a self-deprecating laugh.

Alex smiles. "So Carly and I talked about that idea you two cooked up at Victor's party. Mostly because that dinner was *horrible* and we were hiding and a threesome is random and more hilarious than that trainwreck was."

"Yeah?"

"Yeah. I like her. I mean, it would never occur to me, but if that's a thing you want to do, it's not something I'd want to do with someone other than her instead."

"What about with boys?" Paul asks.

"I think that's a whole different conversation."

"Agreed," Paul says with relief.

Alex laughs. "One thing at a time, and do not assume that by adventure I mean fucking. Or only mean fucking. Or mean a lot of fucking. Or something. Oh, wow, Paul, I love you, but so awkward, our lives are so awkward, and I have no idea why we've been convincing ourselves we're the normal ones in the face of all of everything that happened tonight."

Paul lifts a hand and pushes it through Alex's hair. "I love you too. Normal is relative, but I still kind of feel like we have a lock on it anyway."

"But the *awkward*."

"Yeah, definitely awkward. So is this Carly thing something you're actually interested in, or are you just trying to be generous?"

"I'm not going to fuck someone I don't want to fuck," Alex says. Paul needs to get his head around that, and also start believing Alex when he says things. About anything.

"Well, obviously." Paul's equally spiky. "But have you been thinking about it?"

"I just had this conversation with her," Alex points out. "Also, I am offering you a threesome, and you are being difficult."

"I'm trying to prevent us from making bad choices."

"Yeah, and that's how we got into this mess," Alex says. "Look, doing this with her feels safer while we're still a little bit fragile and not fixed. Like it's allowed to cause problems, and so that way, maybe it won't? I want a trashy dumb Hollywood experience to brag about, although I never will. I want to see things about you you'll never tell me. And I want everything we do to only involve people we actually like regardless of whether it's in bed or not. So yeah, Carly."

"And I want us to have ill-advised adventures," Paul says with a smile. "So do you want to call her, or should I?"

"I've passed my quota of brave about this," Alex says, pressing his face into Paul's shoulder. "It's all you now."

Hanging out at Gemma's house is always strange for Alex because Gemma's house is Paul's house. He's never gotten over the cognitive dissonance of seeing his best friend living in a place that holds such critical memories for him.

"Can we not?" he asks as Gemma dumps the popcorn into a bowl and starts toward the stairs to what is now her bedroom.

She gives him a judgmental look. "Roommate night, Alex, we need the popcorn."

"No, not that. The popcorn's fine."

"What is it?" Gemma props a hand on her hip and gives him a curious and concerned look. "You've been off all night, is everything okay with you?"

"I'm fine," Alex says shortly. He really does not want to have to explain his current aversion to hanging out in her bedroom. Particularly considering the topic he's certain they're going to end up discussing. As uncomfortable as it makes him, that's part of the reason he's here.

"Okay. What gives?" Gemma asks, as Alex takes the bowl off her and heads into the living room instead. It takes several rounds of badgering on Gemma's part and prevarications on Alex's before he finally starts to stammer out the story.

"I don't get famous, I don't get rich, *and* I don't get to have a threesome? This shit is getting seriously annoying," Gemma says. "I also don't know if I'm hurt or relieved you didn't choose me."

"Shut up."

"Promise that if it were you and Liam, it would have been me?

"OH MY GOD, SHUT UP." Alex knows she's teasing. He can laugh at the suggestion in a way he wouldn't have been able to in the past, but he still feels embarrassed and vulnerable. Gemma knows he has none of the power and confidence he pretends to in this world.

She cackles and digs for more popcorn. "We would have been really hot."

"Gemma," Alex says warningly.

"Okay, okay. So, like, are you just here to confess or do you have questions about pussy?"

Alex looks around for a throw pillow to hide in. "Everything you told me about anal sex was wrong. At least make up for that and be useful now?"

"That was perfectly good information."

"It really wasn't. Just — no."

"So." Gemma's grin is evil. "What do you need to know?"

◆

Paul lifts his hand to knock at Carly's apartment. "How are you doing?" he asks.

Alex is saved from having to declare how awkward he feels when Carly answers the door with a ridiculous come-hither pose and two full shot glasses balanced in one hand. "Drinks, boys?" she says in a voice as ridiculous as her pose.

Paul laughs, and Alex grins at her. Silly isn't what he imagined for this encounter, but that might be the tone that makes it work.

"Wouldn't want to leave you without," Paul says even as he liberates them from her clutches and passes one back to Alex as they walk into the apartment. Alex is grateful for the at least momentary distraction from the business at hand.

"I think I can handle pre-gaming in my own house, thanks," she says as they knock back the drinks.

"Where's Liam?" Alex asks. He doesn't want or expects him here. He just wants everyone accounted for.

"Was he invited?" Carly raises an amused eyebrow at him.

"You know what I mean."

"He's at Victor's. Negotiating."

"What's that supposed to mean?" Alex asks.

"Depends how it goes, doesn't it? Now," she says, taking charge again. "Are you okay?"

"I get less okay every time someone asks. Otherwise, I'm fine."

"Excellent. Do I need to be a good host or can you and Paul just, like, make out and be hot? I mean, unless there are any more logistics we haven't covered?"

Alex shakes his head. She and Paul have been through all their various agreements and concerns regarding this evening pretty exhaustively. Largely because of Alex's insistence on not engaging that process and everyone's willingness to humor him.

"No, and thank you for the tequila, but this is really awkward," Alex says.

"It'll pass."

Alex gives her a look.

"What, do you want me and Paul to make out instead?"

Alex nods, a little bit frantic and a little bit nervous. He retreats into an armchair, folding his legs up under him.

Carly gives him a suit-yourself shrug and holds a hand out to Paul. He looks at Alex a little nervously.

"I'll tell you if I'm not fine," Alex says. Paul's assumption that he is going to be unable to handle the sight of Paul making out with Carly because of jealousy is annoying.

"Paul," Carly says sharply. "One of the ways you prove you can respect *no* is by respecting *yes*."

Alex has to stop himself from slapping the arm of the chair and shouting *thank you*. Finally, someone gets it.

"Are you saying yes?" Paul flirts with her.

"Actually, I think I'm saying I'm impatient, and I haven't made out with you in a really long time."

Alex finds the sight completely bizarre. He's never really thought of Paul being with someone who wasn't him. The whole debacle with Craig was something he's avoided thinking about entirely. Meanwhile, Paul's history with Carly is something he's wondered about, but has very little information on.

Paul takes up a lot more space than Carly. Alex is fascinated by how instantly they look like every heterosexual narrative in every TV show or movie he's never cared about. But it's also weird how much they don't. They're both his people in a way; no matter what they are doing with each other, renders them always and deeply queer to him.

Carly is either naturally a talker too or knows how to play Paul. Alex can't tell. As soon as his mouth drifts to her jaw and her neck, she's narrating to him what Alex looks like watching them. The whole thing is a bit *turtles all the way down*, and Alex really needs to know what to do next. Because while he can picture Paul sitting here jerking off to him and Carly making out, he's not so sure that's going to work for him in reverse.

She must be able to sense something of his uncertainty. Before long she stops Paul with a hand on his chest and crooks a finger at Alex. "If you want, baby boy. He's all yours."

Alex is saved the trouble of pointing out that that is not quite the point by Paul, who turns his head to smile at him. "C'mere, Alex. Time for something new."

Bizarre as this situation is, Paul always has pushed Alex past his comfort zone in the best of ways. And that is the point. So Alex goes.

Kissing Carly is different. Her mouth seems so small he's not even really sure how to kiss her. Also, although Alex has never noticed it before, she's short, which is just a hassle. Mostly, losing himself to a moment that is all about asking himself, over and over again, if he's feeling what he's supposed to feel, is a challenge. He finds himself grateful that he spent so much of high school hiding from everyone with work and surliness. To have had to fake this at sixteen would have been a type of misery he's committed to working hard to never imagine.

The warm weight of Paul pressed against his back, though, is another matter entirely. Things may be better between them, but they're still not sharing space or fucking as much as Alex wants, and he feels hyper-aware of everywhere Paul is. He shivers when Paul kisses the back of his neck. Paul whispering in Alex's ear about how Alex and Carly look together is the least surprising thing in the world. It's also incredibly hot.

While it's not quite like a switch has been flipped, Alex finds it impossible not to follow Paul's directions when he tells Alex to start undressing her. Carly, however, must sense whatever hesitation remains and takes a step back.

"You fumbling with my bra like any of us is in high school is decidedly not sexy," she says with a laugh. "I should get naked. And you two should make out and then join me."

She stalks off into her bedroom.

"Carly's nice," Alex says to Paul dopily.

"You're really relieved about the bra thing, aren't you?"

Alex nods vigorously.

It takes a while for the awkward to pass. What ultimately helps the most though, is Alex realizing that none of this is any more awkward than the first time he slept with Paul. He's not even as drunk. It should be weirder, and it just isn't.

Besides, once he's naked and between them, the whole idea of *threesome* feels like a misnomer, because it's all about him. Carly and Paul are absolutely focused on keeping him interested, and he is very interested indeed.

If Paul has consistently been about getting Alex close and pulling him back from the edge since the very first time they hooked up, this is a thousand times worse. Everything Alex's body wants is at a price, many of them easy to provide. If he stops kissing Carly, Paul stops touching his dick. If he wants more or faster or harder, or Paul's fingers grazing over his hole, he better be paying attention to far more than Carly's mouth.

Eventually, Alex stops asking for things with words or whines. He's painfully hard and he'll go where he's put and do as he's told because he has no sense left to think of any reason not to. Paul always gets Alex where he wants to go. Eventually.

When Paul presses Alex's head down between Carly's spread legs and tells him to lick, that he's damn well going to make her come before he even gets to beg for anything for himself, he almost comes right then and there. The only thing that stops him is Paul yanking hard on his balls and Carly's delighted laugh. For half a second the laughter and the drunken ridiculousness of it all makes Alex thinks of Liam.

Going down on a girl is unfamiliar and a little strange, but Carly is responsive and Paul is encouraging. He strokes his thumb along the back of Alex' neck and up into his hair while he keeps up the filthy litany.

After Carly comes, Paul drags Alex back up by the hair and kisses him wet and deep. Alex whimpers. He is ready to come himself right the fuck now.

"Paul, please," he manages.

♦

"What do you want?" Paul asks.

Alex just whimpers in response.

"Do you want to fuck me, baby boy?" Carly asks.

Paul cracks up and leans his forehead against Alex's shoulder. He's not surprised when Alex says *yes*. Alex never does anything halfway.

He helps Alex with the condom, both because Alex is too lost to everything to focus on anything and for the gasp Alex gives when Paul runs his fingers down Alex's dick.

"You want me to get on top?" Carly asks.

Alex shakes his head. Paul flops down next to Carly with a laugh. "He's very predictable."

"Not predictable," Carly chides. She tugs Alex closer and reaches between their legs to guide him into her. "The rest should be easy, sweetheart."

Alex swears.

♦

Easy is too small a word for it, Alex thinks. Because yes, the act is familiar, but it's also different and really at this point all that matters is that he's fucking someone. That he's fucking a girl he'll freak out about later. Right now, he's just pissed off that Paul and Carly are too busy kissing each other to kiss him while he pumps into her.

Alex doesn't realize he's said as much out loud until Carly giggles. Paul leans up on an elbow to kiss Alex. Everything is perfect then, if not as sex, than as attention.

After Alex comes, he wants nothing more than to curl up in the warmth of Carly's bed and pass out.

Processing this can wait until. Carly, however, is having none of it.

"You're heavy," she says after letting him rest for a moment. She taps her fingers against his back. "We've also been neglecting Paul."

Alex lifts his head briefly and snorts.

"Mmmmm, none of that." Carly shifts Alex off of her. She gives a little gasp as Alex slips out. "You want it to be like before?" she coos at him. "You want me to tell you what to do?"

She helps Alex find his knees and guides his face down between Paul's legs. Paul makes an obscene sound.

"I know you can go deeper than that," Carly says with a wink to Paul. She presses Alex's head down to suck Paul's dick until he chokes on it.

Alex whimpers and mewls, and Carly doesn't let up in her narration. It's exactly what gets Paul off and exactly what helps Alex disappear in the best way he knows how.

♦

After Paul comes, Alex flops down face-first into the pillows and lies there, apparently dazed with it all. Then before he curls up small and pressing his face against Carly's side as Paul rubs his back.

"He gets like this sometimes," Paul says softly after a few minutes of the puzzling intensity that sometimes rolls off Alex after sex.

"You okay there, baby boy?" Carly asks Alex. She gets little more than half a nod and a vague sound, before he presses against her tighter while fumbling for Paul's arm. He clutches it too tight around him once he has it. Paul's heart melts.

Carly looks at Paul, her face thoughtful. "He's ridiculously lovely. I'm sure you know that, though."

Of course Paul knows that. It's one of the central facts of his existence. But he still has concerns. "He worries me, sometimes, when he's like this."

Carly frowns at him. "That's because you're an idiot and trust neither your judgment nor his. You're smarter than Paul, aren't you?" She turns her attention back to Alex.

He nods against her.

"You stay down there as long as you need," she says to him. "We've got you, and I know you feel real nice right now. You were so good for us."

Paul watches her with a little bit of awe, a little bit of desire, and more discomfort than is useful. She meets his eyes briefly but says nothing. She returns her attention to Alex until he seems to relax into the bed, probably more interested in sleep than care.

"So," Carly says, pulling her hair out of her face. "You two are lovely and hot and all sorts of sexy, but, wow, could I use a cigarette."

"Go for it." Paul shrugs.

"Would if I could," Carly says.

"Did you seriously leave cigarettes off your shopping list for this adventure?"

"Pregnant!" Carly blurts.

Alex snorts comically and lifts his head out of Carly's side to gape.

Paul stares but recovers faster. "Seriously?"

"No, I just wanted to see your reactions. Yes, seriously, asshole," she grins.

"Jesus Christ, Carly," Paul shakes his head. Alex still looks dumbstruck. "Congratulations." He feels no jealousy; the relationship he and Carly had was a long time ago. He pats himself on the back mentally for not being weird about the situation.

"Thank you," she says to Paul before turning her attention to Alex. "Don't worry, honey. It's not yours. You can go back to sleep."

Alex chuckles and grumbles something about not having failed high school biology before closing his eyes and snuggling against her side again.

"I feel like every single thing I want to say is going to sound really rude," Paul says.

"No, it wasn't planned; yes, my tits are bigger; yes, we are kind of freaking out. Good thing I haven't bought a wedding dress yet!" Carly supplies for him.

"Is Liam okay?" Alex mumbles from beside her.

Carly shrugs. "He's afraid the baby's gonna be like him. Otherwise, yeah."

Alex snorts. "Payback's a bitch."

Paul smiles. There is something sweet and satisfying about the idea of a frazzled Liam facing down his own peculiar offspring.

"Yeah, something like that. We're moving up the wedding, too, so there's full-on logistics battles on all fronts."

"Oh, hey, that's awesome," Paul says. "Have you got a date now?"

"Not yet. Before I might accidentally deliver from excitement. Soon."

"Well, if you need any help."

"Appreciate the thought, but you are way too fucking busy. I'm not marrying into this fucked up life not to be able to pay to make my problems go away."

"Does anyone else know yet?" Paul asks, still trying to get his head around this.

"You mean when are we putting out a press release?" The subject is obviously a touchy one.

"Victor," Alex mumbles by way of translation for Paul.

"Oh. Of course," Carly says.

"How did that go?" Paul asks. As much as he and Victor are increasingly friends, there's a part of Paul that can't help imagining Victor as a particularly petulant housecat determined to suck the breath and soul out of anything that would compete with him for his household's affection. The disaster of the late dinner party aside.

"He's worried about Liam a little, but he's more or less over the moon. God, don't look so surprised. It's a baby, not a cancellation notice. He's not actually evil."

"No, he's just the devil," Alex mutters. "What if he eats it?"

Carly pinches Alex's arm. "You were at dinner," she says. "He's family. For you too. Whether you like it or not."

"The interference is toxic," Alex says.

"It comes from a place of caring."

"Alex isn't wrong," Paul says.

"What authority does he have over you? Any toxic is your own fault in acquiescing where you're not comfortable," she says.

"Not allowed to say no," Alex mumbles. Over his back, Paul gives Carly a significant look.

Carly ignores it in favor of tapping Alex on the shoulder. "Alex," she says, fond but stern. "You have this whole life of yours because you said no at the right time. Don't you get your signals crossed, too."

"You don't understand," he says petulantly.

"I'm a girl. You're never gonna know more about yes and no than me, no matter who or what you think Victor is."

"And to think," Paul says. He wonders if he'll ever stop loving and admiring these two people. "We just came for the sex."

◆

Liam's barefoot when he finally makes himself pad out of his bedroom and into Victor's kitchen. He's drawn by the sound of pans banging around unnecessarily. Victor wants him to get up and doesn't particularly know how to start, or finish, the confrontation from last night.

"Hey. Sorry I was such an asshole last night," Liam says, leaning his hip against the kitchen island.

"I see someone has remembered how to use their words," Victor says snidely.

Liam has no idea if he means to be cruel, or if this is one of those things Victor would say to anyone but lands harder for Liam because of the realities of his life.

"Yeah, thankfully," Liam says as if the remark was merely a casual observation. Last night sucked, and he really doesn't feel like fighting anymore.

Victor opens a cupboard to fish around for some ingredient or other. "I think we're going to have to start doing things differently."

Liam frowns and picks up the metronome sitting on the counter. Victor may not be the only writer to write to a steady beat, but Liam is pretty sure he's the only one that uses an actual physical metronome to find his pacing. And not the electronic kind: The old-fashioned sort that by any measure should live on Victor's piano, not his desk. He slides the little weight up the rod to a tempo he knows Victor likes and sets it going.

Victor looks over his shoulder at him. Liam shrugs.

"In what way?" Liam asks. "That sounds ominous." His own desire to do things differently with Victor had fueled some of last night's terrible; Victor's reluctance to discuss it in any way that had made sense to Liam had fueled the rest.

"Not ominous," Victor reassures him. "But we've both been navigating this issue poorly for months. Since I had to point out to that you getting married was going to change the way you do things with all of the people in your life."

"It doesn't *need* to change anything." Liam is getting exhausted having to point this out.

"No, perhaps not, but things are changing regardless. And now your wedding's getting moved up, you're miserable out of my bed, and I'm miserable with you in it."

Liam's frown deepens. The night he'd spent in bed with Victor after filming Zach's death had been hard, but Victor's care had been vital to him.

"Under ordinary circumstances," Victor adds. "But those facts remain, so we find an arrangement that suits both of us. So if you have a list of what you need from me, now's the time."

"Okay." Liam nods along as he processes all of that. "One. I need to be useful to you. That's hard with you because you're you, and I get that that's how you work even if I don't understand it. It's fine, but it is hard. Two, I need to be able to touch you, because that's how *I* work. You not letting me do that because you're afraid of what else I'll want doesn't make things easier for either of us." Liam frowns at the metronome in his hand, and moves the slider down to make it run faster.

"Three, I have no idea what's changing with this relationship, but something is and has been since Carly and I got engaged. We even talked about it, ages ago, or at least you started the conversation and then went into denial about what, I don't even know. So I need you to acknowledge that this is changing and be specific about what you need and want from me. Also, stop acting like whatever is changing with us is the end of the world. It's not, and you freaking out is freaking me out."

◆

Liam's litany is thorough. He doesn't seem annoyed or spooked anymore. Those are both very good things. But in this moment Victor is impressed most with Liam's capacity to want and feel without any sort of shame at all. It's beautiful, and it's frightening. His confidence — when he's not having a meltdown — in his ability to navigate a situation that's left Victor so often utterly at sea is nothing short of inspiring.

"Okay." Victor turns on a burner under the pan.

"Okay?"

"Yes, something's shifted. Yes, I haven't known what to do about it, and yes, I've made a hash of it every time I've tried to talk to you about it. I am twice your age. I didn't expect to have to reexamine all sorts of things I comfortably deemed irrelevant decades ago."

"Thank you," Liam says, sincere in a way that would be surprising from anyone else.

"I know you hate change, Liam, but that's how people are. They change more than you want or not enough. And you just have to live with it; you have to live with it in yourself and your circumstances too. I need to remember that too, but I'm also never going to be exactly who you want me to be."

"I don't —"

"You do. And I can live with that if you can. So here's the plan."

"Okay." Liam smiles. "What?"

"Take some massage classes. And then you can touch and be useful in the way you need to be, because the stress of this life is going to kill me," Victor says with a laugh.

"I'm going to assume you don't mean *massage* euphemistically," Liam says.

Victor gives him a look. "You know enough to not have to assume."

"Yeah, but I'm not sure you do? Or, like, you did, and now you don't anymore?"

"The rather large space between desiring you and desiring to make you happy hasn't gotten smaller, Liam. Just a little bit more complicated."

Liam shrugs. "Complicated is fine."

"Don't get overexcited," Victor warns. "I'm not always sure, for someone who sleeps with as many people as you do, why you're still here. I adore you, but your sudden bursts of wanting to be the exception to even more rules than you already are is a bit more than I can take."

"I said I was sorry about last night."

"I know, and I appreciate it. Now, if you don't have any other questions, would you care to tell me why I am not currently making breakfast for Carly as well?"

When Liam tells Victor where Carly is, Victor stares and then shakes his head. Yelling about it will do no good, and it's none of his business anyway, but his people never do stop surprising him. Carly will be over later, Liam says.

"She's so fucking amazing," Liam says. Victor nods, very fond, as Liam goes on. "I wish this all were less hard on her."

"The wedding, the baby, or both?"

"The wedding, mostly. She's so much better about the baby than I am."

"Have you made a decision yet?"

Victor sees Liam fold back in on himself and hopes he hasn't done any terrible damage so soon after, mostly, fixing things. "Please stop expecting me to have second thoughts. We're calling it a baby, after all," he says. "If I weren't so worried, I'd be happy. You know that. It'll get better."

♦

After they leave Carly's, Paul and Alex go out for brunch, just the two of them. Alex thinks that having some time on neutral ground is a good idea. But also, he's enjoying simply spending time with Paul. He's barely aware of anyone or anything else as they grin at each other over coffee and share a newspaper.

"So what do we do when we get home?" Paul finally asks.

"Shower. Nap," Alex says lazily. He can't think much beyond that.

"Yeah, but where?" Paul presses.

"We're not going to move back in together the day after one of our crazier joint adventures." He's not surprised that Paul is trying to broach the topic. But he's also not going to budge on the reasonable boundaries they've established.

"Why not?" Paul asks. He stirs his coffee with his straw, not looking at Alex.

"Because I want to sleep. And process. I've got too much to think about as it is without worrying about making the right choice about where you keep your toothbrush."

"I don't want to be your roommate forever," Paul says. "Even a very romantic roommate."

"I know," Alex says softly. "We'll talk about it. Just not today? Because last night I fucked a girl, and now we're having brunch. Everything is very strange and, at the moment, very good."

"I worry about us not talking about things again."

"Believe me, we are not tabling the question indefinitely." He drops his voice, and Paul grins as Alex leans forward enough to be heard. "But oh my God, Paul, you talked me into a threesome. Waiting twenty-four hours for me to deal with that before we talk about our living arrangements is the least you can do."

♦

Carly breezes into Victor's house and slides a box of Krispy Kremes onto the counter along with a fast food bag.

"Did you seriously bring donuts and a burrito into my house?" Victor asks as she gives Liam a loud smacking kiss on the mouth.

"Did you cook anything for me?" she asks, looking at their half-finished meal.

"You know I don't seat late-comers."

"Liam, do you want to surrender the rest of the fried polenta rings to me?" Carly asks.

Liam shakes his head and pulls his plate closer.

Carly cackles. "Hence burrito. We can all share the donuts, even though I need my energy."

"Is that about the baby or the threesome?" Victor drawls.

Carly smacks Liam's arm. "You told."

"You were gonna tell," he says with a shrug.

"Maybe. And now I've missed all the fun. Victor, are you judging me?"

"Always. Mostly you kids and your heartbreaking waste of your low-sleep lives confuse me," he says drily.

"Yeah, but you love us anyway," Liam grins.

Victor grunts.

Carly pulls up the stool next to Liam's. "What else did you boys talk about? Anything I should know? Or brace myself for?"

"No, I don't think so," Liam says softly. Carly thinks that the fact he smiles at Victor as he says it says a lot.

"Well," Carly says in the face of whatever Liam will likely tell her later in private. "Tell me about something." She unwraps the burrito and takes a bite.

"How's the wedding planning?" Victor says benignly.

"Oh my God, Liam, can we just go to city hall with a roll of quarters, because I am sort of over this entire thing."

"If you want. My parents — and my team — will kill me, but like, whatever."

"What's the problem?" Victor asks.

"You ever try renting a venue for a wedding not sixteen months in advance?" Carly asks.

"Remarkably, Carly, no."

"Well, it's impossible."

"You could do it here," Victor says with a shrug.

"Excuse me?"

"Outside. It's not like I don't rent tents and hire caterers for other things. When do you want to do it?"

"Whoa whoa whoa whoa, *No,*" she says. "Why did I buy you donuts?"

"Because you live dangerously."

Carly snorts. "No. Because your territory, your rules. I appreciate the offer, really, but this wedding thing is complicated and difficult enough and involves a whole lot of delicate egos as it is before we bring non-neutral ground into it."

"That's fine. If you're not going to do it here, there are favors I can call in. It's just like booking a location. Network knows, I do that on short notice all the time. Did you have anything particular in mind?"

35

The viewing party for what Alex and Paul have privately been calling the Dead Zach Episode is small. Of the people involved in having shot the more grueling parts of the episode, Victor is the only one with any enthusiasm for it at all.

Alex feels uneasy about being back in Victor's house — this time with low lights, candles, and hors d'oeuvres. He and Liam make wary eye-contact as they work the room. There are barely more than thirty people present, mostly connected to the show. But there's also a journalist there who will be, as far as Alex is concerned, getting only a scoop on him and Liam refusing to watch the episode. He and Liam have already made a pact to step outside for the duration of it.

When he'd told Paul of the plan in the car on the way over, Paul had frowned thoughtfully. "That'll make great apocrypha."

Alex had refrained from saying just how much that made him sound like Victor.

At one point, Alex ends up in a corner with Carly, who's staying out of the crowd and keeping an eye on Liam. Talking with her after recent events isn't awkward at all, which both surprises and gratifies Alex. Everyone, it seems, is going to continue being an adult about that adventure. Which makes Alex feel better about future adventures. In the meantime, Alex is happy to get a hug and three minutes blessedly free of conversation from Carly before he returns to the fray.

Victor is in his element, simultaneously mingling and keeping an eye on his smartphone for whatever social media he's tracking. Alex is sure the internet is already humming in anticipation. He himself has spent a decent chunk of the last week doing media for this episode. Victor's incredibly sketchy secret filming process has been successful: There have been no leaks or spoilers. Alex has taken much delight in telling interviewers and fandom that everyone should watch tonight because huge things are happening for Zach and James and their relationship.

Paul, out of some perverse curiosity, has spent the last week trawling the hashtags for the best of the internet's irrational hopes, dreams, and demands. Alex is far more amused than annoyed. Particularly because Paul hasn't been weird or jealous or anything about Alex and Liam. According to Paul's research, fandom is torn between wanting an engagement or an *I love you*. As much as that pisses Alex off on its own — of the many regrets either James or Zach have, never saying that is not one of them – he can't help but laugh at the wariness with which Paul conveyed this information. Zach and James are fictional. Their relationship, and what the fans want it to be, have no bearing on how Alex feels about whatever mess he and Paul are almost, if not entirely, out of.

◆

"How are you two doing?" Victor asks Paul. Paul startles out of his reverie. Alex is engaged in being sharply charming with someone, and Paul gave up on making his own rounds to watch him fondly.

"I notice you're asking about both of us and not just him," Paul says.

"That's because you're both a mess, and you both still worry me."

"Victor," Paul says, amused and almost but not quite chiding. Victor seems amused. "We're hardly that bad."

"Are you living together yet?"

"Victor."

"What?"

"We share a house. We have always shared a house."

"And a bed?"

"Not your business," Paul says, taken aback. Will Victor ever stop prying? "And last I checked, not your interest."

"You're sleeping with Liam's fiancée. Terribly much my business."

"I disagree. So would Carly," Paul says. "Also, not an ongoing concern."

"Glad as I am to hear it, the question stands."

Paul tries to calculate Alex's possible reactions to anything he says to Victor on this subject ever. "We're working on it," he finally says.

"Work harder," Victor says sternly.

"Oh my God, Victor, sometimes relationships are actually difficult."

Victor looks unconvinced. "You are not telling me anything I don't already know. But you two are making things harder for yourselves than they need to be, and that is simply an absurd waste of effort and potential."

Paul rubs his temple. "Why do you care so much?"

"Because you people are what I have."

♦

At ten to the hour, the room starts to shuffle into seating arrangements in front of the TV. Paul nabs a seat on the couch, and Carly slides in between him and the arm of the couch. Alex walks behind them. He squeezes Paul's shoulder briefly and gives him a little smile. Liam's standing at the door out to the back patio, holding a plate heaped with food. Alex grabs a bottle of wine and two glasses off the sideboard, and together the two of them disappear outside.

Paul thinks he's the only one who sees them go until Carly chuckles softly.

"What?" Paul whispers as Victor takes his own seat and the noise level in the room plummets.

"Thank God those two have each other."

Paul grunts and shifts a little so Ellen can sit down on the other side of him.

"Don't be like that," Carly says, amused but sharp. "I wouldn't want to put up with Liam tonight. Or Alex."

"Speaking as his significant other," Paul starts.

Carly tilts her head to the TV, which Victor has just flicked on. "Hush until you see it. Stop being an asshole, and be glad Alex has a battle buddy."

"Why, have you seen it?"

Carly shakes her head. "Liam told me."

Paul wants to know more about that, but before he can ask anything, he's cut off by the sudden score of the episode's smash opening.

♦

"So what have you been up to?" Liam asks Alex after they get themselves situated at the cafe table out by the pool. He's clearly trying to have, or at least start, a normal conversation. Alex is both surprised and glad. He's had nothing like a normal conversation with Liam in weeks.

Alex picks at the plate Liam's carried out. "Climbing. Media. Looking for work. Trying not to freak out about the last thing any more than I generally am."

"Any good options?"

"Some. I'll know for sure soon. It's not like I can really say anything officially anyway until this is done," Alex nods back toward the house. He's so close now.

"It's cool you're doing new stuff."

"Yeah?" Alex asks.

"Yeah. Like, I love doing *Fourth* and working with Victor. I miss working with you. But like, you wanted something and you're gonna get it. Go you." Liam grins as he reaches for the bottle to uncork it.

They talk quietly for a while about how Alex's movie plans are making things hard with Paul even as other things between them are getting better. Then they talk about Liam's frightened excitement about the baby and more uncomplicated happiness for the wedding.

After about half an hour, the door to the living room slides open. Victor leans out to call to them. "Liam. Alex."

"Yeah?" Liam answers, staring at the glass in his hand.

"You're up. Come see your moment of triumph."

Absolutely not. Alex turns to look at Liam, who turns to look at him at the same time. They both say, "No."

"Was there something you missed about the hiding in your backyard part?" Alex adds. He wants to be very clear and also rub in, again, how awful that filming experience was for both him and Liam.

"You've earned this," Victor says. There's that same peculiar blend of command and pride in his voice that Alex remembers hazily from their discussion when he was in the hospital with heatstroke.

"No," Liam says. He grabs Alex's hand on the table. "We've earned *this*."

Victor disappears back inside with a shrug, sliding the door closed behind him. Alex can tell by the shift of sound that the episode's back on and that everyone is watching raptly. He can hear his own voice on the TV.

"Want to take a walk?" he asks Liam.

Liam nods rapidly.

Together, they wander over to the far side of the pool, far enough away from the door that they can't hear anything. Alex sits down by the fence and Liam flops onto his back and stares up at the sky. When Alex asks him what he's looking at, Liam starts telling him about the constellations he can see, the ones they can't because of pollution, and the various legends that go with all of them.

"How do you know all this stuff?" Alex asks eventually.

Liam shrugs. "You have books. I have people who like to tell me things."

◆

Paul has kept up with watching *Fourth* when he has time, both out of fondness for the show he's spent so much of his life working on, and for the pleasure of watching Alex do what he's so amazing at. At times, that's been awkward. Certainly, he had not handled the James and Zach love scene earlier this year well.

Tonight is a different kind of experience entirely. He's well aware, yet again, that it's all fiction; he knows that Alex shot his parts for this right downstairs in this very house. But Alex had said *remember it wasn't acting* and then had fallen apart when he had gotten home that night. So watching Zach's torture on its own would be disturbing enough, but watching it knowing that it's actually *Alex* breathless and crazed with fear is very close to unbearable.

Carly finds his hand and squeezes it wordlessly.

From his throne, Victor is bathed in the glow of too many screens, solemnly and eagerly watching as much of the reaction of the audience in real time as he can. For all that Paul's been glad to count Victor as a friend, even an often meddling one, all he can see now is someone who took the trust and faith of his people and made them do *this*.

The journalist — Jennie? Jacquie? Paul can't remember — is clearly not happy that her prime subjects aren't actually in the room for her to get a look at their faces while the episode is airing. Paul's never been more sympathetic to Alex's reticence in public than he is right now. She drifts around the edge of the room to the window, through which Alex and Liam are probably vaguely visible. It's really fucking creepy.

When the show goes to commercial, everyone sits quiet and dazed in the interval. Before Paul can say or do something stupid, Carly tugs his hand and whispers in his ear to *go get a girl a drink, already*. Paul feels bad that the best he can do for her is seltzer with a twist.

When the episode is finally over, all Paul can hear is everyone in the room breathing. The atmosphere is incredibly eerie. Even if he had been watching alone and had never known Alex, seeing Zach tortured — psychologically and physically — and then shot in the head is the type of TV that would have forced him out of the house for a run. That's not an option he has right now, unfortunately.

"How could you do that to them?" Paul says softly.

"And Paul speaks for America," Victor says, tapping away at his laptop. When Paul goes to look over his shoulder, it's open to his social media deck, where Victor is probably twisting the knife into the audience with several incredibly injudicious tweets. His username is @TheShowYouHate.

"I still can't believe that's your fucking Twitter handle," Paul says.

"I know. You'd think people would be less surprised when I do things they don't like."

"You're such an ass," Paul says. His tone is good-natured, because they're in public, but he absolutely means it.

"We're going to win all the awards for that," Victor says. "Your boy is going to win all the awards for that."

"He better," Paul says.

"He's also going to be able to do whatever work he wants."

"Less of a comfort than you think," Paul says darkly.

"Feisty," Victor says. He turns to the room at large. "Does someone want to go retrieve the men of the hour and tell them it's safe to come back?"

♦

Liam is in the middle of recounting what Alex thinks is a Greek legend about Cassiopeia when Alex's phone rings. It's Gemma, and he picks up only because she's on his very short list of people he'd remotely consider talking to tonight.

"What's up, Gem?"

"Alex?" she asks. Her voice small.

"Yeah. Are you okay?"

Liam rolls his head over to frown worriedly at Alex. Alex shrugs.

"Yeah, I'm fine. I just....Are you?" she stammers.

"Gemma, why the hell wouldn't I be okay?"

"Mhmm. I know. But I watched the episode…."

Alex has to swallow the entirely inappropriate urge to laugh, especially given his own reaction to filming the episode. "Gemma. It's a TV show," he says as gently as he can.

"I know," Gemma says again. Alex swears he can hear her sniffle. "I just wanted to hear your voice."

"Well, I'm fine." His phone beeps with another incoming call. Alex pulls it away from his ear to look at it in surprise. "Hey, I've got another call, but I'll talk to you later, okay?"

"Yeah, okay."

Alex switches over to the next call with something between amusement and trepidation. Liam plays with Alex's shoelace.

"Hi, Mom."

"Hello, Alex. How are you doing tonight?"

Alex lets his head slump back against the fence. "I didn't know you even watched *Fourth*."

♦

"I'm never, ever going to watch it, you know," Alex says when he and Paul are driving home. It's after midnight. Alex has to be up in less than five hours for morning media on the East Coast.

"You're really good," Paul says. "You probably should."

"Yeah, well, one night of disturbing phone calls from all my friends has been quite enough, thanks. Plus, Liam and I have a pact."

"What are you going to do when they run that clip all through awards season?"

"Don't."

"Don't what?"

"Start spouting Victor's shit about this being my ticket to everything or bitching about Liam or whatever it is you're going to do." He can't take any more of that. Not from Victor, and especially not from Paul.

"You *were* really good," Paul says. "And I know you have good reason to have your hackles up right now, but don't. Because God, the shit I wanted to say to Victor."

"Yeah?" Alex is a little pleased at the thought of Paul defending his honor on this particular point.

"Oh yeah," Paul says. "You're not the only one who's ever wanted to take a swing at him."

"Sure," Alex says. "But I'm still the only one who has."

The media stuff is hard. Some of the hardest Alex has ever done, because he has to balance his own glee at the secret having been kept successfully with the grief, shock, and anger of strangers. Morning shows read him the sort of tweets he's been trying to avoid. Female journalists talk about crying, male ones talk about their wives crying, and everyone wants to know what it was like to shoot. He can't tell the truth any more than he can say, softly, that he'd really prefer not to answer the question. When Liam comes up, he reminds people about how TV magic works. None of that was filmed concurrently. Anything anyone wants to know about Liam, they'll have to ask him.

Which they're having a hard time doing. Liam, for once, skips the limelight. Alex can hardly blame him; having those clips playing everywhere is really not fun. Alex averts his eyes when they're shown if they're on monitors in the studio with him. He and Liam have a promise, and even if it's bordering on petty, he intends to keep it. While Alex is willing to take the brunt of the media attention, Liam's absence doesn't go unnoticed or unremarked on.

The internet is flat-out awful. The fans who think Liam is avoiding everything because he can't bear to talk about his lover being tortured aren't entirely wrong. Which doesn't make the situation any easier to deal with. Liam gets accused of cowardice and of abandoning a friend in a difficult time; Alex gets accused of stealing the spotlight from Liam in his greatest hour and for the worst sort of ingratitude when he doesn't express regret at leaving *The Fourth Estate.*

When he says *Zach is mine now, I get to keep him* to a talk show host, the fandom explodes with rage. Victor sends Alex a congratulatory text. *Right now everyone hates you more than they hate me. Quite the achievement.*

Paul is considerate, soothing, and interested in all of it, often to an extent Alex has to remind himself to find charming. So much of it feels like Paul angling to declare the relationship drama of the last six months over. As much as Alex is willing to do that, he's skeptical of whether the way to do it to return to the way things were. After all, the separate lives, same house, awesome slumber party thing seems to be working out pretty well. Even if Todd objects.

◆

When Alex suggests that being partners with separate bedrooms might be the best way to go forward, Paul is calm, communicative, and having absolutely none of it.

"Lots of artists do it," Alex tells him. They got home late from work, fucked, and are now down in the kitchen, scrounging leftovers for a well-past-midnight snack. Alex is sitting at the island, shirtless in pajama pants and tapping a fork into a Tupperware container. He's absolutely adorable, but he also looks entirely serious when he says, "We're not easy people."

"How many nights have we spent together this week?" Paul asks, shutting the refrigerator door.

Alex shrugs. His shoulders are lovely and dotted with bruises — some from the rocks, but some from Paul. Paul suspects Alex neglected to put a shirt back on just to show them off. The scar from his fall is there too, shiny and pink and extensive. The reminder always makes Paul feel afraid. "Some of those were your idea."

"Yes. And some were yours. This isn't a permanent fix, Alex; we're not built to live this way. I know I don't want it, and I don't think you do either."

"I'm not suggesting an open relationship. I'm suggesting space. So I'm not pissed off when you aren't here because you're trying to work your way through insecurity and so you're not pissed off when I go make a movie."

Paul frowns. "We don't need separate rooms to make that work. I can share a bed with you and deal with you being gone."

"Yeah, but when I'm gone, we're not sharing a bed at all. And when you're here but not *here* I am unhappy."

"Well, maybe I need to get a couch for the office, instead of having an office in the house."

"No," Alex says firmly. Paul is startled.

"What just happened in your head?" Paul asks.

"Assume you get a sofa bed for your office. What happens the next time we start fighting?" He asks. "Two bedrooms, one house," he reiterates. "No sleeping in your damn office."

They're interrupted by Alex's phone ringing. "Shit," Alex says, eyes darting around the room for it.

Paul glances at the clock on the microwave; it's four in the morning. "That's not good."

"No kidding. Help me find my damn phone," Alex snaps.

He's nervous. Paul lets it go as Alex shuffles around things on the counter until he unearths his phone.

"Oh my God, who the fuck died?" Alex says as he glances at the screen. The number has way too many digits; he can't even figure out where he's being called from. "Hello?" he answers tightly.

Paul watches Alex's face nervously. He can't tell if Alex is being awesome at acting or if his brain isn't sending signals to his face properly.

Alex nods rapidly, and then seems to realize whoever he's talking to can't actually see him. "Yeah," he says. Then, "No…no, I didn't….Yes. Thank you. Absolutely. I'll look forward to it." Alex clicks off the phone and stares at Paul unblinkingly.

"I'm going to assume someone didn't die," Paul says cautiously.

Alex finally seems to focus on Paul, his face spreading into a massive grin. "The part's mine," he says, not even trying to contain his excitement.

"At four in the morning?"

"Director's in Japan. He just caught up with his TV viewing and dead, dead, *dead* fucking Zach — so yes, someone died. The lawyers are typing it up, and once I sign it, it's real. I got the paaaaaaaaaaaaaaart."

Alex does a little bounce, his eyes crinkled almost shut.

Paul has never seen Alex be over the moon like this about anything. He's delightful.

"Congratulations," he says, amused and meaning it.

"Oh my God, I got the part. I get to go to Canada." Alex tilts his head. "Is it cold in Toronto?"

Paul laughs. "Do you even have a passport?"

"Have I ever left the country before?"

Paul is struck, in a way he rarely is anymore, by just how surprising Alex's life is for him. The celebrity stuff is strange, yes. But Alex is also someone who never really expected all sorts of commonplace middle class opportunities he currently only lacks time to have.

"You should know, it's only Canada. I mean, you're not even going to the French part," Paul says. "It's kind of like here."

"Paul, don't ruin it!"

"We could go on vacation sometime," he offers softly. "Like, farther than Canada. If you wanted?"

"With what time?" Alex asks, but it's giddy, not bitter.

Paul shrugs. "Twelve weeks isn't forever. And *Winsome* has breaks coming up."

Alex looks at him keenly. Paul can almost hear the wheels turning in his head. "That's a new tune."

"Yeah, well. I'm really happy for you."

◆

Three weeks pass before Alex can tell anyone, but of course a press release featuring sentences he's never actually said goes out first. As much as the process isn't totally unfamiliar, this is a much bigger deal than *Paradise Square* in terms of the size of his role. Having to learn how to navigate the personalities behind a whole new media machine, after so many years of the dysfunctional *Fourth* family, is more than a little frustrating.

Paul, in spite of the loveliness with which he'd taken the news of Alex's offer, goes back to being difficult about the prospect of him being gone for months. Alex finds it irritating and worrying, especially when he starts talking about moving back in together. Again.

"The world is not going to end if I go to Toronto from a different bedroom from you," Alex tells him shortly.

"I was kind of hoping you'd spend the night before with me," Paul says. It's flirty.

Alex grins fiercely. "Yes. Well. We have some time before then. And I appreciate you being happy for me, I do. But that doesn't mean we get to change our living situation on your terms because you were nice about something you should always have been nice about."

"Will you at least go to Liam and Carly's wedding with me?" Paul asks, obviously a little stung but trying to recover.

Alex stares at him. And then bursts out laughing.

"What?" Paul asks.

"Like you were ever going to get out of that? I'd make you go with me even if we broke up tomorrow. Whatever that disaster is going to be, I absolutely blame you for my having to know about it."

"Hey, you know Liam from work," Paul protests.

"And you're the one who's always made that complicated."

37

"Is that a turret?" Alex asks, as they roll up the long, winding driveway to the house that had finally been settled on as the venue for Carly and Liam's wedding.

"A really ugly fucking turret," Paul says.

He's not wrong. It's stone and chunky and looks like a lighthouse grafted onto a Victorian. That's what you get, Alex supposes, when you have two months to plan a celebrity wedding and you let Victor find your venue.

"This is fucked up," Alex says when they get out of the car and Paul hands the keys over to the valet. It's a beautiful December day. The sun is bright and the sky is brilliantly blue. There's a heavy floral scent in the air from the landscaping and the sheer volume of flowers the florists have brought in.

"It's just like a normal wedding with more money," Paul says as they walk around a fountain in the middle of the front lawn that's glinting blindingly in the sun.

"Never been to a wedding, Paul. Don't even know married people," Alex says with a tightness Paul recognizes as nerves. "I mean, like, Raphael, I guess."

"Huh," Paul says. "Weird."

Weird gets a lot weirder incredibly quickly. They climb the steps to the house only to find Victor exchanging enthusiastic greetings with Liam's parents in an incredibly ostentatious foyer, complete with wood paneling and stained glass. Alex feels mildly terrified by the firm handshakes and manly backslapping. For heaven's sake, Liam's dad is a history professor and Victor is gay if he's anything. While still horrifying, at least Victor giving Liam's mom, Kathleen, a kiss on the cheek makes some sort of sense.

"Oh my God, do they know?" Paul hisses way too loudly as Alex grabs his arm in case they need to make a quick getaway.

"I assume they know everything about everyone," Alex whispers back. "His mom made me breakup pancakes."

Paul frowns as Alex starts to pull him further into the house. "I thought he wasn't your ex."

"Did you hear what I just said? The fucked up thing in that is pancakes. From his *mom*."

They decide they can give their respects to Victor later, because Alex, while knowing he will have to face Liam's parents eventually, doesn't particularly want to do it in front of Paul or Victor.

The foyer leads to a hallway, and they follow a stream of people into what looks to be a dining room. Everything is high ceilings and expensive Victorian chic. People are dressed in outfits Alex associates more with awards events than actual people's lives.

He's gone as casual as he possibly could, which means a suit. There was no way he could cope with wearing a tux to Liam's wedding. Paul's doing the suit thing too, and the conversation they'd had about coordinating outfits to avoid clashing — Alex is in gray, Paul in midnight blue — had been very funny. Alex has been doing Hollywood too long to feel out of place now they're here, but it definitely feels particularly foreign to him today. He wonders what his mother would think about it all.

When they round a corner away from Victor and Liam's parents, they run almost directly into another pair of people. At Alex's side, Paul freezes.

Whoever they are, they obviously know Paul; Paul greets them by name and even gets a hug from the woman, although he looks a bit deer in the headlights about it. The man gives him a solid handshake.

When Paul gets his hand back, he puts it on Alex's back. "This is my —" he starts an introduction and then stops.

"Alex," Alex says with a glance sideways at Paul. He is being way too peculiar for Alex to figure out on the spot.

"These are Carly's parents," Paul finishes somewhat pathetically.

Alex is relieved when they eventually escape the small talk and see Raphael and his wife, Irina.

"Oh my God, this is so awkward," Alex blurts. He's relieved to have found someone in the mingling he feels remotely comfortable with other than Paul.

Raphael laughs. "What did you expect?"

"I don't know. At least thirty seconds to acclimate before we had to talk to people."

"How wacky is this for you?" Raphael asks Paul. They both worked on *Fourth* from the beginning, and Raphael must remember perfectly well when it was Paul, not Liam, Carly dropped by the lot to visit.

"It's not except for the part where people keep asking me if it's wacky," Paul grouses. "Why can't you do small talk like a normal person?"

"This is Liam's wedding, and you're asking me that?" Raph says.

Paul sighs. "I need a drink."

◆

Victor is glad that the house is large enough that he can retreat to an empty room and not have to talk to anyone during the pre-ceremony drinking. Which is the best idea Carly has ever had, as far as he's concerned. People should be drunk before they have to sit through the boring and overwrought sentimentality of most people's vows. Also, considering Liam's life and relationships, all two hundred and fifty guests are likely an opportunity for the worst sort of small world theater. Victor remains amazed and slightly cowed by how unreasonably reasonable Liam's parents are about all of it.

He knocks on the open doorframe when he gets to Liam's dressing room and leans into the space without entering. The afternoon sun is slanting in through yet another stained glass window, spilling color onto the gleaming floor and the knotty pine walls and making the whole room glow. Liam's best friend, Charles, is slouched on a couch with his feet up on a coffee table. Victor is relieved to see that he's at least had the sense to take off his suit jacket so it won't wrinkle. Liam is preening — and rambling — in front of an antique, heavy-framed mirror. The composition of the entire scene is perfect, right down to the way the sun is making a halo of Liam's curls.

"Can we have the room?" Victor asks Charles once he catches his breath from the sight.

"Yup," he says good-naturedly as he bounces up and grabs his jacket. "Have fun," he says to Liam as he swerves by him on his way out of the door, shutting it behind him.

Victor and Liam both sigh, and Victor gives a little huff of a laugh, walking over to Liam and turning him away from the mirror.

"Your tie's crooked," he says, realizing that's likely what Liam had been staring at without being quite able to figure out what was wrong.

Liam doesn't say anything, and Victor has a flash of anxiety.

"You cannot decide words are too hard right now," he says sternly. Liam has a script for the ceremony and the working a room thing after should be fine, but, God, he hopes Liam knows that.

Also, as fine — as happy, as relieved — as Victor is about all of this, Liam is looking at him the way he does when he's helpless, in pain, and too damn in love with Victor for his own good. He makes Victor ache in a way that still doesn't entirely make sense in his brain. He can't imagine Liam's wedding day is an appropriate moment for him to tell Liam he's in love with him, too.

"Saving them up," Liam eventually says, looking away.

"Okay, then." Victor unties and reties the tie in silence, tapping his fingers against the knot when he's done. "I'm incredibly proud of you, you know."

Liam merely nods.

♦

Alex has nothing to compare it to at all, but the ceremony itself seems lovely if slightly too long. Carly cries, Liam cries, and Paul holds Alex's hand and smiles. They're all outside, back behind the house, and a breeze stirs Carly's veil and the ribbons on the arbor as the officiant drones on.

Victor is seated across the aisle from them, and when Alex starts to lose interest in the readings his eyes wander to him. He's watching the proceedings with a look that's far away, even wistful, and Alex has absolutely no idea what to make of that. He feels intrusive and turns away.

Alex is still not certain what this marriage is going to mean in the context of Victor and Liam. But an engagement hadn't stopped Carly from having a threesome with Alex and Paul, and Alex knows something about the capacity of Liam's heart.

Paul picks that moment to squeeze Alex's hand. Alex looks over at him to find Paul gazing at him with an expression that's both happy and longing.

Alex mouths *What?* That look, in this context, is both unsettling and gratifying.

♦

Paul shakes his head. Asking Alex, again, to marry him — particularly here, at a public and intensely emotional day that happens to be their best friends' wedding — is a horrible idea. Not to mention terribly clichéd. He very much doesn't want to upset the balance of this day, which has gone so well for them so far.

But he can't stop thinking about a day of their own nearest and dearest, having a ring on his own finger, and getting to call Alex *husband*. He fell too fast and too hard years ago, but there's no way out of it now. Hellish as things have gotten between them this past year, but Paul wants Alex forever.

Some of that must show on his face. Alex gives him a steady look back that goes challenging and then thoughtful before he returns his attention to the ceremony.

♦

At the reception — also outside — the social awkward starts up again. The circle of Liam and Carly's friends, family, and business associates is wide and random. Paul and Alex are seated at a table of people they don't know at all, but starting from the baseline of strange and fucked up Alex is used to from anything Liam-adjacent, it could be so much worse.

Paul gets caught up in a discussion about craft from someone who's apparently a film critic. Alex winds up talking about, of all things, the history of the Safavid Dynasty with one of Liam's dad's connections. The small talk might be the most interesting he's ever made, and he's now grateful for all the background reading he did on Iran for a whole new set of reasons. His conversation partner doesn't even ask about Zach.

♦

Charles, Liam's childhood best friend, gives the toast. Paul leans over to whisper in Alex's ear, "I am so glad there was no awkward sex scene in that story."

Alex nods and mutters back, "Yeah. They've totally been fucking since high school."

"Are you knowing or guessing or do I not want to ask?" Paul says a little weakly.

Alex laughs and bumps their knees together under the table.

Candles and torches get lit as the sun starts to set. Somehow they make the whole lawn, with its white-covered tables, expensive flower arrangements, and guests that are, as Hollywood requires, all better than average looking, seem like one of Nigel's ad campaigns. It's an impression the dancing — music and laughter and swirling dresses — does nothing to lessen, even if Alex is used to his own fairytales being much darker.

◆

The first dances are traditional. But later, once the dance floor is open to everyone, Paul can see them get complicated. Liam and Carly both have a lot of people in their lives for whom this day must be strange or even difficult. Certainly, Paul isn't the only one of Carly's exes here, and he watches as they both, very deliberately, seek certain people out. He assumes himself to be low on the list simply because he and Alex just slept with her. His doesn't need reassurance or attention. As to Liam and Alex, he has no idea what will happen there. He decides to ask Alex to dance before he has to find out. At least he'll be first.

"Dance with me?"

Alex looks at Paul's outstretched hand in consternation. "I don't know how," he says. "Why couldn't they have hired a DJ like on TV weddings? I did not expect the string quartet."

Paul grins at him. "Take my hand, and dance like we usually do. Just less like we're having sex." They both still get grief occasionally for how obvious they were when they danced together at Paul's house at the party where they first hooked up.

"You started it," Alex says.

"Only the first time."

Alex's eyes crinkle up in a smile, and he lets Paul pull him to his feet.

He obviously doesn't know where his hands are supposed to go and then chides Paul for wanting him to lead.

"I *don't know how*," Alex repeats. "You're being stupid."

They laugh awkwardly before they step apart for a moment and then try again.

This time, it works, and they start moving in a little circle. After the first song, Alex squeezes at Paul's arm and leans his forehead into his. Paul gasps. The intimacy of the gesture and the intensity of the look in Alex's eyes make it feel like sex no matter how gentle. Alex smiles softly.

"You little shit," Paul whispers. This is nothing like what he expected from today, and it's absolutely wonderful.

Alex simply says, "I love you."

◆

"You're very good," Carly says, laughing as Victor leads her in a proper waltz. "Why didn't I know this?"

"You weren't paying attention," Victor says lightly. A waltz, when he had grown up with salsa, is very easy. And he'd spent far too much time in his past determined to pass and impress in the circles of rich white people who had the money to fund his projects.

"Well, I should pay more, then."

Victor shakes his head. "You're fine. I'm fine. It's all fine, Carly."

"Is it?"

He shrugs. "Of course it is. A missed date night? He'll make it up to me."

"You haven't danced with him," Carly notes.

"Do you really expect me to?" Victor asks.

"I'm sure he asked."

"He did," Victor allows. "But Liam is unpredictable, and he and I are fine. You two look radiant today. That's all I care about."

"You're a very good liar," she says.

"True," he acknowledges. "But not germane."

◆

Paul and Alex have barely managed to sit down and start chatting with some of Paul and Carly's friends from college when, to Alex's surprise, Liam appears. He doesn't say anything, just grabs Alex's hand and tugs him away from the table toward the dance floor. Alex is a little exasperated but very fond.

Paul, to his relief, only looks amused as Liam drags him off.

They skip the question of who leads with a bit of fumbling to at least mimic something resembling a hold, but they also don't really move at all. Instead, they sway slowly in place. Their feet only catch up to the idea of dancing the one or two times they manage to get off balance and someone has to take a step to prevent them from falling.

Alex expects rambling from Liam, or a list, or at least words. But Liam keeps his eyes down for a while, and Alex decides that this isn't about him at all, but what Liam needs. He can wait it out. In a sea of so many guests, likely no one is paying attention anyway. He hopes Liam gets what he's looking for out of this, before someone among the endless and enthusiastic supply of his friends interrupts.

Eventually, Liam looks up, silent and eyes too bright. The beauty of the look is why he's on TV, and it's unsettling enough that it's why he's good as opposed to just pretty. Liam continues to look at him too intently for a long moment and then puts his head on Alex's shoulder.

Alex sighs, in awe at how simple things between them sometimes are, and tips the side of his head into Liam's.

"I know," he says.

Back at their table, Alex sees Paul look away and sighs in relief. Paul always has been a fundamentally decent guy.

♦

This late in the year the night is cool, but L.A. is never cold, so Paul rolls the windows down as they roll back down the driveway. He feels like they have so much to talk about, after everything that happened tonight and the emotion of the day, but yet, foolishly, talking doesn't seem necessary. It's enough that he and Alex are together.

Alex tucks his feet up and leans his head against the back of the seat. His face is mostly turned away, but the moonlight falls across him beautifully. Paul can tell he's smiling. After the last eight months, they might finally be on the same page again, and a good page at that.

The drive back is silent, peacefully so, and Paul follows Alex up the stairs to the bedroom they once shared when they get home. They kiss as they undress just as silently, and Paul doesn't even feel the need to narrate or tease when they finally go to bed. They laugh a lot. Mostly with relief.

38

The next morning, Paul moves his clothes back from the other side of the house while Alex first pretends to sleep in and then sits in bed reading. He never expected Carly and Liam's wedding, of all things, to be the catalyst for them moving back in together. He's thrilled. But this part of their mess was Paul's fault, and Alex is happy to let him move his own damn crap.

When he's finally done, Paul closes the closet door with a ridiculous amount of self-satisfaction. He turns, folds his hands behind him and leans against it.

"So," he says.

"So," Alex echoes, looking up from his book. Which is the exact moment that Todd chooses to dash into the room and jump up on the bed. Alex and Paul both look at Todd — who immediately curls up on Alex's legs, purring triumphantly — and then at each other. Paul cracks up, and Alex grins as he leans over to scratch Todd's ears.

"Someone's happy," Paul observes.

The look Alex gives him is both coy and content.

"There's a thing I need you to do," Paul says once the mood settles again.

"Yeah?"

Alex doesn't expect it to be about Victor. And when it is, he doesn't expect it to make so much sense. In six weeks he's leaving to go to Toronto for three months. While they can call and visit — and

Paul assures him that will involve mutual advance planning, because they're working hard at not forgetting lessons learned — a lot of Paul's care and feeding is going to be in the hands of other people. And while that means Carly, and Darcy, and apparently even Gemma, it also means Victor.

"I know what you think of him," Paul says. "And I know you're not necessarily even wrong. Or ungrateful. But he's a part of my life that I need. And if you want him to treat you like a real person, you kind of have to treat him like one too."

Alex agrees, because it will make Paul happy and likely change nothing else in his world. But that doesn't mean Alex isn't still the clever and sharp creature Victor discovered three years ago who both America and Paul fell in love with.

So Alex invites him shooting. He considers doing it via Twitter, just to fuck with him, but ultimately decides email is the better option. Victor is, when he replies, predictably appalled. But once Alex gets him on the phone, he can hear him smiling. Some people don't back down from a challenge. He's often like that himself. But Victor seems to take challenges on as an almost delighted form of *fuck you*.

◆

Paul sees him off at the door with an amused, if wary, "Have fun, good luck, don't antagonize the internet."

Alex knows Paul thinks this idea is unwise for any number of reasons. But if he's going to prove he's not scared of Victor by making nice with him, he's going to do it on his own terms. If he's honest with himself, Alex knows he's doing it not just for Paul but for himself. After everything Victor's done to him, Alex has earned the right to exert his own not insignificant power.

There isn't much opportunity for talking on the range, which is fine by Alex. He's darkly delighted that Victor is a miserable shot. Victor has more of a sense of humor about it than he expects.

They finally get a chance to talk in the parking lot. Alex sits on the hood of his car as Victor stands in front of him, hands in pockets, like they're ordinary people used to being in terrible, industrial parts of L.A. He finds himself mostly repeating, word for word, what Paul had said to him.

"I know who you are, Alex," Victor says in response, smiling. "It's you who doesn't know who I am."

It feels, a little bit, like a movie.

But Alex thinks about it on the drive home. About if whether all the times he thought Victor was being malevolent and cruel, he was simply doing what Alex himself does when he's surly: putting on an act to get by in the world. Only with darker consequences.

Victor doesn't control Alex; he just elicits reactions. If Alex has chosen to fall for it, because he's needed a bad guy in his life, that doesn't absolve Victor. But it does point to Alex having chosen too many of his own obstacles. In an existence where everyone fawns over him, of course Alex has needed someone who is anything but giving.

Alex chuckles to himself. He may never forgive Victor for all of the things that he's done, but if Victor of all people doesn't control him then neither can anyone else. Smiling to himself in the car as he turns up onto the steep street to his house, Alex knows a lesson like that is a powerful gift.

♦

"Hey, are you home?" Alex shouts as he walks in the front door.

The shout turns out not to be necessary. Paul's in the kitchen cooking, and he turns, a knife in one hand and half an onion in the other. Alex has to stop himself from laughing uncontrollably, it's so very perfect.

"Me and a pot of soon-to-be vegetable soup. What's up?"

"Ask me again," Alex says breathlessly.

"What?"

"Ask me again."

"Ask you what?" Paul says, clearly puzzled.

"You're gonna ruin it if you make me say it," Alex says.

Paul stares at him, his face shifting from confusion to disbelief to the most cautious, hopeful understanding. "I'm getting the sense I should put down the onion?" he says carefully.

Alex finally lets himself laugh. "Also the knife," he suggests.

Paul complies and wipes his hands on his jeans. He can't take his eyes off Alex's face as he asks like it's the very first time, "So, are you going to marry me?"

All Alex can do is beam and silently nod. For the most important things, he and Paul have never needed words.

More by These Authors

Visit www.Avian30.com to join Erin and Racheline's mailing list and get information about new releases!

The Love in Los Angeles Series

Starling, Book 1
Doves, Book 2
Phoenix, Book 3
More coming soon!

Love in Los Angeles is a queer romance series, with elements of magical realism, set in and around the TV and movie industry.

When J. Alex Cook, a production assistant on *The Fourth Estate* (one of network TV's hottest shows), is accidentally catapulted to stardom, he finds himself struggling to navigate both fame and a relationship with Paul, one of Fourth's key writers. *Love in Los Angeles* is the story of Paul and Alex — and of their friends and family — as they navigate love, and life, both in and beyond Los Angeles.

A Queen from the North

A widowed prince in need of an heir, a not-so-united kingdom in need of healing, and an ancient prophecy that still lingers in the modern world are about to conspire to make Lady Amelia Brockett A Queen from the North.

The Art of Three

Two men. One woman. No love triangles.

The Love's Labours Series

Midsummer, Book 1
Twelfth Night, Book 2
More coming soon!

42-year-old John Lyonel has never been attracted to men before, but falling for 25-year-old Michael Hilliard is actually the least screwed up thing that's happened to him in years. Even if sometimes he thinks Michael's a changeling.

Short stories:

Sample and Hold
Off-Kilter
Lake Effect
Snare
The Omega's Reluctant Alpha
Alpha Bodyguard
The Hart and the Hound

www.ingramcontent.com/pod-product-compliance
Lightning Source LLC
Chambersburg PA
CBHW030519190726

48283CB00006B/1692